Winter's Tales

NEW SERIES: 5

Winter's Tales

NEW SERIES: 5

*

EDITED BY

Robin Baird-Smith

St. Martin's Press

New York

WINTER'S TALES

Library of Congress catalogue card number: 89-62382

ISBN 0–312–03736–8

First U.S. Edition
10 9 8 7 6 5 4 3 2 1

CONTENTS

ACKNOWLEDGEMENTS

The stories are copyright respectively:
© 1989 Graham Greene
© 1989 Paul Sayer
© 1989 Damon Galgut
© 1989 William Trevor
© 1989 Laura Kalpakian
© 1989 Paul Pickering
© 1989 Muriel Spark
© 1989 David Updike
© 1989 Georgina Hammick
© 1989 Norman Thomas di Giovanni
© 1989 Lawrence Scott
© 1989 A. L. Barker

The story by Graham Greene was first published in the *Independent*; that by Muriel Spark in *New Woman*. All the other stories in this collection are original to *Winter's tales*.

EDITOR'S NOTE

It has often been remarked of *Winter's tales* that those who search in it for a common theme do so in vain. The choice of stories always has been, and remains, dictated by the quirks of editorial taste.

And yet in each volume in this new series something resembling a theme does seem to emerge. Last year there was a preponderance of elderly ladies faced with intimations of mortality. This year obsession seems to dominate many stories – often of a neurotic and destructive variety, as in Paul Sayer's tale.

While pondering this, I happened on some words of Frank O'Connor (himself a contributor to the 1955 volume of *Winter's tales*). 'In essence,' he wrote, the short story deals with life's victims – the insulted, the injured, the forelorn and the alienated. It deals with the defeat of human aspirations by brutish circumstances.'

Does this new volume of *Winter's tales* bear out his point? It is true that such defeats, whether violent or mild, are a perennial part of the human condition, providing the kind of drama fiction-writers look for. Perhaps the short story in particular filters down experience to its prime elements of defeat and alienation.

Where space is limited no words can be wasted. An economy of narrative leads to a bleak outlook characterized by a tone of moral bitterness (Laura Kalpakian's long short story this time may be an exception to that rule).

Let me detain the reader no more from what is important – the stories. Apart from established writers such as Muriel Spark, Graham Greene, William Trevor and A. L. Barker (all on top form), there is this year a wealth of new young talent. David Updike, Damon Galgut, Paul Pickering and Paul Sayer have only recently published their first works of full-length fiction. The last has had the unique experience of having his first novel *The comforts of madness* awarded the Whitbread Book of the Year Award. His admirers will be delighted to know that in the story published in this volume is the germ of his new novel.

I hope the stories will please the reader this year, for it is the reader, of course, who is the final judge.

Robin Baird-Smith, 1989

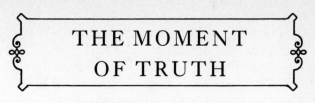

THE MOMENT OF TRUTH

Graham Greene

The near approach of death is like a crime which one is ashamed to confess to friends or fellow workers, and yet there remains a longing to confide in someone – perhaps a stranger in the street. Arthur Burton carried his secret to and fro to the kitchen and back, just as he carried the plates and the orders of the clients, as he had done for years in the Kensington restaurant which was called Chez Auguste. There was nothing French about it except the name and the menu, where the English dishes were given French names, explained at length in English under each title.

Twice in one week an American couple had booked the same table, a small one in a corner under a window, a man of about sixty years and a woman in her late forties – a very happy couple.

There are clients whom one likes at the first encounter and these were among them. They asked Arthur Burton's advice before they ordered and later they expressed their appreciation of his choice. They trusted him even over the wine, and on their second visit, they asked him little questions about himself as though he were a fellow guest whom they were anxious to know better.

'Been here long?' Mr Hogminster asked. (Arthur Burton had learnt his curious name when he telephoned for his reservation.)

'About twenty years,' Burton replied. 'It was a different restaurant when I came called The Queen's.'

'Better in those days?'

[11]

Arthur Burton tried to be loyal. 'I wouldn't say better. Simpler. Tastes change.'

'Is he French – your boss?'

'No, sir, but he's been to France a lot, I think.'

'We're happy to have your help. We don't know all these French words in the menu.'

'But it's put in English, sir.'

'I guess we don't understand that sort of English either. Anyway we'll be along again tomorrow. If you let us have the same table – Arthur, isn't it? I think I heard the boss call you Arthur?'

'That's right, sir. I'll see that you have this table.'

'And your help, Arthur,' Mrs Hogminster said.

He was touched by the use of his first name and the smile of real friendship which he received from Mrs Hogminster. In all his years as a waiter, he had known nothing like it before.

Arthur Burton was in the habit of observing the customers, superficially, if only to keep an interest in his job which it was too late to change. He was alone in life, so there was no initiative for a change and now he was well aware that it was too late. The crime of death had touched him.

Often when he went home at night – if a bed-sitting-room with a shared shower could be called a home – he would remember certain customers: married customers who seemed to lunch together without interest, watching those who came in with a certain envy if the newcomers had words to say to each other: obvious new lovers who paid attention to no one else: sometimes a married young woman (he always looked at the left hand) with a look of anxiety, accompanied by a much older man. She lowered her voice or even ceased to talk when neighbours took the next table and Arthur Burton wished that he could have left

[12]

it empty, so that they would be free to solve their problem.

When he got home that night, he thought of Mr and Mrs Hogminster. He wished he had spoken more to them. He felt that he could trust them, like strangers in the street. He might at least have hinted at the crime which separated him from the manager, the cook, the other waiters, the washers-up – only hinted of course, he wouldn't like them to be distressed.

They were half an hour late the next day for their reservation, and the manager wanted him to give up the table to other guests who asked for it. 'They won't be coming,' the manager argued, 'and anyway, there are three other tables to choose from.'

'But they like this table,' Arthur Burton said, 'and I promised they would have it.' He added, 'They are kind, good people,' but he probably would have been forced to give way if they had not at that moment arrived.

'Oh, I'm so sorry, Arthur, we are terribly late.' He was touched that she had remembered his name. 'It was the Sales, Arthur. We got involved.'

'*She* got involved,' Mr Hogminster said.

'Oh, it will be your turn tomorrow.'

Arthur told them, 'There are restaurants closer to the men's shops. I can recommend one near Jermyn Street.'

'Oh, but it's Chez Augustine that we love.'

'Chez Auguste,' Mr Hogminster corrected her.

'And Arthur. He chooses so well for us. We don't have to think.'

A man with a secret is a very lonely man, and it was relief to Arthur Burton when he could uncover even a small corner of his secret. He said, 'I'm sorry, ma'am, but tomorrow I won't be here. But I'm sure the manager . . .'

'Not here? *Quelle désastre*! Why?'

'I have to go to hospital.'

'Oh, Arthur, I'm so sorry. What for? Is it serious?'

'A check-up, ma'am.'

'Very wise,' Mr Hogminster said. 'I believe in check-ups.'

'He's had four or is it six.' Mrs Hogminster added, 'I think he enjoys them, but it always worries me. What are they checking you for?'

'They've already done the check-up. Now they have to tell me the result.'

'Oh, I'm sure it will be all right, Arthur.'

'I'm happy you've enjoyed yourselves here, ma'am.'

'We have. All thanks to you.'

Arthur Burton said with truth, 'I'm sorry that we have to say goodbye.'

'Oh no – not yet. We'll be here again on Thursday. Tomorrow, we'll take your advice and eat near the men's shops, but we'll be back the day after to have our last meal at Chez Augustine.'

'Chez Auguste,' Mr Hogminster corrected her again, but she ignored him.

'We are flying to New York on Friday, but we'll certainly see you on Thursday and hear your good news, Arthur. I'm sure it will be good news. I'll be thinking of you and crossing my fingers, but I'm sure, quite sure.'

'I have a check-up every six months,' Mr Hogminster said. 'Always satisfactory.'

'Is there anything special you would like on Thursday ma'am? I can ask the cook . . .'

'No, no. We'll take what you recommend. Until then – and good luck, Arthur.'

[14]

Arthur Burton knew that no good luck awaited him. He had known it even before the check-up by the evasiveness of his doctor. He wondered whether a man in the dock could tell the jury's verdict even before they retired from the court in the days when there was still a death sentence: an emanation of shame at what they were going to pronounce. Yet he had a sense of relief because he had at least confessed half his crime to her and she had not rejected him. If, as he believed, the verdict was death, however they wrapped it up in medical phrases of hope, might she be the stranger in the street to whom he could confess the whole? They would never see each other again. She was leaving for New York on Friday.

They had no friends in common to whom she could spread the news of his crime. He felt an odd tenderness for her.

That night Arthur Burton dreamt of her. It was not an erotic dream, nor a love dream, a very commonplace dream in which she played an unimportant part and yet he woke with a sense of relaxation he had not known for many months. It was as though he had spoken to her and somehow she had given him words of sympathy which lent him courage to face his enemies, who were about to disclose the shameful truth.

He had taken a day off his work, though his appointment with the surgeon was not until the evening at five, and then he was kept waiting for nearly an hour. The surgeon asked him to sit down in a tone of such grave sympathy that he was able to guess accurately enough the report which followed. 'An operation urgently required . . . yes, cancer, but you mustn't be frightened by the sound of a word . . . I have known cases as bad as yours . . . taken in time there's always a good hope . . .'

'When do you want to operate?'

[15]

'I would like you to come into hospital tomorrow morning, and I'll operate the next day.'

'If I could come in the afternoon. You see – they are expecting me to be back at work tomorrow morning.' It was not of work he was thinking, but of Mrs Hogminster. She would be expecting news from him.

'I would much rather you had a quiet day in bed. However ... I will be coming to see you with the anaesthetist at six.'

As he lay in bed that night, Arthur Burton thought: doctors and surgeons are not necessarily good psychologists; perhaps, because their interests are so concentrated on the body that they forget the mind, they don't realise how much a tone of voice reveals to the patient. They say 'there's always a good hope', but what the patient hears is 'there is very little hope if any'.

It was not that he was frightened of death. No one could avoid that universal fate, and yet the population of the world was not dominated by fear. All Arthur Burton wanted was to share his knowledge and his secret with a stranger who would not be seriously affected like a wife or a child – he possessed neither – but might with a word of kindly interest share with him this criminal secret – 'I am condemned'. Mrs Hogminster was just such a woman. He had read it in her eyes. Somehow the next day he would find a way of conveying to her the truth, when she asked for the result of the check-up, without words which might involve her husband in his crime. She would ask him: 'What did the doctor say, Arthur?' And his answer? No, no words, a small shrug of the shoulders would be enough to convey, 'It's all up. Thank you for thinking of me,' and the glance that she gave him back would just as discreetly tell him she shared his secret.

He would not go alone into the future.

[16]

'You needn't keep that table,' the manager said. 'Those Americans were in yesterday and I found them one they liked much better.'

'They were in yesterday?'

'Yes, they do seem to like this place.'

'I thought they were going to the men's Sales.'

'I wouldn't know about that. I think you talk too much to the customers, Arthur. Often they want to feel alone.'

He left hurriedly to meet Mr and Mrs Hogminster at the door. Mrs Hogminster nodded and smiled at Arthur as they went by to a little table isolated in a corner of the restaurant. They had no view now of the street outside, but perhaps, as the manager had suggested, they pre-ferred privacy, and perhaps too they preferred to be served by the manager himself.

It was only at the end of their meal after they had paid their bill that Mrs Hogminster called to him as he passed to the kitchen. 'Arthur, do come and have a word with us.'

He went willingly with a lightening of the heart.

'Arthur, we missed you, but the manager was so kind and we didn't want to hurt his feelings.'

'I hope you enjoyed your lunch, ma'am.'

'Oh, but we always do at Chez Augustine.'

'Chez Auguste,' Mr Hogminster said.

'With the Sales you were so right to send us to Jermyn Street. My husband bought two pairs of pyjamas and can you believe it, three – three – shirts!'

'She chose them of course,' Mr Hogminster said.

Arthur Burton excused himself and went on into the kitchen. The problem which he had so feared had not arisen, but the thought gave him no relief from the depression of his secret. He was going to say nothing to the manager: the next day he would simply not turn up.

[17]

The hospital could inform them in due course if were dead or alive.

He spent as little time as he could in the restaurant, though it pained him to see another waiter looking after the Hogminsters and exchanging words with them.

Half an hour later the manager came into the kitchen and spoke to him. He carried a letter in his hand. He said, 'Mrs Hogminster asked me to give you this. They've left for the airport.'

Arthur Burton put the envelope in his pocket. He felt an immense relief. Of course Mrs Hogminster had done the right thing. They couldn't have talked about his secret in the restaurant for others to hear. Now he would be able to carry with him to the hospital her sympathetic question about his secret and read it again next day immediately before the anaesthetist arrived. He felt alone no longer. He would be holding the hand of a stranger in the street. She could never receive the answer to her question, 'What did the doctor tell you?' but she had asked it in her letter and it was that which counted.

Before putting out the light above his hospital bed, he opened the envelope. He was surprised when three five-pound notes came out first.

Mrs Hogminster wrote: 'Dear Arthur, I felt I must write you a word of thanks before we catch our plane. We have so enjoyed our visits to Chez Augustine and shall certainly return one day. And the Sales, we got such wonderful bargains – you were so right about Jermyn Street.'

The letter was signed Dolly Hogminster.

OTHELLO'S SHADOW

Paul Sayer

From the diary I kept of my wife's movements, I note that I first began following her on 3 October last year.

At first I seemed content to see her enter the tube station each morning and leave it at the appropriate time each evening. These particular observations, I recall, meant frantic physical activity on my part. After she had left through the front door (8.40 weekday mornings) I would rush from the rear of our house, sprint down the alley and cross two busy roads to reach a point in the park from where, if I was in time, I would, across a football pitch and distant shrubbery, be able to see her pass from the end of the street into the station. At 5.15 in the afternoon, when I had caught the glimpse of her returning that I craved, my passage back to the house could be perilous if the traffic was heavy and I often had difficulty calming myself for the moment she came through the door, usually just seconds after me. If it had been raining and I was wet and breathless I might say I had just been putting refuse out in the alley, or I had just been to the post-box. And in my heart of hearts, for all my sophistry, I believe she knew something was amiss with me.

By November I was travelling to town on a later train to satisfy myself that she had arrived at the offices where she worked.

At first I would merely pass down the opposite side of the road and glance up at the third floor window of the modern block where I could just make out her green mac on a hat stand by a filing cabinet. Sometimes, delightfully, I might see her in person, turning my face quickly though, in case she spotted me. Then I took to hanging around there, sitting in a café from where I could enjoy an uninterrupted view of the wide, bare office windows. Since there was nothing to stay at home for, and since I felt I then only existed for this odd sense of my *possession* of Susan, I began to go every day.

I would gaze for hours, awaiting her fitful appearances as she stood from the desk I could not see, papers in her hand, perhaps to lift a box file from shelves behind her. Once I had to wait three hours to see her and my concentration had become so intense, my body so poised, that when I did at last glimpse her long hair and the dreamy flow of her ponderous movements, my breath went from me and I stood bolt upright, knocking my long-cold cup and saucer flying across the tiled floor of the empty café. A waitress, who must have been watching me, brought the manager who coolly asked me to leave. I was not offended by his advice; indeed, I returned the next day and on several subsequent days, though I stopped going in there at all when I found a new observation point on the staircase of a multi-storey car park. Although this was further away, I found I could now look down into the office and therefore view all of Susan's movements. I was ignored by passers-by, suffered only occasional, inquisitive glances, though, in truth, I was quite mindless of anyone as I stamped my feet, rubbed the damp from my clothes, made my notes. For 9 December I wrote:

Quiet morning. T. [office manager] seems absent. Horseplay at break time. Telephone activity minimal, though nine-minute conversation at 11.06. Lunch in office. 3.30 – G. [female colleague] pro-

duced a boxed cake from the baker's round the
corner. A celebration?

And later in the entry:

Probed about cake business. Feel unhappy with explanation that it was G.'s birthday.

I might say I was contented in those early days. I felt in
control of the situation, imposing order on my feelings
for Susan, a timetable of hours to fill with my odd
longing for her.

How? When did all this begin?

I don't know for sure.

I loved my wife. No, it was more than that, far from
simple, I realize. My love had many discernible facets.
It was a dark and splintered thing, like a fixed reflection
in the shards of a broken mirror. I can explain nothing,
have only details to offer . . .

When I worked I ran my own one-man graphic
design business from a studio near our Chiswick home.
I once designed the logo for a famous 'Seventies rock
band of whose hit singles anyone under the age of
forty-five could name at least two. I worked for department stores and took sub-contracts from big City agen-
cies. My most lucrative commission was to fashion a
symbol for a young company whose rapid acquisition of
other concerns made my art internationally visible. I
was successful but not happy, not well, had not been for
a while, suffering cruel stomach and back pains that I
despaired of my doctor, to whom I was a frequent
visitor, ever being able to cure. And, in an odd way, I
did not like my professional behaviour: everything was
too neat, too easy. Much weighed on my mind at that
time, a darkness behind all my conscious thoughts and
actions.

One morning, in the summer of last year, I lay in bed and watched Susan dressing. Things are different for women, I thought. They are flexible, adventurous yet central in themselves, less prudish than men who find ways of distracting themselves with money, cars, fetishistic sports. Men do not have to be modern to survive, not the way women must be. Men can always hide behind a woman's resilience, her power, the power a wife like Susan possessed. My head, that morning, suddenly teemed with thoughts like these.

I watched her, morbidly drawn and bewitched by the fine gold curve of her spine, the fatty folds above her hips, her breasts, the steady poise of her grey eyes, the certainty of her movements as she stooped to pick clothing from a drawer.

If I remember correctly, at that very moment I was intensely jealous, not of *her*, not from any sense of *owning* Susan, but of her sex, her womanhood. In those profound seconds I do believe my wish was actually to *be* my wife, to become her, somehow, don't ask me how.

We were both thirty-four years old and had been married for five years. We had made an early pact never to have children. We had our careers and our differences: I disliked her practicality and she resented my 'bitter' intelligence. Yet between us we had created a modern idyll. We had a terraced house, comfortably replete with an expensive chesterfield and Liberty print curtains, which Susan insisted on calling our 'cottage'. Cleverly, perhaps too cleverly, we had also contrived to give each other room to exist independently. It must have been what we wanted. Yet why, once one achieves all one might reasonably hope for in life, does one have to destroy everything? Why must it all go wrong? Why must we make it go wrong?

When Susan had finished dressing and went downstairs I felt a sudden chilling fear, the dread of a baby whose mother has left the room and who cannot comprehend that she has not vanished for good. Not to have Susan still with me at that moment was a devastatingly unthinkable prospect.

Naked, I followed her down to the kitchen. The sight of her filled me with an unbridled relief. I stood behind her, put my hand in her hair then quickly withdrew it, recoiling, repulsed by the intimacy of my action, I don't know why.

'I don't want you to go to work today,' I said.

She turned and smiled, appearing to give no real thought to my presence. She squeezed my balls gently. 'Silly,' she said. 'Plenty of time this evening. If you can wait that long. We'll have a grand supper. Wine too. Yes?' Her smile, pretty as it usually was, seemed threatening, Luciferous.

'No,' I said. 'You don't understand. I just want you to stay here in the house. With me.'

She went into the lounge and I trailed her. 'Are you not going to the studio today?' she asked, drily. 'You're not ill again, are you?'

'No. I don't think so.'

Feeling a tightness in my throat, confused by my own words, by everything, I forced myself to return upstairs to the bedroom where I sat on the bed. Soon she was shouting goodbye and I heard the front door thump as she left. My heart shrank. Somehow, I managed to perform the mundane tasks of shaving, dressing, and went to my studio with a dreadful pain under my ribs. I was a long way from understanding myself.

Such work as I managed that day was cosmetic rather than creative: filing accounts, writing a letter. My stomach felt sore and squeezed and shortly after twelve I locked my studio door and went home to bed.

Over the next few days I felt a little brighter, though Susan was taciturn, distant in her dealings with me. I went to my doctor. 'You again?' he said. 'Yes. Me again,' I replied. We would often laugh, he and I, about my many ailments. He gave me a new brand of antacid which seemed to work for a while. Then, one Friday evening, on my way home, I stopped outside Mr Falik's television rental shop. On each of the twenty or so different sized screens, a man was talking, being interviewed, his face looking to the side of the shop window, a smooth angular face I had seen many times on television (once he had been a presenter of a children's magazine programme). I could not hear what he was saying, but for some fantastic reason I thought he was talking about Susan.

I stepped back on the pavement, the rush hour traffic thundering behind me. How could this be so? What were those evenly-stated words on his lips? Betrayal? Whore? Infidelity? The last offered with a wink and a turn of the mouth?

I hurried home, knowing I must see her, fearing I should need to ask her what all this meant.

All evening I could do nothing but watch her every movement, pretending to read the *Evening Standard*, drinking a red wine that griped my poor stomach. She was embroidering. She could not help but notice the attention I was paying her.

'I wish,' she said, 'you wouldn't keep staring at me like that.'

'I'm sorry.'

'I don't know what's got into you lately.'

'Nothing. I'm fine. Really I am.'

She put down her work, took off her spectacles and knelt in front of me. Each of these actions seemed to disturb me. She smiled coolly, the way my doctor did at the end of my interviews with him. 'Tell me what's on your mind,' she said. 'What have you found out about me that's so suddenly fascinating? Sometimes I think you can't bear to have me out of your sight.' She giggled, unforgivably.

'Odd, isn't it?' I said.

'I'm going to bed now,' she said, feigning a yawn.

'Yes. I'm coming too.'

She wanted to make love that evening but I was very disappointing to her. It put her in a mood for days. Susan had always known more about sex than me and, in the early days, I used to prefer that the sources of her dark knowledge remained secret: it fixed my imagination and inspired me in the lovemaking she enjoyed more than me. Why had I not wanted to know about her sexual past? Perhaps my desired ignorance gave me an excuse for . . . for what?

I began rising at the same time as her, insisting on walking to the tube station with her. She resented this, perhaps seeing her little walk as a private time of her own, before her day began. One morning, after another hopeless attempt at sex the night before, I squeezed her hand and apologized in the street. 'Why mention it?' she said. 'You think too much about it. That's your problem. You think too much about everything.'

'I thought it might be annoying you.'

'I'd quite forgotten about it,' she lied. 'It will come right again soon.'

She shook her white, waxy hand free of my hard grip and marched across the road, dodging cars as I made the almost insuperable effort of turning away towards the street that led to my studio.

My work suffered badly then. I did nothing constructive that I can now recall. More than once I sat in front of a sketch and saw it transform into her face. Often, as if by way of exorcizing her from my imagination, I would draw her deliberately in a dreadful effort to pull myself together. Angry with myself, I might screw up the drawing and throw it in the waste paper basket, though I would soon retrieve the ball of paper, smooth it out on my draughtsman's board and gloat again over the pencilled image, feeling a shame of sorts, deriving an odd comfort from her likeness, weeping a little at times, I don't know why. (And once I woke from an afternoon nap to find a dozen of these pictures hung up about the studio. Try as I might, I could not remember having drawn them or placed them there. Some were simple outlines. Others were dark abstractions with grotesque features that horrified me.)

I tried to explain my feelings to her, but my planned, forced statement came out illogically, incongruously. I told her that I envied her and that I wanted, somehow, to be like her. She seemed very put out and could think of nothing to say in reply. I wished I had not done that for she misinterpreted everything I said, as I realized when, not long after, in an extraordinary mood, she swept into the house with two carrier bags full of outsize women's clothing. In an absurdly contrived dominatrix voice she informed me that I was to shower and change into these things. 'You will wait upstairs,' she said. 'I will be up to inspect you shortly.' The scenario that followed made us both feel very foolish. I crumpled the clothes back in the bags and threw them in the spare room. She was missing the point.

About that time I decided to get rid of my business. I could no longer function, my interest in work had been moribund for a long time. I hived off what small contracts I had to a friendly rival who also made me an offer for some of my equipment. I pressed for, and received, payment on the last two accounts owed to me. The remaining portion of my lease was quickly sold. In all, I raised thirty-one thousand pounds. I still have it, don't seem to need it, don't really want it.

Susan was unsurprised and informed me coldly that I should not expect her to support me when the money had gone. To cheer her up I invented new business ideas which I would pursue as soon as I had had a 'rest'. Neither of us really believed in my suggestions.

Winter passed. Once she remarked, 'Glenda, from the office, said she saw you today. She was late for work. She said she brushed past you in a street near the car park. She said hello but you didn't reply. She thought you were in an awful hurry to get somewhere. Were you down near the office today?'

'I've been here all day?'

She asked again, 'Was it you?'

'No. It wasn't. I haven't seen Glenda for years. She doesn't know me. She must have been mistaken.' I affected an air of steely dismissiveness, bending my head low over the book I had been pretending to read for weeks.

For all that I longed for her, for all that I keened to possess every hair, every sinew, every atom of her body, I could no longer bear to touch Susan. Our attempts at lovemaking stopped altogether. Perhaps I saw that as a way of provoking her, exacting a kind of revenge. For what I cannot explain. When I suggested that I moved into the spare room she surprised me by breaking down in tears. She asked, 'What's got into you? Why do you want to destroy everything we've worked so hard for?' I was unmoved. She was behaving loosely, out of character. I wanted to tell her to pull herself together but she ran from the room before I could speak.

My objectification of her continued unabated and the

reams of notes I made developed into a kind of case history. And yet I often saw the folly in my ways. Occasionally I forced myself not to follow her to work, but my intense anxiety would only be converted into other activities: looking at her possessions, checking dates on bank statements and receipts, disposing of the magazines she read, examining her clothes for, I suppose, signs of infidelity. I might find a hair on a dress or take exception to the way a blouse was folded. Sometimes I buried my face in her clothes, wanting to weep, to beg forgiveness for my monstrous idiosyncracies, knowing I had become incapable of crying and humility. My obsession took on a life of its own. It sustained me, somehow.

There was much, Susan began to say, that she missed from our 'old life'. She asked if I minded if she went out with her colleagues one evening. I threw a depraved tantrum, holding my breath until I went blue. She did not go that time, but the inevitable was soon to happen.

On a hot July day, after many hours spent observing her at work, I dashed home to watch her arrival at the station. But she did not appear.

I ran to the house, trying to convince myself that I might have missed her among the crowd emptying from the trains. The morning mail still littered the doormat, the house was cool inside, and Susan was not there. I ran back to the station, by way of the street this time. I checked the times of the trains and stood midstream against the ebbing tides of irritable commuters. No Susan. After an hour and five trains I returned to the house and rang her office, receiving only the bastard tones of an answering machine in reply. I harangued myself bitterly for not having met her straight from work, as I had been meaning to, once I had found a suitable pretext.

[30]

My anxiety knew no bounds. I can only liken it to sudden bereavement. I ran from room to room. I wanted to break up our home, the fragile objects of our shared life – fine china, mirrors, a glass clock – suddenly acquiring a sinister appeal. I ran to the back yard then returned to the kitchen where I howled filthy, filthy tears. How wretched I became that night.

When she did appear, at midnight, Susan had about her the purposeful air of folly and calamity of someone who has become intentionally drunk. She threw her arms around me and said she wanted to take me to bed. I hated her that moment. I burst from her arms and sent her sprawling to the floor. My head throbbed with dry machine-like sounds left by my wailing. 'How could you do this to me?' I said, many times over. She pulled herself up into an armchair, lilting between composure and unconsciousness. 'At least tell me where you've been,' I demanded, my voice high-pitched, circumscribed with hysteria. She garbled the name of a nightclub, opened her eyes and said, 'I think I'm going to be sick.'

She stumbled up the stairs and I followed, lusting for information about who she had been with, needing facts, motives for the savage betrayal she had visited on me. In the bathroom she dropped to her knees and heaved into the toilet. I picked her up by her arm. 'Let go of me,' she said, tapping my hand away with ease, leaning over the wash-basin to rinse her face. 'Tell me why you did this to me,' I screamed.

'Be quiet,' she said, softly, firmly. 'The neighbours will hear you.'

'Susan!'

'You're sick. Do you know? You're not sane.' She looked sideways at me, supporting herself on the sink, drops of water forming on the ends of swept aside hair.

[31]

'I know you follow me to work. I see you every day. Do you think no one notices you? Everyone in the office knows you're there. How do you think that makes me feel?' She wiped her mouth and eyes with tissue from the shelf above the sink. 'The things they must say behind my back. The excuses I have to make about not being late home. And I know,' she added, 'that you go through my things. You're sick. You need help.'

She looked suddenly beautiful in her quiet distress. I followed her into the bedroom and when she collapsed on the bed I began shaking her hard, feeling confused, not sure that I might indeed want to make love to her. But I did not. Instead I went back downstairs and suffered my anguish long into that hot summer night.

A sense of destiny came over me. Had I initiated all this myself? From a time before I had even met Susan? I could never analyse my syndrome. I knew only simple things: I was capable of intense love and hatred, both of Susan and myself, and I had, ultimately, to destroy one or both of us.

I faltered in my observations of her and the will to behave as I had done before that night, disappeared. I brooded badly in the house and she habitually stayed out at nights.

Three months ago, she announced to me that she had taken a lover. She spoke quietly, kindly even. 'I think . . . I know, deep inside, from the way you've been acting, that, in some way, don't ask me how, this is what you've been wanting me to do.' She had just come in from work. I was still in bed. In a rage I rose up and ripped to shreds each item of bed linen about me. Susan screamed at me to stop. I flung my fist at her, in a backward sweep, and she fell to the floor, catching her head on the pine dressing-table. She whimpered oddly before closing her eyes. A little blood issued from her ear.

My head was light and devoid of thought. I dressed at lightning speed and ran from the house. I careered through the suburbs, down to the river, whooping, filled with a bizarre, unearthly joy. I went into pubs, drank beer and lager, leaving half-filled glasses before moving on to the next, undetermined place. Drinking was something to do, something everyone did, though I have never much cared for it. The brilliant, released energy in my veins drew me on through unknown terraced streets, past an industrial estate where dogs barked at the locked mesh gates, down bright shopping arcades peopled by tramps, junkies, hard young men I did not fear. How high was the moon that night!

At last I felt the exhaustion I hungered for and made my way, instinctively, back to the house, feeling outside of myself, beyond time and sensation. I entered, fully expecting to find Susan's corpse where I had left it.

But there was no sign of her, only the fluffy detritus of my outrageous anger – clouds of duvet filling, shreds of brown pillowcases – and three coins of blood on the stone-coloured carpet. I checked the other rooms, found them empty, then returned to the lounge where I lay on the sofa and fell into a comatose sleep.

When I woke it was late afternoon. There was a presence in the room, a tall man standing in front of the cold gas fire. He looked down at me. He seemed modern-looking, clean-shaven, worldly. 'Are you a policeman?' I asked.

'No.'

'Then you must be the lover.' I began to laugh. Flippancy came easily for I was still possessed of the histrionics of the previous night. 'I thought my wife's tastes might be more sophisticated. What's your line of business? Estate agent? Used cars? MP?'

'Scum,' said the man. He took a step towards me. 'I should take your limbs off for the way you've behaved towards Susan.'

'Ah, Susan, Susan,' I said wistfully, seating myself upright. 'I take it she's all right then?'

The man seemed to snarl. I giggled.

'I am taking her things to her and you are not to follow. Not ever. Do you understand?'

I could not help but laugh. I went into the kitchen and made coffee and toast which I ate with great relish. This oafish man went upstairs and slammed drawers, carting armfuls of Susan's clothing away to his car outside. When he had gone I tidied up a little and watched television. But I was restless, excited for no obvious reason. I washed, changed my clothes, and set off once more to the streets I had found so agreeable the night before.

I know that Susan has left her job. Enquiries I made to her family as to her whereabouts were met with her father's morbid aggression and threats of informing the police about me. The days pass and I know I want her still. I love her in my own fashion and I cannot bear the thought of this love.

Each morning I set out from the house that is cold and disorderly since she went. If the sun is bright I simply follow my shadow, adoring its outline, its relentlessness, believing, dimly, in rare moments of insight, that I have become that shadow and am no longer the being that forms it.

[34]

CLOETE'S REVENGE

Damon Galgut

We didn't dislike him. (There is that about men to be admired: we can be vile, mean, unconscionably cruel, but if circumstances demand it, we can get on with each other.) He was a spotty, red-headed boy with warts on his shoulders and a skew, discoloured front tooth. His name was Daniels, and he came from Paarl.

There were twelve of us in that tent and we'd been there two months. After basic training, as in armies world-wide, we had been posted out to bases and installations all over the country, becoming the temporary inhabitants of sentry-boxes and guard-huts, barracks and messes. Two years, we were told, is a short time to serve your country; but it is long enough to be moved to a lot of places while you wait. (It is also long enough to die in, but that is another matter.) I had been moved to three different camps before this one: Phalaborwa in the Eastern Transvaal, Bethlehem in the Free State, Upington in the Cape.

It was at the end of my first year that I was posted once more: northward this time, to the border. *The Border*, of course, was that of South-West Africa; famous once as the site of real war, it had been superseded by the myriad other borders drawn now inside the country. (I speak, naturally, of the townships, but that too is another matter.) People still died there, but their deaths were remote.

We lived in a smallish camp, far from the larger bases that dotted the bush. We slept in tents and shat in holes. There was something primitive about our existence here, as though we had moved closer to nature. Even our clothes – the standard browns – were camouflaged. We were temporary beings in an enduring landscape. In a very strange sense, so far from civilized life, our plight was metaphysical: I became aware of distance and of time. I knew the reason for my – and all of us – being here: war, death and pain. We had purpose after all.

Daniels slept two beds down from me. He'd been sent up from a camp near Bloemfontein; his posting, he told me once, was a punishment for some imagined offence. He was a silent presence in the tent: modest, mild. The only activity that set him apart from the others was an obsession with chess, which he seemed to play against himself, pointlessly, on a faded board.

I went over to him. 'Would you like to play me?'

He looked up, startled.

'Do you . . .?'

'Yes,' I said. 'A bit. My brother's quite good.'

He set up the board. I lost.

We played, after that, quite often. He was a better player than I, and mostly he beat me. I'm not a good loser by nature, but I didn't mind this: the game was the point. We were bored there, in our kingdom of veld. There was nothing to relieve the tedium, the implacable ennui of being alive. We stood guard from time to time. We walked patrol. But, for the rest, we were soldiers off duty and we spent our time as soldiers do: getting drunk, telling jokes.

I had other things to occupy me. My aspirations were poetic: I wanted to write verse. Every night, braving the scorn of my illiterate compatriots (some of them well-nigh speechless in their bid to escape language), I hammered out rhymes in a wire-backed notebook that I kept for the purpose in my locker. They were not good poems and I knew this in my heart; I was, in those days, not lonely enough.

Daniels and I were companions. I use the word advisedly: there was no friendship on the border, and we didn't share secrets. (I have even forgotten his first name, if ever I knew it.) But we accompanied each other on the numerous little missions that go into maintaining a life in the bush: washing clothes, standing guard. Once he showed me a photo of his lover, a tall, thin girl with braces. She was at high school still.

We did not dislike him. There were odder people in the tent than he, but even towards them we displayed no animosity. Normal laws did not apply in the bush: we had, all of us, been sent up here for varying periods of penance, and we had no choice but to endure each other. There was no love, but there was tolerance.

So it was that all of us were witness to a most unlikely battle. When I first arrived at the camp, our tent was under the control of a fat but gutless man by the name of Retief. Corporal Retief was due to finish his four-year (Permanent Force) contract in a month; he had no interest in discipline, and he viewed the world through tiny eyes dimmed with benevolence. We stood no inspections. At night, gently drunk, Corporal Retief would lurch into the tent. Balancing himself on uneasy legs, he would lower his distended bulk onto a nearby bed and regale us with tales from his past. Most dull they were too; but they reminded us of a world beyond this one, where people wore civilian clothes and did not carry guns. Under his aimless authority, our morale rose high. Dust collected in our lockers. We slept in our beds and made them up, in the mornings, as carelessly as we would at home.

We could not imagine that he would leave. But he did: on a certain day, bearing cases of whisky bestowed on him in parting, Corporal Retief departed the camp in a lumbering Dakota as heavy and shapeless as himself. And in his stead, the very next night, Corporal Cloete arrived.

Let me describe this man. He was small of build, thin, with a luminous scar on his cheek. His eyes were too close together, set deep in his skull. Ginger hair receded from his forehead. His teeth were many and large and perfect, showing, when he smiled, as a bright gash in his face. And his hands – for some reason his most memorable feature – were delicate and small, like the hands of a pianist.

But he played no music. He had been on the border for several years past and in that time had collected into his soul a portion of the dark bush that would never entirely leave him. You could see it in his face. Those close, unblinking eyes gazed out with a single stare, like that of a cyclops.

He despised us, I think. Not because we belonged to him, but because we were alive. From the time that he arrived, our tent was a different place. Every morning, at five a.m., we stood inspection. He would appear, promptly on time, as scrubbed and spruce as a man who'd been awake for hours. With an intense, demonic energy he would pass through our ranks, scrutinizing every surface for the smallest wisp of dust. Our rifles, newly-cleaned, would lie dismantled on our beds. Though our boots were clean, our shirts starched, he would contrive to find, in some cranny beyond the reach of our fingers, a trace of dirt that was our downfall. Then his clear, high voice would sing:

'PT!' he cried –

– and all of us were fumbling, in the half-dark, to change into shorts and vests. Under the rising sun we would

[40]

assemble, glowering in anticipation of what was to come. For two uninterrupted hours we were at his command: running round tents, rolling across the earth, doing push-ups. He stood by, devoid of emotion, watching our little strivings like a god. Eventually, bruised and cut, swimming with sweat, we were permitted to return to our tent.

He knew Daniels from before. On that first night – the night he arrived – he came walking down the central aisle of the tent, between the beds where we stood at rigid attention, and came to a stop in front of Daniels. There was a silence before he laughed, very softly, to himself.

'You,' he said. 'You.'

'Yes, Corporal.'

'*Wat maak jy hier?*'

'I was posted here, Corporal.'

'Ah,' said Cloete. 'Aha.' And he walked towards me, sucking his beautiful teeth.

After he'd left, vanishing into the night like a wraith, we crowded round Daniels. 'Where do you know him from? What's he like?'

But Daniels wouldn't answer. He only said, 'He also lives in Paarl,' and turned away to his chess-board, a solitary player tonight.

Soon after that, as we stood guard together at the gate of the camp, Daniels kicked at a stone in the road and said, 'I want to ask you something.'

'Mm?'

'Do you believe in revenge?'

'What do you mean,' I said, 'by *believe*?'

'Do you think there's something . . . holy about it?'

'No,' I said. 'No.'

I didn't know what he meant. The moon that night (our shift was late) was full; it shone above us, cold and

[41]

clear and white. All around us was the bush: unsleeping, black, the whispering skin of a continent.

Cloete hated Daniels. The hatred he had for the rest of us was general: the collective animosity he dispensed to the human race as a kind of benediction. But he hated Daniels with a very particular, highly inspired hate. 'Daniels is slacking, boys,' he would shout at PT. 'Another ten push-ups for all of you!'

Or: 'Daniels isn't drilling properly, *manne*. You can all take a run round the camp!'

He never spoke directly to Daniels. The punishments he inflicted on him were inflicted on all of us. When he referred to him, he did so in the third person, as though he wasn't present. Thus: 'Daniels hasn't prepared for inspection!'

Or: 'Daniels hasn't shaved properly! Ten star-jumps for every bristle I can find on his chin!'

And in time we all came to look on Daniels as the cause of our misfortune. In the tent at night, when Cloete had retired to his room, we would remonstrate with him: 'Daniels, come on . . . Pull your weight, man . . . Don't get us in shit, Daniels . . . .' Even I, his chess companion, had my say.

'You've got to try harder,' I told him.

He stared bitterly at me. 'I try,' he said.

'I *know*, but you've got to try more. Look,' I said, weakening, 'we all know it's not you. He's got it in for you, we can see that. But you've got to do better than us so he can't catch you out.'

'He's going to get me,' Daniels said. 'He's going to get me good.'

Daniels had harmed him in the past. This was clear to all of us. Some awful deed had taken place for which Corporal Cloete was exacting revenge. I tried to imagine what this deed might be: Daniels had crippled his brother. Daniels had stolen his car. Whenever these things crossed my mind, however, I would look across the tent at Daniels – sitting on his bed, alone in thought – and know that they couldn't be true.

Imagine, then, my surprise when I discovered that the cause of this relentless retribution was the thin and bloodless girl in the photograph he'd shown me.

'It's Ilana,' he confessed one night as we walked back together from the bar. 'She's the problem.' Three years before, Daniels had stolen Ilana from the clutches of Corporal Cloete – who was then not a corporal, but a boy down the street, the same age as Daniels. Stefan – for Cloete had a first name, I learned – had never forgotten.

It was bizarre: twelve of us, stuck out here in the wilderness, suffering endless persecution for the sake of this high school girl we'd never met.

'And I don't even love her,' moaned Daniels.

We walked on together through the dark.

Then came the patrol.

We had walked patrol before then; it was, of course, the reason for our presence in the camp. Laden with rucksack, radio, sleeping-bag and rifle, we would set out in small groups to prowl the veld. Walking silently, in a long sideways file, we tramped for miles through the dry waist-high grass. At night we slept in a circle, the corporal in the centre. These were longish missions – a week, sometimes – and we would always return to camp exhausted, battered, hollow with fear. Even the benign leadership of Corporal Retief could not lighten our load: if we encountered *them* as we walked on patrol, it was kill or be killed. Suddenly the enemy was a presence with a face, with a uniform like ours. Indeed, I had seen the face of this enemy several times: every now and then a group out on patrol would return, shepherding prisoners ahead of them with their rifles. These – the prisoners – were young black men, sweating as we did in the raw glare of sun. Their hands held high, their faces blank, they were taken to the cell at the heart of the camp; there, behind cold iron walls, they were interrogated one by one. Cries could be heard from that cell, echoing dimly through steel. It was not a good place.

Sometimes these men were brought in as corpses. Helicopters, rushing over the trees like birds, flew in and out with their gruesome cargo. I had seen these too: shattered bodies, stiff in death, unloaded like pigs from the side of the chopper. Consigned to black bags, they too were ferried away, but to where I never found out.

I had never had a contact on patrol. I dreaded this: the nameless exchange of shots in the dark. I was a poet, but I wanted nothing to do with death.

Cloete's first patrol. 'Six of you,' he said, grimacing with mirth,' are coming with me.'

Two days later we climbed aboard a chopper and were flown north-west, across the border into alien land. Daniels, of course, was with us; he sat beside me on the flight, his knee against mine. I believe he was trembling.

'*Is jy bang*, Daniels?' Cloete called. 'Are you scared?'

'No, Corporal,' Daniels muttered. We flew on.

We were dropped twenty kilometres into Angola, in an area that had been full of sporadic fighting the past week. As the helicopter flew off, trailing its sound behind it, the wide world opened about us, buzzing with insects and heat. I lay where I had hidden after dropping in the grass, one cheek pressed against an ant-hill. *Please*, I thought. *Don't let me die*.

[44]

'All right, *boytjies*,' Cloete said. 'Let's move.'

In a line, on booted feet, we tiptoed like dancers through the veld.

Three days later, a few hours before we were due to return: I raised my eyes to the horizon and saw above it a rising trail of smoke, like the fumes from a witches' coven. Then the radio hissed. An enemy encampment, surprised by our planes; it had happened barely ten minutes before. We were heading south, towards home and safety; this was not supposed to happen now.

It was just after dawn; the air was cool. The moon was up, a thumb-print on the sky. Our rifles held across our chests, we ran from bush to bush, bent double, carrying on our backs the invisible weight of death. Daniels was beside me.

Like our nightly bivouac, theirs was circular: in this formation, as if at the height of some obscure ritual, they'd died. It was not, as I've said, my first sight of corpses. But it was my first encounter with death so recently bestowed; the earth still smoked. They lay between trees, gnarled and seemingly hard, like coal discharged from the ground. One man (over whom I almost tripped) was still in his sleeping-bag, curled up like a foetus in eternal repose. There was a charred stench in the air.

'One alive here, Corporal!' Daniels' voice was trembling on the air.

'Don't let him move!'

As I too, approaching another of these bodies, saw life: a black hand scuttling like a crab across the stones. 'You!' I screamed, swinging my rifle up: we stared at each other down the shaft of steel.

He was blasted, hurt; his lower body red. His round

eyes, somehow, were yellow, like yolks in his head. 'Another here,' I called.

'Don't let him move!'

I stood, statuesque, in the hardening light, holding my rifle in my hands. The man below me was as still; lying propped on one arm, as if disturbed in bed, he watched my face with those amazing yellow eyes.

Behind my back, the scuffling ceased. They had scoured the area and found nobody near. Already poems were rising in me, winding what I'd witnessed into a mesh of words. Cloete crossed to me. He knelt beside me, peering into the black man's face. He looked lower, prodding at his leg. The eyes before me closed briefly, like a light snapping off. Cloete rose. He took his pistol from his holster. He flicked the catch. He shot the man in the centre of the forehead.

(Always I will see this: the body falling back, brains bright as coral.)

I stood, mesmerized, my useless rifle pointing, keeping watch over something senselessly departed, gone. The noise of the shot could not penetrate my skull.

'He was too badly wounded,' Cloete said.

He crossed to the other prisoner, lying, like mine, at Daniels' feet. Here too he knelt; performed his perfunctory examination. He stood again. The pistol was still in his hand; he pointed it. A pause. He lowered it once more.

'Daniels,' he said. 'Shoot him.'

'No,' Daniels said.

Cloete was turning away already, feigning indifference. He stopped in mid-stride, his back to Daniels.

'Shoot him,' he said.

'Please, Corporal . . . '

'I'm giving you an order.'

[46]

They faced each other now. We stood about them in a circle, silently, watching them.

'Shoot him,' said Cloete again, steadily.

Daniels pressed his rifle to the forehead of the man. He shot. A bird rose in terror from a tree nearby, whirring into the sky.

We left them there as we had found them and jogged away through the bush. *It doesn't matter*, I told myself; *nothing matters at all*. Our lives are gestures inscribed upon the void. Like flares fired up into the night, our arc burns brightly for a while, fades quickly, and goes out.

Revenge is a transaction: Cloete was finished with Daniels. After the incident on that first patrol (about which we never spoke), the persecution was over. We continued to stand inspection; we continued to suffer the punishment of PT; but these were never again inflicted in the name of Daniels. Corporal Cloete's enmity remained unchanged, but it had become impersonal: a prejudice directed at us all.

We walked patrol often after that, of course. I saw the action I had dreaded, and even wounded a man. But on these occasions we took our prisoners alive, and bumped them ahead of us into camp on the ends of our rifles.

I never played chess with Daniels again. We barely spoke, in fact, after that; but I woke once in the night and heard him crying. Time, the priest, absolves us all: the year went past like a season and we found ourselves dispersed once more, southward, become civilians overnight. I met Daniels a year or two after, in the bar of a small Transvaal town where he was a shop assistant and I had stopped overnight on my travels. He had been married, he told me, and divorced. 'To Ilana?' I asked.

'Who?' He blinked. 'Oh, her. No. No. To somebody else.'

We had a drink together; talked about our time up north. I had written many poems meanwhile, some of them published in literary magazines in Jo'burg. One of these – my first 'successful' poem – was about Daniels and that first patrol with Cloete. On impulse, feeling generous with booze, I scribbled it on the back of a serviette and passed it to him. He read it, frowning, then passed it back to me. 'No,' he kept saying. 'It wasn't like that.' I was drunk and irritable, and we parted on bad terms. As I recall it, he vanished down the road in the rain, while I lurched behind, telling him that poetry was beyond him. But I suspected, even then, he was right: it hadn't happened the way I'd written it, and there were things in life beyond the reach of words.

IN LOVE
WITH ARIADNE

William Trevor

Images cluster, fragments make up the whole. The first of Barney's memories is an upturned butter-box – that particular shape, narrower at the bottom. It's in a corner of the garden where the grass grows high, where there are poppies, and pinks among the stones that edge a flowerbed. A dog pants, its paws stretched out on the grass, its tongue trailing from its mouth. Barney picks the pinks and decorates the dog with them, sticking them into its brindle fur. 'Oh, you are bold!' The hem of the skirt is blue, the shoes black. The hat Barney has thrown off is placed again on his head. He has a stick shaped like a finger, bent in the middle. It is hard and shiny and he likes it because of that. The sunshine is hot on his skin. There is a baby's perspiration.

Barney's mother died three years after his birth, but even so his childhood was not unhappy. In the garden at Lisscrea there was Charlie Redmond to talk to, and Nuala was in the kitchen. *Dr G. T. Prenderville* the brass plate on the wall by the hall-door said, and all over the neighbourhood Barney's father was known for his patience and his kindness – a bulky man in a tweed suit, his greying hair brushed straight back, his forehead tanned, a watch-chain looped across his waistcoat. Charlie Redmond made up doggerel, and twice a day came to the kitchen for cups of tea, leaving behind him a basket of peas, or beetroot, or whatever was in season. Because of the slanderous nature of his doggerel, Nuala called him a holy terror.

Lisscrea House, standing by the roadside, was

covered with Virginia creeper. There were fields on one side and on the other the Mulpatricks' cottage. Beyond that was the Edderys' cottage, and an iron gate which separated it from Walsh's public house – single-storeyed and white-washed like the cottages. Opposite, across the road, were the ruins of a square tower, with brambles growing through them. A mile to the west was the Catholic church, behind white railings, with a shrine glorifying the Virgin just inside the gates. All the rooms at Lisscrea were long and narrow, each with a different, flowered wallpaper. In the hall the patients sat in a row of chairs that stretched beween the front door and the stairs, waiting silently until Dr Prenderville was ready. Sometimes a man would draw up a cart or trap outside, or dismount from a bicycle, and the doorbell would jangle urgently. 'Always listen carefully to what's said at the door,' Dr Prenderville instructed Nuala. 'If I'm out, write a message down.'

When Barney was seven he went to school in Ballinadra, waiting every morning on the road for Whelan's cart on its way to Ballinadra creamery with churns of milk. The bread van brought him back in the afternoon, and none of that changed until he was allowed to cycle – on Dr Prenderville's old Rudge with its saddle and handlebars lowered.

'Up the airy mountain,' Miss Bone's thin voice enunciated in the schoolroom. Her features were pale, and slight; her fingers stained red with ink. *There goes Miss Bone*, Charlie Redmond's cruel doggerel recorded, *She's always alone*. Miss Bone was tender-hearted and said to be in love with Mr Gargan, the school's headmaster, a married man. '*Quod erat demonstrandum*,' Mr Gargan regularly repeated in gravelly tones.

On the Sunday before he made the journey to school on the Rudge for the first time Barney found his father listening to the wireless in the drawing-room, a thing he never did on a Sunday morning. Nuala was standing in the doorway with a dishcloth in her hand, listening also. They'd have to buy in tea, she said because she'd heard it would be short, and Dr Prenderville said they'd have to keep the curtains drawn at night as a protection against being bombed from an aeroplane. Charlie Redmond had told Barney a few days before that the Germans ate black bread. The Germans were in league with the Italians, who ate stuff that looked like string. De Valera, Charlie Redmond said, would keep the country out of things.

The war that began then continued for the duration of Barney's time at school. Lisscrea was affected by the shortages that Nuala had anticipated; and De Valera did not surrender the will to remain at peace. It was during those years that Barney decided to follow in his father's and his grandfather's footsteps and become the doctor at Lisscrea.

'How're the digs?' Rouge Medlicott asked, and the Pole, Slovinski, again beckoned the waitress – not because he required more coffee but because he liked the look of her.

'Awful,' Barney said. 'I'm moving out.'

When he'd arrived in Dublin at the beginning of the term he found he had not been allocated a set of College rooms and had been obliged to settle for unsatisfactory lodgings in Dún Laoghaire. Greyhounds cluttered the stairs of this house, and broke into a general barking on imagined provocation. Two occupied a territory they had made their own beneath the dining-room table, their cold noses forever investigating whatever flesh they could find between the top of Barney's socks and

[53]

the turn-ups of his trousers. Rouge Medlicott and Slovinski shared College rooms and at night pursued amorous adventures in O'Connell Street, picking up girls who'd been left in the lurch outside cinemas or ice-cream parlours.

'Why doesn't she come to me?' Slovinski demanded crossly, still waving at the waitress.

'Because you're bloody ugly,' Medlicott replied.

Students filled the café. They shouted to one another across plates of iced buns, their books on the floor beside their chairs, their gowns thrown anywhere. Long, trailing scarves in black and white indicated the extroverts of the Boat Club. Scholars were recognized by their earnest eyes, sizars by their poverty. Nigerians didn't mix. There were tablefuls of engineers and medical practitioners of the future, botanists and historians and linguists, geographers and eager divinity students. Rouge Medlicott and Slovinski were of an older generation, two of the many ex-servicemen of that time. Among these were GI's and Canadians and Czechs, a couple of Scots, a solitary Egyptian, and balding Englishman who talked about Cecil Sharp or played bridge.

'You meet me tonight,' Slovinski suggested in a peremptory manner, having at last succeeded in summoning the waitress. 'What about tonight?'

'Tonight, sir?'

'We'll have oysters in Flynn's.'

'Oh God, you're shocking, sir!' cried the waitress, hurrying away.

Barney had got to know Slovinski and Rouge Medlicott through sitting next to them in biology lectures. He didn't think of them as friends exactly, but he enjoyed their company.

Medlicott had acquired his sobriquet because of the

colour of his hair, a quiff of which trailed languorously over his forehead. There was a hint of flamboyance in his attire – usually a green velvet suit and waistcoat, a green shirt and a bulky green tie. His shoes were of soft, pale suede. He was English, and notably good-looking. Slovinski was small and bald, and still wore military uniform – a shade of blue – which Medlicott claimed he had bought in a Lost Property office. Slovinski could play part of Beethoven's Fifth Symphony on his teeth, with his thumbnails.

'I heard of digs,' Medlicott said, 'out near the Zoo. That Dutch fellow was after them, only he decided to go back to Holland instead.'

It was in this casual way that Barney first came to hear about Gogarty Street, and that evening he went out to inspect the lodgings. A woman with an orange-powdered face and waved black hair, kept tidy beneath a net, opened the door to him. A discreet smear of lipstick outlined her lips, and there was a hint of eye-shadow beneath her myopic-seeming eyes. She was wearing a flowered overall, which she apologized for as she removed it in the hall. Beneath was a navy-blue skirt and a cream-coloured blouse that had a fox-terrier brooch pinned to it. She folded the overall and placed it on the hallstand. Normally she would not take in boarders, she explained, but the house was too large, really, for herself and her mother and her daughter, just the three of them. A pity to have rooms and not use them, a pity to have them empty. The trouble was that smaller houses were usually not in districts she cared for. She led the way upstairs while still speaking about the house and household. 'It's a residence that's been in the Lenehan family for three generations,' she said. 'That's another consideration.'

The door of a room on the second floor was opened.

'Fusty,' Mrs Lenehan said, and crossed to the window. The bed was narrow, the bedstead of ornamental iron. There was a wash-stand with an enamel basin on it and a shaving mirror above it on the wall. There was a wardrobe, a chest of drawers, two holy pictures, and a chair. Patterned, worn linoleum partially covered the floor, leaving a darkly varnished surround. There were net curtains and a blind.

'The bathroom and WC are off the landing below,' Mrs Lenehan said. In Mr Lenehan's childhood there were two maids and a cook in this house, she went on, and in her own day there'd always been a single maid at least, and a scrubbing woman once a fortnight. Now you couldn't get a servant for love nor money. She noticed Barney glancing at the fireplace, which contained an arrangement of red tissue-paper. She said that in the old days there'd have been a fire laid in the grate every morning and coal blazing cheerfully every evening. Now, of course, that was out of the question. 'Thirty shillings would be fair, would it? Breakfast and six p.m. tea, the extra meal on a Sunday.'

Barney said he thought thirty shillings was a reasonable rent for what was offered.

'Of a Friday evening, Mr Prenderville. In advance would be fair, I think.'

'Yes, it would.'

'Best to have a clear arrangement, I always say. No chance for misunderstandings.'

Two days later Barney moved in. When he'd unpacked his suitcases and was waiting for the gong which Mrs Lenehan had told him would sound at six o'clock there was a knock on his door. 'I'm Ariadne,' Mrs Lenehan's daughter said, standing in the doorway with a bar of yellow soap in her hand. 'My mother said give you this.' She was dark-haired, about the same age as

[56]

Barney. The rather long mauve dress she wore was trimmed with black, and snowy-white beads were looped several times around her neck. Her lips were painted, her hands and wrists delicately slender. Large brown eyes surveyed Barney frankly and with curiosity.

'Thanks very much,' he said, taking the bar of soap from her.

She nodded vaguely, seeming to be no longer interested in him. Quietly she closed the door, and he listened to her footfall on the stairs. As light as gossamer, he said to himself. He was aware of a pleasurable sensation, a tingling on the skin of his head. The girl had brought to the room a whiff of perfume, and it remained after she'd gone. Barney wanted to close the window to keep it with him, but he also wanted just to stand there.

The sounding of the gong roused him from this pleasant reverie. He had never much cared for the appearance of the girls – women sometimes – whom Medlicott and Slovinski admired in cafés or on the streets. Ariadne was different. There was an old-fashioned air about her, and an unusualness. As well, Barney considered her beautiful.

'Fennerty's the name,' a small, jaunty old woman said in the dining-room. Wiry white hair grew tidily on a flat-looking head; eyes like beads peered at Barney. 'Fennerty's the name,' she repeated. 'Mrs Lenehan's mother.'

Barney told her who he was. The last occupant of his room had been employed in Clery's bed-linen department, she replied, a youth called Con Malley from Carlow. Now that someone had replaced him, the house would again be full. There had been difficulty in regularly extracting the rent from Con Malley. 'Mrs Lenehan won't tolerate anything less than promptness,' the old woman warned.

A man of about fifty, wearing a navy-blue belted overcoat and tan gloves, entered the dining-room. 'How're you, Mr Sheehy?' Mrs Fennerty enquired.

Divesting himself of his coat and gloves and placing them on the seat of a chair by the door, the man replied that he wasn't so good. He had a sharply receding chin, with features that had a receding look about them also, and closely clipped hair, nondescript as to colour. The removal of his coat revealed a brown pin-striped suit, with a row of pens and pencils clipped into the top pocket, and a tiny badge, hardly noticeable, in the left lapel. This proclaimed Mr Sheehy's teetotalism, the emblem of the Pioneer movement.

'I had a bad debt,' Mr Sheehy said, sitting down at the table. Mrs Fennerty vacated a rexine-covered arm-chair by the fire and took her place also. Ariadne entered with a laden tray, and placed plates of fried food in front of the three diners. Mrs Fennerty said the thick York-shire Relish had been finished the evening before, and when Ariadne returned to the dining-room a minute or so later with a metal teapot she brought a bottle of Yorkshire Relish as well. Neither she nor her mother joined the others at the dining-table.

'Did you know Mattie Higgins?' Mr Sheehy enquired of Mrs Fennerty. When he spoke he kept his teeth trapped behind his thin lips, as though nervous of their exposure. 'I sold him a wireless set. Three pounds fifteen. I had the price agreed with him, only when I brought it round all he had was a five-pound note. "I'll have that broken into tonight," he said. "Come back in the morning." Only didn't he die that night in his bed?'

Swiftly, the old woman crossed herself. 'You got caught with that one,' she said.

'I was round there at eight o'clock this morning, only the place was in the hands of five big daughters. When I mentioned the wireless they ate the face off of me. A good Pye wireless gone west.'

Mrs Fennerty, still consuming her food, glanced across the room at the radio on the dumb waiter in a corner. 'Is it a Pye Mrs Lenehan has?'

'It is.'

'I heard the Pye's the best.'

'I told that to the daughters. The one I sold him had only a few fag burns on the cabinet. The five of them laughed at me.'

'I know the type.'

'Five fat vultures, and your man still warming the bed.'

'Strumpets.'

The rest of the meal was taken in a silence that wasn't broken until Ariadne came to clear the table. 'I meant to have told you,' she remarked to Barney, 'your window gets stuck at the top.'

He said it didn't matter. He had noticed her mother opening the bottom sash in preference to the top one, he added conversationally. It didn't matter in the least, he said.

'The top's stuck with paint,' Ariadne said.

Mrs Fennerty returned to her place by the fire. Mr Sheehy put on his navy-blue overcoat and his gloves and sat on the chair by the door. Skilfully, with the glass held at an angle, Mrs Fennerty poured out a bottle of stout that had been placed in the fender to warm. On her invitation, accompanied by a warning concerning hasty digestion, Barney occupied the second rexine-covered armchair, feeling too shy to disobey. Mrs Fennerty lit a cigarette. She was a boarder the same as Mr Sheehy, she said. She paid her way, Mrs Lenehan's mother or not. That was why she sat down in the dining-room with Mr Sheehy and whomever the third boarder happened to be.

'Are you at Dowding's?' She referred to a commercial college that offered courses in accountancy and book-keeping, preparing its students for the bank and brewery examinations.

'No. Not Dowding's.' He explained that he was a medical student.

'A doctor buries his mistakes. Did you ever hear that one?' Mrs Fennerty laughed shrilly, and in a sociable way Barney laughed himself. Mr Sheehy remained impassive by the door. Barney wondered why he had taken up a position there, with his coat and gloves on.

'Six feet under, no questions asked,' Mrs Fennerty remarked, again laughing noisily.

Dressed to go out, Mrs Lenehan entered the dining-room, and Mr Sheehy's behaviour was explained. He rose to his feet, and when the pair had gone Mrs Fennerty said, 'Those two are doing a line. Up to the McKee Barracks every evening. Sheehy wouldn't part with the price of anything else. Turn round at the barracks, back by the Guards' Depot. Then he's down in the kitchen with her. That's Ned Sheehy for you.'

Barney nodded, not much interested in Mr Sheehy's courtship of Mrs Lenehan. Nevertheless the subject was pursued. 'Ned Sheehy has a post with the Hibernian Insurance. That's how he'd be selling wireless sets to people. He calls in at houses a lot.'

'I see.'

'He's keen on houses all right. It's the house we're sitting in he has designs on, not Mrs Lenehan at all.'

'Oh, I'm sure—'

'If there's a man in Dublin that knows his bricks and

mortar better than Ned Sheehy give me a gander at him.'

Barney said he didn't think he could supply the old woman with such a person, and she said that of course he couldn't. No flies on Ned Sheehy, she said, in spite of what you might think to look at him.

'She made a mistake the first time and she'll make another before she's finished. You could turn that one's head like the wind would turn a weathercock.'

Ariadne came in with the *Evening Herald* and handed it to her grandmother. Barney smiled at her, but she didn't notice. Mrs Fennerty became engrossed in the newspaper. Barney went upstairs.

In time, he heard footsteps in the room above his, and knew they were Ariadne's. They crossed the room to the window. The blind was drawn down. Ariadne crossed the room again, back and forth, back and forth. He knew when she took her shoes off.

Handwritten notes clamoured for attention on the green baize of the board beside the porters' lodge: love letters, brief lines of rejection, relationships terminated, charges of treachery, a stranger's admiration confessed. The same envelope remained on the baize-covered board for months: *R. R. Woodley*, it said, but R. R. Woodley either did not exist or had long since ceased to be an undergraduate. *It is hard to find myself the way I am, and to be alone with not a soul to turn to*: a heart was laid bare within the dust-soiled envelope, its ache revealed to the general curiosity. But other notes, on torn half sheets of exercise-paper remained on the green board for only a few hours, disappearing for ever while they were still fresh.

Within their fire-warmed lodge the porters were a

suspicious breed of men, well used to attempted cir-
cumvention of the law that began where their own rule
did. They wore black velvet jockey caps; one carried a
mace on ceremonial occasions. They saw to it that
bicycles were wheeled through the vast archway they
guarded, and that female undergraduates passed in and
out during the permitted hours only, that their book
was signed when this was necessary. In the archway
itself, posters advertised dances and theatrical produc-
tions. Eminent visitors were announced. Societies' account sheets were published. There were reports of
missionary work in Africa.

Beyond this entrance, dark façades loomed around a
cobbled square. Loops of chain protected tidily shorn
lawns. The Chapel stared stolidly at the pillars of the
Examination Hall. Gold numerals lightened the blue
face of the Dining Hall clock. A campanile rose fussily.

Barney attended the lectures of Bore McGusty and
Professor Makepeace-Green and the elderly Dr Posse,
who had been in the medical school in his father's time.
Bore McGusty was a long-winded young man, Professor Makepeace-Green a tetchily severe woman, who
particularly objected to Slovinski reading the *Daily
Sketch* during her lectures. The students of Barney's
age keenly took notes and paid attention, but the recent
shedding of years of discipline by the ex-servicemen left
them careless of their academic obligations. 'Listen,'
Slovinski regularly invited, interrupting Bore McGusty's dissertation on the functioning of the bile-ducts by
playing Beethoven on his teeth.

The medical students favoured certain public
houses: the International Bar, Ryan's in Duke Street,
McFadden's. After an evening's drinking they danced
in the Crystal Ballroom, or sat around pots of tea in the
café attached to the Green Cinema, where the private

lives of their mentors were breezily speculated upon, and for the most part scorned. On such occasions Slovinski spoke of his wartime liaisons, and Medlicott retailed the appetites of a baker's widow, a Mrs Claudia Rigg of Bournemouth. For Barney – years later – this time in his life was as minutely preserved as his childhood at Lisscrea. And always, at the heart of the memory, was Mrs Lenehan's household in Gogarty Street.

'You've maybe not come across the name Ariadne before,' Mrs Lenehan said one morning in the hall, adding that she'd found it in a story in *Model Housekeeping*. Had a son been born instead of a daughter he'd have been christened Paul, that being a family name on her own side. As soon as she'd seen *Ariadne* written down she'd settled for it.

Barney liked the name also. He thought it suited Mrs Lenehan's daughter, whom increasingly he found himself thinking about, particularly during the lectures of Bore McGusty and Professor Makepeace-Green. Ariadne, he soon discovered, didn't go out to work; her work was in her mother's house and it was there, during the lectures, that he imagined her. She assisted with the cleaning and the preparation of meals, and the washing-up afterwards. She was often on the stairs with a dustpan and brush; she polished the brass on the front door. Every morning she set the dining-room fire, and lit it every evening. Once in a while she and her mother cleaned the windows.

Mrs Lenehan occasionally sang while she performed her household tasks. Ariadne didn't. There was no trace of reluctance in her expression, only a kind of vagueness: she had the look of a saint, Barney found himself thinking once, and the thought remained with him. In the dining-room he was usually the last to finish breakfast, deliberately dawdling. Ariadne came in with a tray and, seeing him still at the table, absorbed the time by damping the fire down with wet slack and picking up the mantelpiece ornaments and dusting them. Her elegant hands were as delicate as the porcelain she attended to, and her clothes never varied: the same shade of mauve combined repeatedly with mourner's black. 'Good evening, Mr Prenderville,' she sometimes whispered in the dusk of the hall, a fleeting figure passing from one closed door to another.

After he'd been in the lodgings a month Barney was familiar with every movement in the room above his. When Ariadne left it and did not return within a few minutes he said to himself that she was washing her hair, which he imagined wrapped in a towel, the way Nuala wrapped hers before she sat down to dry it at the range. He imagined the glow of an electric fire on Ariadne's long, damp tresses. Staring at a discoloured ceiling, he invaded per privacy, investing every sound she made with his speculations. Would she be sewing or embroidering, as Nuala did in the evenings? Nuala pressed flowers between the pages of the medical encyclopaedia in the dining-room at Lisscrea, pansies and primulas she asked Charlie Redmond to bring from the gardens. Barney wondered if Ariadne did that also. He guessed the moment when she lay down to sleep, and lay in the darkness himself, accompanying her to oblivion.

He didn't tell Rouge Medlicott and Slovinski, or anyone else, about Ariadne. In his letters to his father he mentioned Mrs Lenehan and Mrs Fennerty and Mr Sheehy: Ariadne mightn't have existed. Yet in the noisy cafés and the lecture-halls he continued to feel haunted by her, and wished she was there also. He left the house in Gogarty Streeet reluctantly each morning, and hurried back to it in the evenings.

'Ariadne.'

He addressed her on the first-floor landing one Sunday afternoon. His voice was little more than a whisper; they were shadows in the dim afternoon light. 'Ariadne,' he said again, delighting, while they were alone, in this repetition of her name.

'Yes, Mr Prenderville?'

Mrs Lenehan and Mr Sheehy spent Sunday afternoons with Mrs Fennerty in the dining-room, listening to the radio commentary on a hurling or Gaelic football match, the only time the dining-room wireless was ever turned on. When it was over Mr Sheehy and Mrs Lenehan went to the kitchen.

'Would you like to come for a walk, Ariadne?'

She did not reply at once. He gazed through the gloom, hoping for the gleam of her smile. From the dining-room came the faint sound of the commentator's rapid, excited voice. Ariadne didn't smile. She said:

'This minute, Mr Prenderville?'

'If you are doing nothing better.'

'I will put on my coat.'

He thought of her mother and Mr Sheehy as he waited. He didn't know which direction the McKee Barracks and the Civic Guards' Depot lay in, but wherever these places were he didn't want even to see them in the distance. 'I'm ready,' Ariadne said, having delayed for no longer than a minute. Barney opened the front door softly, and softly closed it behind them. Damp autumn leaves lay thickly on the pavements, blown into mounds and heaps. When the wind gusted, more

[65]

slipped from the branches above them and gently descended. Ariadne's coat was another shade of mauve, matching her headscarf. There'd been no need to leave the house in that secret way, but they had done so nonetheless, without exchanging a look.

'I love Sunday,' Ariadne said.

He said he liked the day also. He told her about Sundays at Lisscrea because he didn't know how else to interest her. His father and he would sit reading in the drawing-room on a winter's afternoon, or in the garden in the summer. Nuala would bring them tea, and a cake made the day before. His father read books that were sent to him by post from a lending library in Dublin, novels by A. E. W. Mason and E. Phillips Oppenheim and Sapper. Once, laying one down when he had finished it, he changed his mind and handed it to Barney. 'Try this,' he said, and after that they shared the books that came by post. Barney was fourteen or fifteen then.

'Your mother is not there, Mr Prenderville?'

'My mother died.'

He described Lisscrea to her: the long, narrow rooms of the house, the garden where Charlie Redmond had worked for as long as Barney could remember, the patients in the hall. He mentioned the cottages next to Lisscrea House, and Walsh's public house, and the ruined tower he could see from his bedroom window. He repeated a piece of Charlie Redmond's doggerel, and described his prematurely wizened features and Nuala's countrywoman's looks. He told Ariadne about school at Ballinadra, the journey on the milk cart when he was small, the return by the bread van in the afternoon, and then the inheriting of his father's old Rudge bicycle. She'd never known a town like Ballinadra, Ariadne said; she only knew Dublin.

'It isn't much,' he said, but she wanted to know, and

he tried to make a picture of the place for her: the single street and the square, O'Kevin's hardware, the grocers' shops that were bars as well, the statue to the men of '98.

'A quiet place,' Ariadne said.

'Oh, a grave.'

She nodded solemnly. She could see the house, she said. She knew what he meant by Virginia creeper. She could see his father clearly.

'What would you have done if I hadn't suggested a walk?'

'Stayed in my room.'

'Doing nothing, Ariadne?' He spoke lightly, almost teasing her. But she was still solemn and did not smile. Maybe tidying her drawers, she said. She called him Mr Prenderville again, and he asked her not to. 'My name's Barney.'

'Just Barney?'

'Barney Gregory.'

Again she nodded. They walked in silence. He said, 'Will you always help your mother in the house?'

'What else would I do?'

He didn't know. He wanted to suggest some work that was worthy of her, something better than carrying trays of food to the dining-room and sweeping the staircarpet. Even work in a shop was more dignified than what she did, but he did not mention a shop. 'Perhaps a nurse.'

'I would be frightened to be a nurse. I'd be no good at it.'

'I'm sure you would, Ariadne.'

She would care tenderly. Her gentleness would be a blessing. Her beauty would cheer the melancholy of the ill.

'Nuns are better at all that,' she said.

'Did you go to a convent, Ariadne?'

She nodded, and for a moment seemed lost in the memory the question inspired. When she spoke again her voice, for the first time, was eager. 'Will we walk to the convent, Barney? It isn't far away.'

'If you would like to.'

'We have to turn right when we come to Prussia Street.'

No one was about. The front doors of the houses they walked by were tightly closed against the world. Their footsteps were deadened by the sodden leaves.

'I like that colour you wear,' he said.

'An aunt left me her clothes.'

'An aunt?'

'A great-aunt, Aunt Loretta. Half of them she never wore. She loved that colour.'

'It suits you.'

'She used to say that.'

That was why her dresses, and the coat she wore now, were rather long for her. It was her clothes that gave her her old-fashioned air. Had she no clothes of her own? he wondered, but did not ask.

The convent was a cement building with silver-coloured railings in front of it. The blinds were drawn down in several of its windows; lace curtains ensured privacy in the others. A brass letter-box and knocker gleamed on a green side-door.

'Did you walk here every morning?' he asked.

'When I was small my father used to take me. It wasn't out of his way.'

She went on talking about that, and he formed a picture of her childhood, just as, a few months ago, she had of his. He saw her, hand in hand with her father, hurrying through the early-morning streets. Her father had worked in Maguire's coal office in East Street.

Sometimes they'd call in at a shop for his tobacco, half an ounce of Digger.

When they crossed the street he wanted to take her arm, but he didn't have the courage. They could walk to a bus stop, he suggested, and wait for a bus to O'Connell Street. They could have tea somewhere, one of the cinema cafés that were open on a Sunday. But she shook her head. She'd have to be getting back, she said.

They turned and walked the way they'd come, past the silent houses. A drizzle began. They didn't say much else.

'God, there's talent for you!' Medlicott exclaimed in the Crystal Ballroom, surveying the girls who stood against the walls. Slovinski conveyed a willowy woman of uncertain age on to the dance-floor, from which, a few minutes later, they disappeared and did not return. Some of the girls who were standing about glanced back at Medlicott, clearly considering him handsome. He approached a lean-featured one with hair the colour of newly polished brass, not at all pretty, Barney considered.

Because he had no knowledge of dance-steps, the partners Barney chose usually excused themselves after a minute or two. 'What line are you in?' a plump one, more tolerant than the others, enquired. He said he worked in a dry-cleaner's, Slovinski having warned him not to mention being a student in case the girls took fright. 'You can't dance,' the plump girl observed and commenced to teach him.

When the end of the evening came she was still doing so. Medlicott had remained attached to the lean-featured girl, whom he confidently reported he had 'got going'. Outside the dance-hall Barney heard him com-

plimenting her on her eyes, and felt embarrassed because he didn't want to have to tell the plump girl that
she, too, had lovely eyes, which wouldn't have been
true.

Instead, he asked her her name. 'Mavis,' she said.

Medlicott suggested that they should go out to Goatstown in a taxi, since the city bars were closed by now.
There were fields in Goatstown, he reminded his companions: after they'd had a couple of nightcaps they
could go for a walk through the fields in the moonlight.
But Mavis said her father would skin her if she got in
late. She took Barney's arm. Her father was fierce-
tempered, she confided.

The lean-faced girl didn't want to make the journey to
Goatstown either, so Medlicott led her into an alleyway.
They kissed one another in a doorway while Mavis and
Barney stood some distance away. When her father
went wild, Mavis said, nothing could hold him. 'All
right,' Barney heard the lean-faced girl say.

A battered Ford car was parked at the far end of the
alleyway next to a skip full of builders' rubble. Medlicott and his companion approached it, she teetering on
gold-coloured high heels. Medlicott opened one of the
back doors. 'Come on in here, darling,' he invited.

It was difficult to know what to say to Mavis, so
Barney didn't say anything. She talked about her brothers and sisters; half listening, he imagined Ariadne at
Lisscrea. He imagined being engaged to her, and introducing her to Nuala in the kitchen and Charlie Redmond in the garden. He saw himself walking along the
road with her, and waiting while she attended mass in
the nearby church. He showed her Ballinadra – the
rudimentary shops, the statue to the men of '98 in the
square.

He glanced at the car and caught a glimpse of brassy

hair through the back window. He would introduce her to the tender-hearted Miss Bone. He imagined Miss Bone dismounting from her bicycle outside O'Kevin's hardware. 'Welcome to Ballinadra, Ariadne,' she murmured in her gentle voice.

Three men had turned into the alleyway, and a moment later shouting began. A door of the car was wrenched open; clothing was seized and flung out. One of the lean girl's gold-coloured shoes bounced over the surface of the alleyway, coming to rest near the skip. 'Get that hooer out of my car,' a voice furiously commanded.

In spite of what was happening, Barney couldn't properly detach himself from his thoughts. He walked with Ariadne, from the town to Lisscrea House. On the way he showed her the Lackens' farm and the hayshed where the Black and Tans had murdered a father and a son, and the ramshackle house at the end of a long avenue, where the bread van used to call every day when he got a lift in it back from school, where mad Mrs Joyce lived. Weeds flowered on the verges; it must have been summer.

'Get out of that bloody car!' The garments that lay on the ground were pitched into the skip, with the shoe. Medlicott called out incomprehensibly, a humorous observation by the sound of it. 'D'you want your neck broken?' the same man shouted back at him. 'Get out of my property.'

'I'm off,' Mavis said, and Barney walked with her to her bus stop, not properly listening while she told him that a girl who would enter a motor-car as easily as that would come to an unsavoury end. 'I'll look out for you in the Crystal,' she promised before they parted.

On the journey back to Gogarty Street Barney was accompanied by an impression, as from a fantasy, of

Mavis's plump body, breasts pressed against his chest, a knee touching one of his, the warm perspiration of her palm. Such physical intimacy was not the kind he had ever associated with Ariadne, but as he approached his lodgings he knew he could not let the night pass without the greater reality of seeing her face, without – even for an instant – being again in her company.

When he arrived at Mrs Lenehan's house he continued to ascend the stairs after he'd reached the landing off which his room lay. Any moment a light might come on, he thought; any moment he would stand exposed and have to pretend he had made a mistake. But the darkness continued, and he switched on no lights himself. Softly, he turned the handle of the door above his, and closed it, standing with his back to the panels. He could see nothing, but so close did the unspoken relationship feel that he half expected to hear his name whispered. That did not happen; he could not hear even the sound of breathing. He remained where he stood, prepared to do so for however many hours might pass before streaks of light showed on either side of the window blinds. He gazed at where he knew the bed must be, confirmed in his conjecture by the creeping twilight. He waited, with all the passion he possessed pressed into a longing to glimpse the features he had come to love. He would go at once then. One day, in some happy future, he would tell Ariadne of this night of adoration.

But as the room took form – the wardrobe, the bed, the wash-stand, the chest of drawers – he sensed, even before he could discern more than these outlines, that he was alone. No sleeping face rewarded his patience, no dark hair lay on the pillow. The window blinds were not drawn down. The bed was orderly, and covered. The room was tidy, as though abandoned.

Before the arrival of Professor Makepeace-Green the following morning, the episode in the alleyway and Slovinski's swift spiriting away of the willowy woman from the dance-hall floor were retailed. Barney was commiserated with because he had failed to take his chances. Rouge Medlicott and Slovinski, and several other ex-servicemen, gave him advice as to amorous advancement in the future. His preoccupied mood went unnoticed.

That evening, it was the old woman who told him. When he remarked upon Ariadne's absence in the dining-room she said their future needs in this respect would be attended to by a maid called Biddy whom Mrs Lenehan was in the process of employing. When he asked her where Ariadne had gone she said that Ariadne had always been religious.

'Religious?'

'Ariadne's working in the kitchen of the convent.'

Mr Sheehy came into the dining-room and removed his navy-blue overcoat and his tan gloves. A few minutes later Mrs Lenehan placed the plates of fried food in front of her lodgers, and then returned with the metal teapot. Mr Sheehy spoke of the houses he had visited during the day, in his capacity as agent for the Hibernian Insurance Company. Mrs Lenehan put her mother's bottle of stout to warm in the fender.

'Is Ariadne not going to live here any more?' Barney asked Mrs Fennerty when Mr Sheehy and Mrs Lenehan had gone out for their walk to the McKee Barracks.

'I'd say she'll stop in the convent now. Ariadne always liked that convent.'

'I know.'

Mrs Fennerty lit her evening cigarette. It was to be expected, she said. It was not a surprise.

'That she should go there?'

'After you took Ariadne out, Barney. You follow what I mean?'

He said he didn't. She nodded, fresh thoughts agreeing with what she had already stated. She poured her stout. She had never called him Barney before.

'It's called going out, Barney. Even if it's nothing very much.'

'Yes, but what's that to do with her working in the convent?'

'She didn't tell you about Lenehan? She didn't mention her father, Barney?'

'Yes, she did.'

'She didn't tell you he took his life?' The old woman crossed herself, her gesture as swift as it always was when she made it. She continued to pour her stout, expertly draining it down the side of the glass.

'No, she didn't tell me that.'

'When Ariadne was ten years old her father took his life in an upstairs room.'

'Why did he do that, Mrs Fennerty?'

'He was not a man I ever liked.' Again she paused, as though to dwell privately upon her aversion to her late son-in-law. 'Shame is the state Ariadne lives in.'

'Shame?'

'Can you remember when you were ten, Barney?'

He nodded. It was something they had in common, he'd said to Ariadne, that for both of them a parent had died. Any child had affection for a father, Mrs Fennerty was saying.

'Why did Mr Lenehan take his life?'

Mrs Fennerty did not reply. She sipped her stout. She stared into the glow of the fire, then threw her cigarette end into it. She said Mr Lenehan had feared arrest.

'Arrest?' he repeated, stupidly.

[74]

'There was an incident on a tram.' Again the old woman blessed herself. Her jauntiness had left her. She repeated what she'd told him the first evening he sat with her: that her daughter was a fool where men were concerned. 'At that time people looked at Ariadne on the street. When the girls at the convent shunned her the nuns were nice to her. She's never fogotten that.'

'What kind of an incident, Mrs Fennerty?'

'A child on a tram. They have expressions for that kind of thing. I don't even like to know them.'

He felt cold, even though he was close to the fire. It was as though he had been told, not of the death of Ariadne's father but of her own. He wished he had taken her arm when they went for their walk. He wished she'd said yes when he'd suggested they should have tea in a cinema café. Not so long ago he hadn't even known she existed, yet now he couldn't imagine not loving her.

'It would have been no good, Barney.'

He asked her what she meant, but she didn't answer. He knew anyway. It would have been no good because what seemed like a marvel of strangeness in Ariadne was damage wrought by shame. She had sensed his love, and fear had come, possibly revulsion. She would have hated it if he'd taken her arm, even if he'd danced with her, as he had with Mavis.

'Ariadne'll stay there always now,' the old woman said, sipping more of her stout. Delicately, she wiped a smear of foam from her lips. It was a silver lining that there'd been the convent kitchen to go to, that the same nuns were there to be good to her.

'She'd still be here if I hadn't taken the room.'

'You were the first young man, Barney. You couldn't be held to blame.'

When Barney returned to Dublin from Lisscrea at the

beginning of his second term he found, unexpectedly, that he had been allocated College rooms. He explained that in Gogarty Street, and Mrs Lenehan said it couldn't be helped. 'Mr Sheehy and myself are getting married,' she added in the hall.

Barney said he was glad, which was not untrue. Mr Sheehy had been drawn towards a woman's property; for her part, Mrs Lenehan needed more than a man could offer her on walks to the McKee Barracks. Mrs Lenehan had survived the past; she had not been damaged; second time round, she had settled for Mr Sheehy.

In the dining-room he said goodbye to Mrs Fennerty. There was a new young clerk in Ned Sheehy's office who was looking for digs, she said. He would take the vacant room, it wouldn't be empty for long. A student called Browder had moved into Ariadne's a week or so after her going. It hadn't been empty for long either.

It was snowing that evening. Huge flakes clung to Barney's overcoat as he walked to the convent, alone in the silence of the streets. Since Ariadne's going he had endlessly loitered by the convent, but its windows were always blank, as they were on that Sunday afternoon. Tonight, a dim light burned above the green side-door, but no curtain twitched as he scanned the grey façade, no footsteps disturbed the white expanse beyond the railings. In the depths of the ugly building were the strangeness and the beauty as he had known them, and for a moment he experienced what was left of his passion: a useless longing to change the circumstances there had been.

While he was still in Mrs Lenehan's house he had thought that somehow he might rescue Ariadne. It was a romantic urge, potent before love began to turn into regret. He had imagined himself ringing the convent bell, and again seeing Ariadne's face. He had imagined himself smiling at her with all the gentleness he possessed, and walking again with her; and persuading her, when time had passed, that love was possible. 'You'll get over her,' his father had said in the holidays, guessing only that there had been some girl.

A bus creeps through the snow: years later, for Barney, there is that image, a fragment in the cluster that makes the whole. It belongs with the upturned butter-box in the grass and the pinks in the brindle hair of the dog, with Rouge Medlicott and Slovinski, and the jockey-capped porters, and the blue-faced Dining Hall clock. A lone figure stares out into the blurred night, hating the good sense that draws him away from loitering gloomily outside a convent.

LAVEE, LAGAIR, LAMORE, LAMAIRD

Laura Kalpakian

The morning Mabel Judd left for France, bunting billowed from the railroad cars and the station roof; the high school band oompahed lustily while recruiters for the Red Cross and the Army, as well as the city council, the Mormon bishop and the Methodist pastor took turns addressing the crowd on behalf of sacrifice, unstinting valour and Liberty Bonds. Their words caught on the same dry breeze that fluttered the American flag, intertwining it symbolically with a makeshift French tricolour and a British Union Jack. Admittedly, Mabel Judd looked rather odd amongst her France-bound compatriots: three dozen youths '... the cream of St Elmo's young manhood ...,' who had volunteered to fight the Hun Over There and about a half-dozen volunteer nurses, girls of good character. Mabel looked odd because her character was (by St Elmo standards) questionable and by no means could she be considered a girl. Fortyish, stout, clad in a stiff blue travelling suit, she wore an out-of-date hat with a long rusty plume that blew about in the desert wind, occasionally tickling the cheeks of those who stood closest to her. Her face was round, reminiscent of a fishbowl, the effect enhanced by thick glasses over her heavy-hooded eyes. She listened to the speakers impassively, as though neither the grand words, nor the solemnity of the occasion, nor the prospects of War itself moved her beyond her usual expression – benign, distracted, unsuitably wistful for a woman her age.

Her sister and brother-in-law and several of their

children and grandchildren (the youngest a babe in arms) had brought Mabel to the station that morning in the clattering family Dodge and they stood by her, listened attentively, clapping when applause was indicated. Mabel's sister (universally known as Dumpling) held her baby grandson, but cast baleful glances towards her fifteen-year-old daughter Cordelia who had shamelessly thrown herself into the arms of Eldon Whickham, one of the departing recruits. Dumpling also kept an eye on her youngest son, Clarence, who, at seventeen seemed ready to bolt towards the Army recruiter so that he too might be showered with flowers, bathed with praise, kisses and tears from the bevy of admiring maidens. That her son should go Over There was not on Dumpling's agenda. If someone in the family must court death (for that's how Dumpling saw it), then let it be Mabel. The thought made Dumpling sniffle and shifting the baby to her other ample hip, she took her sister's arm. 'Oh Mabel, if only Pa and Ma were here to see you. They'd be so proud of you.'

'I think Miss Savage would be proud of me too. I think Miss Savage would be glad to know that finally, thirty years later, I can put her teaching towards a noble cause. At last I'm going to get to speak French.'

'I'm just sure Pa and Ma are looking down from heaven on you this very day, Mabel,' Dumpling replied, returning to her initial premise.

'Yes, and probably Miss Savage is dead too by now. You suppose she's looking down from heaven too, Sarah?'

'Probably not the same heaven,' said Dumpling dubiously.

'Heaven is a singular place,' Mabel informed her, 'not plural.'

Theological hair-splitting was not Dumpling's forte. She said, 'We're all very proud of your sacrifice, Mabel.'

'I haven't made any sacrifice. Yet,' she added as an afterthought.

'Yes, Mabel,' Roy chimed in, 'we'll, all of us, the family, the church, we'll remember you in our prayers every day. It's a long long way to Tipperary.'

'About six thousand miles,' she replied, speaking over the band's rendition of this very tune.

Irritated, Roy made an awkward noise, privately cheering the war, any war for that matter, that would spare him Dumpling's eternal dithering over her unmarried sister, that could relieve him of the unstated, but very real burden of Mabel Judd's presence in his family.

The mother of one of the nurse-volunteers came up to them, her daughter, Ellie, in tow. Her face awash with tears, Bertha Dewitt embraced Mabel and begged her to look after Ellie. 'Oh Mabel, you'll be her friend and companion, won't you? You'll look after Ellie. Oh, all those foreigners! My heart breaks!'

Mabel cast a frankly appraising glance to the twenty-three-year-old Ellie. Clearly, Ellie's heart was not breaking. Mabel turned to Bertha. 'In France we will be the foreigners, Bertha. And don't forget the war.'

'Oh, this terrible, terrible war!' cried Bertha, who, since 1914 had scarcely read beyond the headlines before confidently tucking her *St Elmo Gazette* at the bottom of her canary's cage. Even after the April announcement of America's entry into the war, the European conflict remained mercifully distant till Ellie announced she was volunteering to be a Red Cross nurse, spurred romantically on by the uplifting song, 'The Rose of No Man's Land'. Naturally Bertha (like every other parent of these girls of good character) had forbade her daughter even to think of such a thing. No unmarried girl of good character could dream of handling men's bodies, even men's blasted, bloodied bodies. But in wartime, values change; at least Ellie's values changed, Bertha's did not. 'Oh Mabel, I hope I can rely on you to look after Ellie and –'

'You can't,' Mabel replied without blinking. (Dumpling always shuddered when her sister was so cruelly blunt.) 'I am going to France as part of the war effort, to translate for the Allies and I shall certainly not have time to think of Ellie. You know I'm the only person in this town who can speak French, impeccable French, thanks to our governess, Miss Savage. Isn't that right, Sarah?'

Dumpling murmured something vaguely affirmative. Bertha Dewitt who, as a married woman had every right to feel superior to Mabel Judd and who (democratically) sniffed at the very idea of a French-speaking governess, muttered something dubious, snatched Ellie's elbow and led her away through the crowd.

'Oh Mabel,' Dumpling moaned, 'did you have to say it just like that?'

'Like what? Was Bertha offended?'

The train whistle sliced through Mabel's question as well as the Mormon bishop's concluding remarks and for an instant, before the high school band launched into 'The Battle Hymn of the Republic', the buzz of conversation and farewell ceased and the platform was eerily quiet. Then the weeping began in earnest. The boys shouldered their new kitbags and began boarding the bunting-draped train (especially provided as a patriotic gesture on the part of the railroad). This train would take the recruits and Red Cross volunteers to Los Angeles where they would be put on yet other trains, eventually on boats, braving the submarine-infested waters of the Atlantic to arrive in war-ravaged Europe where they would make short work of the horrible Hun. Railway workers began stripping bunting from the cars. The look of manly pride in the eyes of the young men faltered; second thoughts flashed across the faces of the Red Cross volunteers, but they all got on the train just the same.

Dumpling flung herself against her sister till Roy extricated her and Mabel gave them all (including the baby) a perfunctory kiss and hug. She refused Roy's offer to carry her bag on board with the observation that in wartime women must shoulder new responsibilities as well as their own bags. She stepped aboard.

'Oh Roy,' Dumpling wept against her husband, squeezing the baby between them as Mabel's back vanished into the car. 'What if Mabel dies Over There?'

Roy patted her back ineffectually. 'She going to translate, Dumpling, not to fight.'

'But so much can happen in wartime.'

'Not to Mabel Judd,' he replied with rather more emphasis than need be. 'Nothing ever happened to her and nothing ever will.'

'But what if she dies?' Dumpling wailed. 'You know how the church feels about . . .' She daubed the baby's head where tears had fallen, '. . . marriage, Roy. I mean if Mabel dies unmarried, she won't . . . she can't . . . she'll be denied the Celestial Kingdom.'

'Oh, that. Well, who knows, Dumpling? Maybe she'll get married.' He chuckled. 'A wartime romance. Why, just look at all these good Mormon boys in uniform!'

Dumpling drew away from him indignantly. 'How can you make fun of my sister? How can you say such a cruel thing when Mabel is making sacrifices for her country and –'

'All I'm saying is that whatever your sister had to sacrifice, she gave it up a long time ago.'

The whistle split the air again and the train heaved to life, its wheels making those first uncertain revolutions forward, gathering courage and conviction slowly. Just then Mabel Judd stuck her head out the window, the silly plume in her hat twitching in the wind and cried out, 'Goodbye St Elmo! Hello Paree!'

Prior to that day in January, 1918, Mabel Judd was the librarian at the St Elmo Public Library, a post she had held for many years and an occupation which suited her since she was educated, bookish, organized, unmarried and required to earn her own bread. That she should be unmarried was odd because, particularly in the days of Mabel's youth, men outnumbered women in St Elmo two to one, and even a plain girl could count on two or three (equally plain and probably poor) suitors, but suitors nonetheless. Mabel's spinsterhood was all the more remarkable because she was a Mormon; for Mormons, marriage is the only state imaginable, as much an edict as an institution. Mabel's family was poor and they were not a clan graced with beauty, but neither poverty nor plainness stopped her sisters from marrying. Nothing stops a Mormon girl from marrying. Before each of them was twenty, the other Judd girls all wed: Agnes to the feckless Zeke (eight children), Molly to the dour Willis (six children) and Sarah to Roy who worked for the railroad and who had dubbed her early on with the name Dumpling and by whom she had five children.

When Mabel was young (and even then, blunt and bookish) friends and relatives would inquire lightly when she intended to marry, citing (sometimes subtly, sometimes not) her duty to God and to all the little souls awaiting bodies which she could endow them with once she was properly wed. To these inquiries, Mabel inevitably replied that she had her eyes on Higher Things (which accounts perhaps for her slightly befuddled expression). Whatever these Higher Things were, no one else in St Elmo could see them and gradually Mabel passed into ossified eccentricity, the object of both mirth and pity. Mabel alone seemed unaware of her incongruous, anomalous, impossible situation in the family, the church, the community itself.

Mabel worked at the library and, until their deaths, lived with her parents, Ephraim and Leona, in their little rented house on C Street. When they died, rather than moving in with one of her married sisters, or taking a room in some respectable boarding-house, Mabel continued to live alone in the C Street house. That house was destroyed in the terrible floods of 1917 and even then Mabel declined the shelter of her sisters' roofs. She moved the few things she'd salvaged from the flood into the back room of the library, set up a cot and lived there. She worked day and night to redeem the flood-ravaged books; she had few needs and fewer wants, so she was happy.

By August of 1917, the Library Board decided she could not live there any more, but not until September did they muster enough courage to give Mabel Judd sixty days' notice, which she ignored. When, more forcefully, in November, the Library Board members came to call (after hours so as to spare everyone embarrassment), they softened their outrage saying they would be happy to find suitable accommodation for a maiden lady. Mabel heard them out and then announced she would be giving up her post, that she had volunteered to use her command of the French language for the betterment of the Allied Cause against the Hun. They didn't believe her. She assured them it was so, saying (as she had said to the recruiting officer – having anticipated his objections) that the Allies could ill afford to spurn her contribution merely on the basis of her age and sex.

When she announced her decision to her sisters and their husbands, they were unanimously aghast and declared she could not go. In her bland, blunt way, Mabel reminded them she had not asked for their approval. She added, 'Of course I am eager to use my abilities and education to defeat the brutal Hun, but I must say, I'm looking forward to seeing England and France. Miss Savage believed in me and I want to –'

'Don't say that woman's name in my hearing!' cried Agnes. 'Don't mention that – that –' Agnes glanced to Molly and Sarah to supply the word, but even their faces were mute. Agnes coloured and concluded grandly, 'I can't bear to hear that name.'

As the eldest of the Judd girls, Agnes could well remember the day the impecunious Miss Savage entered their young lives. Agnes was seventeen when the girls and their mother, dressed in their finest, had driven the family rig down the single street of Leona, California to the dock at the gold mine to meet the supply train that came thrice-weekly bearing food, water, mail, payroll for the miners, liquor for the two saloons, and any other necessary contact between this distant desert and the rest of the world. Any passengers had to squeeze themselves behind the engineer and the stoker because the narrow-gauge train only pulled a few supply cars, boasted no particular place for passengers, but then, not many people came to Leona, California. The sounds of this thrice-weekly train, its clank and rattle, were the only punctuation to the incessant thump and throttle of the smelting mill, and the gold mine which beat through the desert air sunup to sundown like a doleful tattoo. It sounded behind Leona Judd and her four daughters now as they got out of the rig and walked up the platform to the unshaded dock to await the train.

That Leona Judd should take the rig to meet the train was itself worthy of note. That she should take her four daughters with her was virtually a civic event. Leona Judd made every effort to shield her daughters from the rough and tumble life of this desert mining town, never mind the town bore her name, as did the gold mine itself, as did the Dry Goods store and the boarding-house run by Mrs Skaggs, wife of the mine foreman. Naturally the saloons and the grimy cafe were not graced with Leona's name. However, Leona, California was strictly a man's town, populated by a few inscrutable leftover Indians, a handful of insidious Chinese and a great many miners, men who worked hard, drank hard, lived hard and occasionally shot one another in brawls contesting the affections of a handful of whores who – other than Mrs Skaggs, Mrs Judd and the four Judd girls – were the only white women in town. So new, so raw, so committed to gold was Leona, California, there was not even a church, Mormon or otherwise and certainly there was no school. Even if there had been, Leona Judd could not possibly have sent her daughters, (monied young women with gilded prospects) to be educated with the children of the unsavoury Indians, the heathen Chinese and the vulgar brats begot upon the whores. Clearly, the daughters of Ephraim and Leona Judd required an education suitable to their gilded prospects and through the mails, the services of Miss Savage of San Francisco had been engaged.

Standing on the loading dock that day in 1887, Leona

[89]

and her four daughters watched the supply train coming into view from a far distance, the sight wavering, slippery, silvery, slick as mercury in the waves of heat, congealing finally into discernible shape which could only with certainty be called a train when the clack and rattle could be heard, snapping down the narrow gauge tracks. The train heaved in and disgorged its single passenger who climbed down the ladder, carrying a carpet-bag and muttering, 'Bloody hell. Bloody heat,' as she alighted on the dock. She turned and looked at the five of them gathered there, blushed very slightly at her oath and then, tossing her skirt emphatically behind her in a theatrical manner, strode up to Leona with the words, 'Mrs Judd, I presume.'

Still rather undone by the unmistakable oath, Leona murmured in the affirmative.

'And these are the girls?'

Leona nodded. 'Miss Savage?'

'Who else?'

Never in all their limited lives had the Judd women beheld anyone quite like her. Of indeterminate age, Miss Savage was not particularly small, but so pathetically thin and bony that she seemed tiny and the substantial Judd women appeared to tower over her. She had a small, sharp face, sharp nose, sharp, hollowed-out cheekbones, sharp little teeth in her small mouth. Her brown eyes were shrewd and from beneath her flamboyant (and now dust and cinder-crêped) hat, she had a crop of the reddest hair imaginable.

Miss Savage appraised them quickly, from the seventeen-year-old Agnes to the nearly twelve-year-old Mabel. She turned from them and rested her gaze on the desert which lay in every direction, the hot, wavering landscape encircled by very distant mountains which looked like black ash heaps smouldering in the

white distance. Her eyes travelled back along the track
that stretched into the uncertain past and then down
towards the collation of frame buildings, shacks, the
single street that constituted the town of Leona. She
brought her gaze back to the family and to the rhyth-
mically thumping, throttling mine and mill emblazoned
with faded, ornate lettering, LEONA GOLD MINE. She
was visibly, grossly, grievously disappointed.

'Have you had a tiring journey, Miss Savage?' asked
Leona.

'How could it be otherwise?' Miss Savage replied in a
manner the Judds would come to recognize: whenever
possible, Miss Savage answered questions with yet
another question.

In the family rig (Leona, Mabel and Miss Savage in
front; the other girls in the back) they drove down the
single dusty street, past the Leona Gold Mine offices,
the Leona Room and Board, the Leona Post Office,
Telegraph and Land Claims, past the Golden Grotto
Cafe and the Gold Camp Laundry (both of these run by
Chinese), past the Golden Nugget Saloon and the
Golden Floss Saloon (this last named in honour of a
misunderstood Golden Fleece), but for all the insist-
ence on metallurgic substance, all that glittered here
was not gold. All that glittered were dust motes, raised
by the rig as it traversed the unpaved street. Dust
gleamed golden in the sunlight as Miss Savage and the
Judds rolled past tin-roofed shacks and blanket-doored
lean-tos and the other squat, hastily assembled buildings that sheltered Indians, pigtailed Chinese and miners, many of whom loitered in what shade there was to
be had, squatting, smoking, spitting. 'Vulgar,' Miss
Savage announced.

'Ain't it?' said Mabel, breathing in the scent of Miss
Savage's cologne, overripe and fruity despite the dust

and dirt of travel. 'That's our house, down yonder. Best house in the whole town.'

'In the whole county,' added Leona before the obvious *that's not saying much* could be uttered.

They pulled into view of a grand, galleried, rambling, two-storied wedding cake of a house, set so high off the ground a dozen shallow steps led to the broad porch, its roof upheld by eight slender white posts, grooved and lovingly worked with pineapple formations at the tops. The cornices and balustrade of the roof and balcony were festooned with intricate bric-a-brac, half-hubs of lacy wheels, so elaborate one might have believed them spiders' webs worked in wood. The eight windows fronting the street were graced not only with real glass, but pale lace curtains and the door was heavy with bevelled, leaded glass that caught the light and ricocheted it everywhere.

A Chinese servant came out to hold the horse and rig while the ladies stepped down and went inside, Mabel hurtling forward to be the one to hold the door for Miss Savage. 'My Pa and Ma say nothing's too good for us,' said Mabel, ushering the governess into the large foyer, complete with gilded mirror and a coat tree of smooth, polished mahogany and bin for workingmen's boots. Miss Savage regarded the boots in the bin. 'Bourgeois,' she declared.

She moved into the parlour, decorated with huge potted palms and rich red velvet tasselled valances over the lace curtains in the windows. In open contradiction to the unmerciful heat, the Judds' parlour testified to the best of taste, everything clothed, dripping, mantled in gold tasselled velvet hangings, the red velvet settee and matching chairs equally gold tasselled; gold tassels framing the mantel while the obese legs of the grand piano were shrouded beneath a white silk shawl, also hung with gold tassels. Miss Savage flipped open the keyboard and fingered out a little tune. 'Lovely,' she remarked.

Agnes was instructed to lead Miss Savage to her room and the other three followed in tow as they walked down the long hall towards the kitchen where they encountered a pigtailed Chinese man plucking a singed pullet and chattering to a virtually genderless Chinese woman peeling potatoes. The smell of burnt feathers lingered in the kitchen. Miss Savage wrinkled her nose. 'Disgusting,' she stated unequivocally.

Off the kitchen, they opened the door to a small room papered in a faded gay rosebud print with a narrow bed, a spindly washstand and a wardrobe with a cracked mirror. Miss Savage walked directly to the window and pulled aside the thin curtains which offered a view of the back porch jutting off the kitchen, a shack sheltering the washtub (also used for bathing), the privy, a clothesline strung between the shed that housed the horse and buggy and another shed where the Chinese servants slept, as well as a shaded chicken-house and rabbithutch. Miss Savage turned back and regarded her room. 'Adequate,' she said, baring her small white teeth.

As was his custom, Ephraim Judd came home for the midday meal. Although he owned the gold mine, Ephraim still wore heavy boots (which he threw into the boot bin and donned a more genteel pair of shoes), thick workingman's pants and a collarless cotton shirt. He put on a collar and washed the ink and dirt from his hands before he was introduced to Miss Savage. Ephraim Judd was an unlikely rich man. Genial, tolerant, shiftless in his youth, his slack ways and uncertain means had been the bane of his thrifty Mormon family. Ironically, his very lack of character and Mormon convictions had made him rich. He had won the gold mine in a poker game in Ma Grant's Saloon and Pleasure Palace eighteen years before, playing a gnarled prospector named Fitzhenry who had hunkered over this claim for years, shooting at all comers, reduced finally to gambling in a desperate attempt to secure more capital so that he might wrap his scrawny hands around veins of gold. But the winning cards that day were in the loose, lazy rawboned hands of Ephraim Judd.

Of course Ephraim could never so much as indicate to his Mormon relatives that he had been playing cards in Ma Grant's Saloon and Pleasure Palace and he put off their inquiries with vague references to hard work and self-denial, which indeed were qualities he came to practise once he got the gold mine. The full weight of his Mormon ancestry rose up within him and he was, in a manner of speaking, transformed by his wealth into an upright, hard-working, thrifty, steadfast man. On the basis of that single hand of cards, he not only got the gold mine, but sufficient prospects to ask Leona's father for her hand in marriage and thus claim the girl he had always loved. He named the mine and the town after her. For the first two years they lived in the mine office; then they moved to one of the tin-roofed shacks, thence to a clapboard house with a real cookstove and glass windows. They had moved into their fabulous white wedding cake of a home when their youngest, Mabel, was three. Mabel remembered nothing of the earlier hardscrabble life and the rest of them quickly forgot.

For all his easygoing ways, Ephraim Judd was shrewd enough to hire (and pay well) the skilled mining engineer Skaggs to oversee the day-to-day operations of the mine and later, the mill. Ephraim was respected by his miners and beloved by his family; he had no airs and no affectations and for a man whose mine brought in several hundred thousand yearly, he still sometimes put his food into his mouth with his knife rather than his fork. A fact Miss Savage did not fail to note.

'I'd no idea you were this isolated,' said Miss Savage in her crisp curling accent as the Chinese woman collected their plates and delivered dessert, a pudding of doubtful origin.

'Not nearly as isolated as we used to be before the telegraph,' said Leona.

'I can see your daughters are certainly in need of education befitting the children of a man who owns a gold mine.' Miss Savage was appalled as she spoke these words to see Ephraim rub his nose with his napkin. 'Otherwise, they would be forced to marry miners.'

'Forced?' Leona's voice quavered slightly.

'Of course. A girl with money but wanting suitable education, refinements and accoutrements, a girl who can neither play the piano, nor speak French, nor draw, a girl who knows no poetry or literature, who lacks manners and postures and social graces, who else can such a girl marry except a miner?' Miss Savage took a petite uncertain bite of the pudding. 'She could marry a drover, I suppose. A clerk, possibly. A railroad man might suit. A farmer wouldn't be out of the question. A –'

'Oh no,' said Leona hastily. 'That would never do. Our girls must marry well.'

'Latter-day Saint men,' Ephraim added with an internal nod to his ancestors.

Leona was not as committed to the faith of her mythical sons-in-law as she was to their prospects. 'We want our daughters to choose their husbands from the very best society.'

'Exactly,' Miss Savage daubed her lips. 'I hope you will not think me too bold if I suggest we begin today.'

[95]

'Oh, Miss Savage, you must rest today. It's such a tiring journey and –'

'I intend to rest today. I was not referring to beginning legitimate instruction today.' (She said the word 'legitimate' with a sort of fierce affection.) 'I meant I hoped you would not mind if I say to Molly that her elbows do not belong on the table, that Agnes ought not to bite her nails and Sarah ought not to chew her hair. Sit up, Mabel. You must sit up straight and carry yourself with a posture commensurate with your expectations in life.'

'What?' said the gawky Mabel.

'You will never be a tall woman. That much is clear. You might as well get used to enhancing what you have. Sit up straight. Shoulders set. Do not allow your back to touch the chair. Carriage. Courage.' Miss Savage turned to Leona. 'I have a motto, Mrs Judd, by which I have instructed girls of the best society from London to San Francisco.'

'London? England?' said Agnes breathlessly.

'Isn't London the only civilized city in the world?'

''Zat why your voice sounds so, so funny and curlied up?' Molly asked.

'That is why your voices sound so funny – and flat – to me,' Miss Savage replied coolly. 'Your remark, Molly, further illustrates your need for suitable education. I shall imbue you all with my motto.'

'And what's that?' asked Ephraim, leaning back gracelessly in his chair and picking his teeth with his fingernail.

'That young ladies may best advance themselves in this world by keeping their backs straight, their mouths shut and their eyes on Higher Things.' With that, Miss Savage rose, excused herself and left the family dumbstruck in the dining-room, with only the constant thrump and throttle of the mine and the mill echoing gently through the open windows.

Beginning the very next day, the life of the entire Judd family underwent an often painful, resoundingly thorough reconstruction. The woman who had been hired to provide the niceties for the daughters, refitted them all to their prospects in life and in the course of this undertaking assumed – usurped – a power within the family not at all in keeping with her hired status. Miss Savage was critical, high-handed, demanding and unfailingly correct. Should Leona Judd be so bold as to object to the governess's plans, methods, goals, values or assumptions, Miss Savage bowed immediately to Mrs Judd's judgement. Then, within the course of the next few hours, Miss Savage found occasion to refer (in passing) to miners, drovers, clerks, railroad men, farmers and the like, whereupon Leona inevitably took her aside and said that she had rethought whatever was under discussion and clearly, clearly Miss Savage was right.

Ephraim was too tolerant and malleable to object outright, but he resisted Miss Savage in his own way with the result that within three months of her arrival, the Judd girls too were appalled at his table manners, though in keeping with the Savage motto, they kept their mouths shut.

The girls themselves never got the hang of Mama and Papa and continued to address their parents as Ma and Pa, but on the whole they were obliging pupils and followed the Savage regime dutifully. They practised their scales on the piano and worked over the sole piece of music in the house, 'The Battle Hymn of the Republic'. 'The Battle Hymn' practised by each of the four girls in turn wafted through the house and out the open windows to the street, punctuated by the thrump and roar of the mine and the mill and the thrice-weekly clank and rattle of the supply train. His Truth Went Marching On.

If the Judd girls had heretofore been innocent of music, they were equally innocent of literature, the sole books in the home being the usual hoary tomes: the Bible, the Book of Mormon, the Doctrine and Covenants. Early on Miss Savage presented Mrs Judd with a very long list of books to be ordered from St Elmo and brought in by the supply train. (And brought to the house in three separate trips with the rig, the Chinese servants and a couple of miners heaving and perspiring under the heavy crates.) To begin with, the girls did not read these books. They walked with them. They lined up and walked back and forth across the gold-tasselled parlour with books on their heads so as to perfect their posture, while, acceding to the metronomic drumbeat of Miss Savage's ruler, they recited English poetry, particularly Scott's 'Young Lochinvar' and Shelley's 'Ozymandias'. They had not the least idea what the latter was about and only Mabel cared. Even Miss Savage did not seem to care. She stated emphatically that a lady need not understand poems, only recite them, that the ability to pull a line of poetry quickly from a seemingly endless well of erudition was the mark of a lady and that these lines could be used to cover virtually any sort of situation. 'Like what?' asked Mabel.

'Time enough for that,' replied Miss Savage while her ruler beat time against her hand and the girls continued to march up and down the room, reciting with the books upon their heads. 'Remember your rhythm, remember your cues,' Miss Savage intoned.

So from nine to one and then again from two-thirty to five on any given day, one girl thumped out 'The Battle

Hymn of the Republic', while, sitting, rising, walking with books on their heads, the other three chanted 'Young Lochinvar' and 'Ozymandias' and the house had the air of a persistent dress rehearsal for some monumental production that never quite came to pass.

In art, Miss Savage pronounced them hopeless and curtailed instruction in watercolour after their first outdoor painting expedition when she fainted from heat prostration and the girls returned dehydrated and spent. Miss Savage had to be helped to her bed where the girls hovered around wringing out wet cloths for her head. 'The art of painting will have to wait till you have perfected other things,' said Miss Savage still in the grip of a killing headache. 'Besides, in this vile climate, this beastly desert, there are no colours. There's only white sand and white sky and grey mountains and pale dust. Everywhere. How can you paint what's not there? Where are your colours? I ask you?' (She always phrased her statements as questions.) 'Where are your delphiniums? Where are your daffodils? Where are your tulips and peonies and primroses? Where are your poppies? Where are your lilacs and lilies? Where?'

The girls did not know where. The Judd girls would not have recognized these flowers, nor their colours, if they had suddenly marched down the main street of Leona, California, stalk by stalk. The girls shrugged. Miss Savage, even lying heat-prostrated, flattened by the bloody heat and aridity, admonished them for shrugging. 'A lady never shrugs. It's bourgeois.'

The Judd parlour served for piano, posture and recitation. The dining-room served as schoolroom with Miss Savage usurping Ephraim's place at the head of the table and the girls lined up, the two oldest on one side, Mabel and Sarah on the other. Here they studied English literature (the only literature worth knowing)

[99]

and the French language (the only language worth speaking). French, Miss Savage was fond of asserting, is the single accoutrement essential to anyone who would call herself a civilized being. She went on to catalogue the many accomplishments of the French race, adding that they had managed to achieve all this despite their being Catholics.

'What's that got to do with it?' asked Sarah.

'It means they have no morals,' Miss Savage declared. 'They simply confess their vile acts to the priest and think themselves forgiven, so naturally they have no morals and Sarah, the next time I see you put your hair to your lips, I shall call in the cook – with his cleaver – and instruct him to chop off your hair at the neck. Is that understood?'

Miss Savage used no text in her French instruction, but relied upon the same principles of memorization and recitation she brought to 'Young Lochinvar'. She began with polite greetings and had the girls address one another till they had got it right. Then she moved on to polite conversation, most of which (at first) consisted of observations on the weather and asking to be passed certain items present at the table. She gradually moved on to forms of address, directions, descriptions and increasingly convolute expressions of feeling and taste, pleasure and displeasure, affirmative and negative. She perpetually prefaced her French lessons with the injunction, 'Inflection and conviction! Inflection and conviction are everything!' She kept the ruler always handy to snap at the girl who was deficient in one or both.

Only Mabel seemed to have the necessary ear and quickness of tongue to correctly inflect and convict. Miss Savage approved of Mabel. Her approval was worth having. Ruler in hand she instructed the other girls to emulate Mabel's pronunciation, 'Toot Sweet, Agnes! Metnaw!'

At the end of one particularly dispiriting session, Agnes skulked away from the dining room table muttering unflattering aspersions on her youngest sister, on the French, on the learning of French, on Miss Savage's French in particular. Swiftly, as though galvanized by an electric current, Miss Savage (and her ruler) came between the girls and the door. 'You have forgotten the central tenet of our motto, Agnes. You have forgotten to keep your mouth shut. Whatever you may think,' (she said this last word with a kind of mocking asperity), 'silence is the better part of valour. Keep your own counsel. One's own thoughts, one's own words never enhance a lady. Are you blind, Agnes? Are you so dismally deficient, all of you, that you fail to understand *why* I have waxed such efforts that you should know poetry? That you should recite? That you should have at your disposal any number of appropriate, oblique well-known phrases?' Abashed, the girls did not reply; by this time they knew Miss Savage did not expect replies, that she clad her wolf-like demands in the sheep's clothing of questions. 'Never speak your own words when someone else's will do. Never betray your feelings or your ignorance. Never allow your heart or mind to act quicker than your tongue. No one in society does that sort of thing,' she added, cooling somewhat. 'It's bourgeois.'

February, 1918
Enroute to Europe

Dearest Sarah, Roy, and family,

Last night I dreamed of Ozymandias. I recited it in my dream and heard the mine and mill behind my voice, but I could not see them. I could not see Miss

Savage either, but I am certain she was there, as we were all there, four of us as we were in our precious youth. How strange it is that as I traverse these treacherous seas, I should be drawn back to our desert girlhood. Though, perhaps, not strange at all. At last I shall see Miss Savage's England. At last I shall see France, but not alas, the France of yore, but embattled France. Pray for France and Victory.

'Frogs,' said Roy.
'What?'
'Mabel's asking us to pray for Frogs, ain't she?'
'For victory, I think,' said Dumpling, scrutinizing her sister's letter more carefully. Maybe Roy was right and there was something she had missed.
'Don't Aunt Mabel have anything to say about the boys on the ship? You know, the soldiers?' asked Cordelia, gnawing a piece of cornbread.
'I haven't finished the letter yet,' her mother replied.
'Don't she even ask about us here at home?' said Clarence.
'Mabel's going to the Western Front!' cried Dumpling. 'How can St Elmo compare to that?'
'Now, Dumpling,' Roy said genially, 'no need to get angry with Clarence. Just read on.'

If the Hun has his way, we shall all go down in the watery deep, but our cause is just and true and I shall trust in God to keep us safe from U boats, trust I shall mail this letter from English soil, that green and glorious, emerald isle we only imagined as we listened to Miss Savage read to us. The only other translator is a man so I am billeted here on the ship with four young Red Cross volunteers from Michigan who think my enthusiasm unwarranted and faintly comic.

How can I tell them they are too young, too callow, to
know that we shall soon be walking on the very soil
that nourished Shakespeare and Shelley, the very
fabric of literature itself.

'You'd think Aunt Mabel's going on the stage, 'stead of
going to war,' Clarence observed.

'Mabel doesn't know anything about war,' said Dumpling, 'but she knows literature. We never had any
history when we were growing up because Miss Savage
said that what people did was vulgar. It was what they
thought and imagined that was important,' she added
with a little grimace; Dumpling was unaccustomed to
voicing her own thoughts.

'Pass me another fritter there, Clarence,' said Roy. 'If
you ask me, all you Judd girls woulda been a lot better
off if your Pa and Ma had sent you to school like regular
folks. 'Course in those days, you weren't regular folks,
were you?'

Dumpling shrugged and glanced out the window, to
the scrap of brown lawn and, the squat oleander that
graced her frontyard. She paraphrased the rest of the
letter and slid it in her pocket, closing her eyes for a
single moment, sharing with Mabel, the dream and
memory of their precious youths, their desert girl-
hoods, saw her parents' dining-room, the lace curtains
blowing back with the inferno breeze, the black ash
mountains in the white unbroken distance, the thump
and throttle of the mill and mine, the sand blowing gold
off the unpaved street and Miss Savage transporting
them far far from gold and brass and fire, from the
smelter, the squalor, carrying them on the tide of her
declamatory voice, propelling the girls to the lush leas of
England where meadows and moors rolled down to
turgid, slow-moving rivers, green and thick with water

lilies and heavy-boughed willows wept into the water, to the brawny, wild mountains of Scotland where Sir Walter Scott characters fought and roved and loved, to the swarming fetid streets of Dickens' London: Miss Savage, regaling them with the unquenchable vivacity of her ringing voice, fictionally instructing them in the ties of obligation and responsibility that bound king to subject, captain to clown, Miss Savage tearing her hair, smiting her breast as she recited Lear's speech on the wild heath.

'I shall assume you are literate,' said Miss Savage, embarking on their first lesson in literature after the three crates of books had arrived from St Elmo. 'Am I correct?'

The girls nodded in unison. If the words weren't too big, it was a fair assumption that they were literate.

'Very well. We shall dispense with reading and begin enhancing your listening skills. All young ladies who wish to marry into good society must be accomplished listeners. The ability to listen well is concomitant to keeping one's mouth shut, is it not?' (The girls all nodded.) 'Elbows off the table, Molly. In the vulgar parlance, one might be said to keep one's ears open and one's mouth shut. Agnes, would you like to listen with the Book of Mormon on your head?'

'No.'

'No?'

'No, Miss Savage.'

'Then sit up straight or you certainly shall. Carriage. Courage. They go together. Now, listen.'

They listened. Miss Savage did not simply read. Miss Savage enacted, declaimed, incited the girls to tears and laughter, sighs and exquisite, unbearable tension as she

made her way through the works of Scott, the Bröntes,
Dickens, Thackeray and Shakespeare. They were in
thrall to the power of the governess's voice, to her
flawless inflection and conviction. She never formally
concluded these classes. She simply came to the close of
an appropriately dramatic chapter and closed up the
book, left it on the table; tossing her skirt theatrically
behind her, she exited the dining-room as though gas
light flickered, as though applause and a descending
curtain would certainly follow. Every time.

One afternoon when Miss Savage had been in their
employ for nearly a year, Ephraim Judd was consider-
ably surprised to see Leona marching up the street of
the town that bore her name, directly into his office
adjacent to the thumping mine and throttling mill that
likewise bore her name. She burst in, closed the door
behind her, flung herself in a chair and began to weep
for a full five minutes before Ephraim could console her
into telling him the problem.

'Unthinkable!' she gasped. 'Horrible! With my own
ears, Father! Our daughters' virtue, Father! She is –'

'What happened, Mother?'

'I was walking past the dining-room and I heard her
reading to them, some piece of – of filth! Something
about a woman who had a son for her cradle before she
had a husband for her bed! And I stepped right in and I
said, "Miss Savage, really! This is not the sort of thing
for young ladies!" And you know what she did, Father?'

Ephraim shook his head, removed his glasses, and
rubbed the bridge of his nose.

'She gave me one of her awful looks. Her awful, awful
looks. Oh, I hate that look, Father! You know how she
raises one lip so you can see her horrible little white
teeth? And she says to me, "*King Lear*".'

'King who?'

'Lear. Shakespeare. She said it was Shakespeare and I wasn't to interrupt till she got to the end of the first act and I was being rude and vulgar – I tell you, it's got to stop!'

'Well, you do what you think best, Mother.'

'You tell her.'

'Tell her what?' Ephraim swung in his squealing chair, away from the rolltop desk cluttered with ledgers and oceans of papers, accounts due on emblazoned stationery bearing the names of faraway firms.

'You are the head of the family. You dismiss her.'

'It's true, she ain't exactly a pleasure to have around the house.'

'She's a – she makes me feel . . . she makes us look . . .'

'Well, she's done some good, Mother. Agnes don't chew her nails anymore.'

'She dipped Agnes's hands in ground pepper.'

'And Sarah don't bite her hair.'

'She called Wu Chan in with his cleaver to cut it off. She actually let that heathen lift his cleaver over the neck of our daughter!'

'Well, I'm sure you're right, Mother. I don't have too much experience with young ladies, 'cept for you, Mother, and you're just about perfect.' He winked affectionately.

Leona gave him a wan smile. 'Maybe it's time to see the proof of the pudding, Father. Maybe it's time to take the girls into society.'

'Where would that be, Mother?'

'Well, somewhere. Somewhere where there's society and all that. The girls are accomplished. We have money. Maybe it's time for husbands.'

'Mabel's mighty young for a husband, Mother. She's only thirteen.'

'Agnes is eighteen.'

'Well, you and me didn't marry till you was almost twenty-one.'

'But I was *waiting* for you, Ephraim. Agnes has to meet someone before she can fall in love. Anyway,' Leona sniffed, 'Mabel's the one I worry about most. Mabel adores Miss Savage. Just adores her.'

'Well, she'll get over that. Mabel's a sensible girl. Now, I think if I was to worry, I'd worry about Sarah. I took Sarah to the Dry Goods t'other day and asked her to tally a few things and bless me if she couldn't add.'

'Adding is bourgeois. It's not a refinement,' said Leona, unthinkingly quoting Miss Savage.

'Well, that may be. Like I say, I don't know much about what ladies do. What do they do, Mother?' he asked earnestly. 'I mean, 'sides play 'The Battle Hymn of the Republic' and talk about Young Lochinvar coming out of the west. What do you reckon these girls are going to do with all this learning?'

'They're going to get married, of course. They're going into society and meet rich young men and marry them.'

'Well, yes, but what then?'

'I don't know what you mean!' she replied so as to make it clear that she knew exactly what he meant and she refused to comment.

'I don't mean that.' Ephraim's tanned leathery face crinkled into a blush. 'I mean – why're we educating them up like this? What're they going to do with French? Why don't they read them books 'stead of carrying them on their heads?'

'Well, I – they –' Leona's own background had not exactly fitted her for such a question. The daughter of a St Elmo livery stable worker, her girlhood had certainly not been graced with French and Young Lochinvar. Leona had gone to school like other children, but like most girls, her real education took place at home: canning fruit, rolling dough, mixing mush, boiling, stewing, baking, bluing, washing, starching, all those undertakings guaranteed to make her dauntless in the war against dirt. Leona began to cry.

Ephraim patted her hand. 'If these girls grow up to be half the woman their mother is, they'll be lucky. My hope for these girls is that they grow up to be like you, Mother.'

'But I want them to have every advantage,' Leona wailed.

'Having you for a mother, why, that's all the advantage they need.' Ephraim covered the papers on his desk, the rolltop clattering down. He wiped the ink from his hands. 'Let's go home now and have that heathen Wu Chan make us a lemonade 'afore supper.'

She rose and took his arm and through the glaring heat, the dust motes glowing golden in the afternoon light, they ambled the length of Leona, California, to their high white galleried mansion. As they approached the front door, through the open windows of the dining room, they heard Miss Savage declaim, 'How sharper than a serpent's tooth it is to have a thankless child!' They glanced in to see Miss Savage smite her breast and the girls weeping unabashedly.

March, 1918
London!!!

Dearest Sarah and Roy and family –
I cannot begin to tell you of the joy that greeted our ship as we steamed into sight of England. From the decks we would see the American colours flying and hear the people on shore singing American songs and welcoming us with such fervour as it is beyond my

[108]

poor pen to describe. We are the saviours of Europe and we are universally loved. I am proud to be an American and to be lending my small efforts on behalf of civilization, peace and democracy.

But Sarah, my dear, I digress beause I originally took up my pen to tell you the most wonderful thing! England! England, Sarah. I am here! I feel like Cordelia returning to assume her battered birthright.

'My battered what?' asked Cordelia, spearing a chunk of potato from the meatless stew.

'That's a different Cordelia,' Dumpling replied. 'Someone you don't know.'

'Well, go on, Ma.'

I recognize this place, Sarah! Though I have never been here. Ah, but I have! You have. We have. On the tide of Miss Savage's voice we have visited this green isle, though we grew up in the white desert. We have seen the effulgent spring though everywhere around us was the unrelenting desert. Miss Savage led us out of that desert, Sarah. Miss Savage led us to these greener pastures.

'I thought that was Jesus's job,' snickered Roy. 'Imagine that – Mabel Judd in Limeyland and all she can talk about is Miss Savage.' He shot an arch, conspiratorial look to his wife. 'And we all know what she was.'

'What was she, Pa?' asked Clarence.

'She was a governess,' said Sarah quickly.

'Well, go on, Dumpling,' Roy chuckled.

Green. Greener. Greenest. Such colour, Sarah. Although it is but the very verge of spring, my eye delights, revels in the colour and life swirling every-

[109]

where. The very vineyard of colour, Sarah. The evening dews and damps! And here, in London, the glowing lamps send their radiance into the softening fog. Oh, Sarah, it is not at all new and strange, but just as I imagined it. As good as memory. This is the country of the imagination, as the desert is the country of memory. Oh, to be a free citizen of both.

Of freedom, I must also add that I have had my hair cut. Bobbed, as they say. Several of the young nurses have done so. At the front we must be constantly prepared and alert. We cannot be bothered with useless hair. I must tell you, Sarah, you ought to have let Wu Chan chop your hair off. It is so satisfying. So liberating.

'Aunt Mabel's cut her hair!' cried Cordelia with a shriek. 'Oh, can you just imagine what she looks like!'

Clarence laughed out loud. 'Who's Wu Chan, Ma? Were you really going to bob *your* hair?'

'Mabel cut her hair as a sacrifice to the Allied Cause,' said Sarah stoutly.

'Don't sound like a sacrifice to me,' said Clarence,. stifling another guffaw. 'Sounds like she's having a great time.'

Sarah gave her son a hard look. 'Your aunt is going to the Front, Clarence. I don't see anything funny in that.' She returned to Mabel's letter.

Shortly I shall leave for beleaguered France, for Picardy. I am to act as translator to an American colonel working in liaison with French officers. Oh, Sarah, standing as I am at the border of the country of memory and the country of the imagination, I know it is all the more imperative that we bring down the hideous Hun or he will crush the finest flowers of both of our great countries. It's as though mine eyes have seen the glory of Western Civilization, Sarah dear, nay, all mankind. Just as Miss Savage said, *Lavee, Lagair, Lamore, Lamaird*. Oh, let us pray for *Lagair* soon to end forever and for *Lamore, Lavee* and *Lamaird* to reign supreme.

'What's all that mean?' asked Cordelia.

Sarah folded the letter and tucked it in the pocket of her green checked apron. 'It means, Life, War, Love, and Peace.'

'In Froggy,' added Roy.

Sarah drew herself up with injured dignity. 'I don't think any of you understand what Mabel is going through. This is war.'

'And it was made for Mabel Judd, Dumpling. She'll come back and we won't hear of nothing else till the day she dies, but Limeyland this and Froggy that. She'll come back talking Froggy and 'spect us to understand her every word.'

Of the Judd girls, only Mabel mastered Froggy. In fact, early on and without doubt, Mabel was the star pupil: Mabel, who could recite 'Young Lochinvar' and 'Ozymandias' without a slip or a hitch, Mabel, who could best thrum out the stirring chords of 'The Battle Hymn of the Republic', Mabel, who (after Miss Savage had closed the book and left it on the dining-room table) snatched the book, who read as well as listened, who ingested whole chunks of Shakespeare and Dickens and Scott and the terrible Bröntes. Mabel alone could walk the entire length of Leona, California with a book on her

[111]

head, who in fact, on a taunting dare from Agnes, did just that and not merely with one book, but three.

With a look of unconquerable disdain (which she had learned from Miss Savage), Mabel stepped out of the family mansion and raised her chin to the correct level. Acting unofficially as her second, Sarah handed her the three books and she placed them, one at a time, on top of her head. While her sisters gathered on the porch, Mabel Judd walked down Leona, California's single street, that sole navigable avenue of the country of memory, the metronomic thump and throttle of mill and mine beating time, waves of sound, cresting in the waves of heat. Mrs Skaggs, her Chinese and Indian servants stopped work in the middle of the afternoon to peer from their windows; on the street itself, Indians gathered to gawk and the Chinese came out of the Golden Grotto and the Gold Camp Laundry; drunken miners and hard-bitten whores tumbled from the swinging doors of the Golden Nugget and the Golden Floss to hiss and whistle. Mabel Judd did not heed them in the least. Fourteen years old, her brown hair curling down her back, her white blouse gleaming in the fiery heat, her narrow shoulders set, her chin erect, the books perfectly balanced, her eyes on Higher Things, Mabel Judd commanded herself to inflection, conviction, courage, carriage. As she passed, guffaws died on the lips of heathen, whore and drunk alike, taunts blew away on the desert wind. They could not have been more silent and respectful if fair Ellen or Young Lochinvar strode the gold-dusted street, if Mabel's parade had been orchestrated with lutes and harps rather than mine and mill.

Mabel's prowess clearly endeared her to Miss Savage and, just as clearly, Molly and Agnes resented her for it, thinking it unseemly that the last should be first, as bad as if Mabel had got married before they did. Sarah, ever her younger sister's champion and confidante, did not share these ungenerous attitudes; Sarah remained happily in awe of Mabel. On those rare occasions when Mabel did not perform up to Miss Savage's standards, Molly and Agnes snickered audibly, downright enjoyed it when Miss Savage snapped at Mabel, and then ordered the rest of them out of the room, closing the dining-room doors and pouncing on Mabel for some infraction.

'I expect perfection of you, Mabel,' Miss Savage declared on one of these occasions. Mabel hung her head. 'The standards are higher for you than they are for the others. You may actually do something with your life, Mabel, other than merely get married. To get married and buried in the same breath.'

Mabel looked up. 'Is that why you never got married, Miss Savage?'

'It is very rude to ask personal questions.' Miss Savage ran her hands over her abundant and still fiery red hair; two years in the desert had not dimmed that hair. She sat down across from Mabel and clasped her hands neatly before her; the prim gesture could have easily turned to wrought emotion with a turn of the wrist.

'Is it a tragic story, Miss Savage?' asked the undaunted Mabel (hoping it was). 'Was he very beautiful, your lover? Was he like Young Lochinvar – you know, so stately his form, so lovely her face? Did you kiss the cup and let him drink?'

'You are too young to be thinking of lovers.'

'Can I think of lovers when I'm as old as Agnes and Molly?'

'Agnes and Molly will never think of lovers, Mabel. Agnes and Molly will think of husbands. Husbands and

lovers are mutually exclusive terms. Men are unre-
liable. At best. Higher Things, Mabel. It is best to think
of Higher Things.'

Spurred on by Miss Savage's skirting so close to some
brilliant, tragic, unimaginable truth, Mabel recklessly
confessed, 'But I'm dying to know what it's like to be
kissed, Miss Savage. That's what I want. I want to
be kissed. Can't I think of Higher Things after I get
kissed?'

'After that,' she replied tautly. 'it is increasingly difficult to think of Higher Things.'

Higher Things were continually under discussion
amongst the elder Judd girls. Not higher in the same
sense that Miss Savage used the term, or as Mabel
understood it, but in the more immediate sense of
getting out of Leona, California, getting into society
and getting husbands. There was talk of Leona and the
girls moving to Pasadena. Leona had heard there was
society in Pasadena worthy of the educated daughters of
a man who owns a gold mine.

Miss Savage pooh-poohed the notion of Pasadena.
She made casual, cavalier reference to New York,
Boston, London. She added that rich American girls
were all the rage in London now, and indicated with a
peculiar tilt of her chin that a title might not be wholly
out of the question, or at the very least (as she briefly
explained the legal concept of primogeniture to the
Judds) younger sons were always eager for rich, accomplished American girls.

'London's impossible,' said Leona, effectively
squashing the subject. (Agnes ran from the table in
tears.) The announcement rather surprised Leona herself, as never in her wildest dreams had she thought she
might have occasion to say those words, or anything
vaguely like them. She quickly put the memory of the

livery stable from her mind and glanced at her beloved husband. 'I wouldn't dream of going that far away from Father. Never. My place is with you, Father.'

'Well, Mother,' Ephraim scratched his nose in a contemplative fashion, 'maybe I can go with you and see what all this society is about. I just need to get a few things settled here at the mine and then, well by golly, I'll go too, if you girls won't be too ashamed of your old Pa.'

'When, Pa?'

'Well, I got a man from an eastern syndicate coming out here next month to have a little look over our operations and if it all goes like I reckon it, well I think he'll buy me out for a pretty good bunch of money. Yessir, a real good chunk of money, so's I can come with you and make sure my girls get real men for husbands.'

'Will you come too, Miss Savage?' asked Mabel. 'Please say you'll come.'

'Indeed I will not. I have done what I set out to do here.' The flash of her sharp teeth lit a fleeting smile. 'I have other offers. Quite good offers.'

'How could you?' asked Molly. 'You never get a speck of mail. All the time you been here, I reckon you haven't got half a dozen letters and you said all those were from your sister in England.'

'It is as rude to comment on other people's mail as it is to read it. Back straight, *mouth shut*, Molly. Eyes on Higher Things. Whatever I do when I leave this abominable desert, is none of your concern.'

'I want to go with you, Miss Savage,' Mabel cried.

'Mabel!' Leona remonstrated.

'But I do!' she wailed. 'I don't want to go into society! I'm too young for a husband!'

Leona was about to further chastise her youngest when Ephraim cut in saying all this was just a lot of jawing till the man from the eastern syndicate arrived and the few things from the mine got settled.

With the arrival, the following month, of the man from the eastern syndicate, a good deal more than that got settled. In the vulgar parlance, Miss Savage's hash got settled once and for all when Mr Charles Norby, representing Empire Mining and Milling, a cartel of eastern bankers and industrialists, arrived on the supply train, bringing with him a fair young man named Pilch. Abner Pilch. A recent graduate of the Colorado School of Mines.

Abner Pilch was about twenty-five, six feet tall and weighed in at about 180 pounds of muscle and fur (the latter easily left to the imagination, given the luxurious blond hair on his head and the thatch of hair on the back of his big, capable hands). He was (as the girls managed to discover by inquiring after Mrs Pilch) unmarried. And so, for Abner Pilch, the girls' education came to its finest fruition; they burst into gilded flower, befitting the children of a man who owned a gold mine. On Abner Pilch was bestowed two years of sweating and straining and reciting and piano-pounding and posturing, two years of having their manners retooled and their language enhanced. Lavished on Abner Pilch were two years of mottoes and admonitions and injunctions and French, their eyes continually on Higher Things as they endured the sharp sting of the ruler on their wrists, the pain of gnawed nails thrust in ground pepper, the wink of Wu Chan's cleaver blinking over the mane of hair. The finest flower of young womanhood bloomed forth in the Judd parlour after dinner as Agnes rendered 'The Battle Hymn of the Republic' and Molly recited 'Young Lochinvar' (with special loving emphasis donated to the maidens more lovely by far 'who would

gladly be bride to young Lochinvar'). Sarah rose to
bring that traveller from the antique land, the 'shattered
visage' of 'Ozymandias', king of kings, the heartbreak of
'that colossal wreck, boundless and bare' right into the
Judd parlour. Mabel was called upon to recite from
Shakespeare and (inappropriately) chose Lear's speech
on the heath, beating her young breast in the manner of
Miss Savage. The girls shone brilliantly for Abner Pilch
while Ephraim and Leona looked on proudly. While
Miss Savage eyed Mr Norby.

Mr Norby was about forty years old. By the same
subtle means used on Mr Pilch, the girls discovered
there was no Mrs Norby, but this was not of any enduring interest. Compared to the beautiful Mr Pilch, Mr
Norby was of small concern, though he was attractive in
a florid, well-fed way, his manner both affable and
crisp. Mr Norby had indicated during dinner that great
things lay before him with Empire Mining and Milling,
that he would not long be traversing these antique
lands, these boundless, barren deserts, doing business
in the killing heat. He wore a real suit and a massive gold
watch on a chain draped across his torso and he occasionally patted the watch as though to reassure himself his time in boundless bareness, these desert dump
towns, was finite.

The windows in the parlour were open to admit such
breeze as there was, though the breeze was unkind,
bringing with it the smelting odour of the mill and the
grit and sand and unlit dust from the street. It was
intolerably hot and Miss Savage got out her hanky,
daubed the moisture from her face. The hanky slipped
from her hand and Mr Norby, with the gallantry Young
Lochinvar himself might have envied, reached to

retrieve it. Their fingers brushed momentarily, and they both excused themselves.

The gala evening ended with everyone singing 'The Battle Hymn of the Republic' and then Ephraim said that he and Mr Norby and Mr Pilch had a long day before them and everyone had best get to sleep. However – and here Ephraim's brow furrowed as he realized that the town boasted no hotel and he did not think the boarding-house could accommodate two men, not when they had been expecting Mr Norby alone. Of course, there were the rooms above the saloon, but prudently, Ephraim did not mention these.

'It don't matter to me,' said Mr Pilch genially. 'I slept with mice and I slept with lice. I can sleep any old where.'

The girls thought this wonderfully witty, and Molly suggested why didn't the family put both men up, that she and Agnes could double-up with Sarah and Mabel. Mr Pilch and Mr Norby could have their bed. 'I mean,' Molly flushed, 'our room.'

'Yes,' Agnes chimed in, positioning herself strategically behind Mabel, 'Mr Pilch can sleep in our room just fine.' And then, swiftly, before Mabel's objections could spring to her lips, Agnes dealt her an emphatic kick.

'Perhaps Miss Savage might be kind enough to give up her room for the night,' Leona said sweetly. 'I'm sure that Wu Chan and Li Chun can go – well, somewhere for the night. They're Chinese,' she added as though this explained everything. 'Miss Savage could sleep in their quarters outside.'

'Out of the question,' said Miss Savage, biting down sharply on the *not bloody likely* that fluttered just under her tongue.

A good many offers and counter-offers and objections and proposals flew around for at least twenty minutes till at last it was decided that the girls would indeed double-up, that a pallet on the floor could be made up for Mabel while the three older girls shared the big bed and Mr Norby and Mr Pilch could have Agnes and Molly's room. Miss Savage would keep her own quarters.

It was a restless night. Leona lay awake wondering if Abner Pilch were good enough for her daughters and if so, whether Agnes or Molly ought to get him. Ephraim lay awake worrying that he had not reckoned on Mr Pilch at all. He had reckoned on dealing with an easterner, a man who would content himself with talk of money and tonnage and contracts and ore quality. Talk only. Not a mining engineer. Not a graduate of the Colorado School of Mines. Not a man who could probably sniff out the declining quality of the ore with his nose. Ephraim lay awake wondering how he could gracefully alert his foreman, Skaggs, before the morning, decided it could not be done gracefully, but it must indeed be done, that he must rise before dawn and go to Skaggs, warn him, coach him as to what could be said – and what could not.

Mabel lay awake twisting and turning on the narrow pallet on the hard floor, thinking it patently unfair that she should be assigned the pallet simply because she was the youngest, wishing she could have traded quarters with the Chinese. At least they had beds. She tossed and turned, slept fitfully, waking often, wondering finally if she might not be more comfortable on the red velvet settee in the parlour, knowing that if she took her blanket and pillow in there, she would have to wake before dawn and be back on the pallet before the rest of the house was up and about. Her mother would die of shame to find her in the parlour in her nightdress when men were present.

The very idea of men present kept the other girls awake, giggling over the muffled question of which side of Agnes and Molly's bed would Mr Pilch lay his fair head and if, in the morning, they might find some token of his esteem lying beneath that pillow.

Mr Pilch slept like the dead.

Mr Norby decided to have a cigarette, got out of bed, pulled on his pants and braces, buttoned his shirt halfway up, took his papers, tobacco and some matches and stepped quietly out of the door of his room, tiptoed down the long hall till he found the kitchen. He crossed the kitchen and stepped out on the back porch where he lit up and listened to the nocturnal desert creatures scurry about the godforsaken brush. He inhaled and looked to the star-spangled sky, chips of light grated unevenly over the unrelenting blackness.

Miss Savage put on her nightdress and took down her savage red hair. She took her candle to the cracked mirror on the wardrobe where she met her reflection, skewered and oddly angled, as though the two sides of her face would forever disagree. She touched the knobs of her collarbones gingerly and stared at her bony hands. At the sound of footsteps, she blew out the candle and made her way across the tiny room, parting the thin curtain, looked out to the back, to the endless desert and the outbuildings, clustered close in, like moths snuggling up to the white flame of the house. Her gaze lingered on the shack where the Chinese slept (and smoked opium) and she muttered something deprecating about the very bloody idea of Leona Judd's offering her the Chinamen's bed. She was about to drop the curtain when a glow caught her eye from the porch, a tiny fiery gleam piercing the darkness, moving swiftly upwards. To a man's lips.

A few minutes later, Mr Norby wheeled about. 'Miss Savage! You startled me!'

'I saw you smoking from my window,' she said, clutching her shabby calico wrapper against her white nightdress. 'I wondered if I might trouble you for a cigarette.'

Mr Norby's eyes lit with surprise. Even in the darkness she could see the surprise. He said by all means. He rolled her a cigarette.

'A cigarette now and then is civilized,' she declared defensively.

'I'm not like some men,' he assured her, 'I say if men can smoke, why not women?'

'Why not indeed?'

He lit the match and cupped his hands protectively around the thin flame; Miss Savage bent into the light which, for that moment illuminated her sharp face, her wild red hair. Mr Norby held the match till it burnt his fingers. 'There ain't much civilized out here. A lady like you, I don't know how you bear it.'

'One must eat, Mr Norby. One must live.'

'Here?' He gestured to the desert beyond the puny, clustered buildings.

'We are villains by necessity, fools by heavenly compulsion.'

'What?'

'Shakespeare.'

'Oh.' They continued to smoke silently, standing side by side till Miss Savage shivered slightly. 'Now if I'd known you was to join me, Miss Savage, I'd have worn my coat and I could offer it to you. Hot by day and cold by night, this godforsaken hell. Excuse me, I mean –'

'Do not excuse yourself, Mr Norby. I am not Agnes

[121]

Judd, a green girl. God was right to forsake this country. God showed more sense than men.'

Mr Norby flicked the butt of his cigarette into the
brush.

'You mustn't do that,' she cautioned him. 'You must
be sure to put it out completely. It's very dry. Things
burn here. They burn.'

He stepped off the porch and retrieved the glowing
butt, ground it under his heel. He turned back to look at
her, her nightdress gleaming white where the shabby
wrapper was undone, her bright hair illuminated by
starlight, the veil of night itself kind to the hard planes
of her taut face. Miss Savage finished her cigarette,
watching Mr Norby who moved closer and remarked
that her feet were bare. 'Let me put that out for you.'

'Please.'

He took the butt, stomped it out in the dust, mounted
the porch steps and stood close by her. 'It's a hard life
out here for a lady beautiful as you.'

'A woman, Mr Norby,' she replied, her husky voice
reverberating in her narrow chest.

He touched her hair, took her in his arms, astonished
to feel her fragility, astonished that such a tiny woman
could answer his hands and lips with such fire and
vivacity; as his hands sought the rounded tips of her
breasts, the calico wrapper gave way under his eagerness. Miss Savage thrust herself against his eagerness,
knowing exactly where and how to thrust so that she
might enjoy, exacerbate the throbbing impact of his
body. Mr Norby groaned against her hair, laced his
arms across her back and pulled her high to meet his lips
again and again.

'Not here,' she said at last, whispering harshly, 'not
here.'

'Where then?'

[122]

'My room. Let me go first. I'll open the window for you. Can you come through the window?'

'I'll do anything. Anything you ask.'

Miss Savage slid down his body, splaying her hands across his shoulders. 'What is your name?' she murmured, placing her forehead against his ample chest.

'Charles. What's yours?'

'Flora.'

May, 1918

Darling Sarah –

I have seen the fearful lightning of His terrible swift sword. I have seen such things as my pen refuses to describe. Such carnage. Such putrefaction. Such horror, Sarah darling, but not, alas, wholly the horrors of war. You cannot know, nor guess the degradation I have endured. The disgrace. The humiliation. The shame. Oh Sarah, I burn to think of it. And visited not simply on my head, but implicating you, dear sister, implicating Molly and Agnes and our dear dear parents whom death hath mercifully spared this revelation.

'What's your parents got to do with the war? Shut that baby up!' Roy barked. 'Can't a man come home without hearing a baby wail? Shut him up.'

'Her, Roy. The baby is a her.'

'I don't care what it is! A man's entitled to some peace at home. You took care of your children, Dumpling. Why can't your daughter look after hers? She's a married woman. Why don't she keep them at home?'

'Cordelia, you go in and soothe your niece.'

'I want to hear Aunt Mabel's letter. I want to hear about disgrace and degradation.'

[123]

'Keep your back straight and your mouth shut, Cordelia and do as I ask.'

'Yes, Ma.'

'That's better,' said Roy, unlacing his boots as the baby's wails softened from the other room. 'Now go on. What's Mabel talking about? I swear, Dumpling, I never could understand a word that woman says.'

'Mabel means well.'

'I'm not saying she don't. Now, go on, what's all this about disgrace?'

But Sarah's eyes had already quickly traversed the page as best she could, given her limited literacy skills and she paraphrased Mabel saying that the conduct of the war was a disgrace to all right-thinking Americans which would have included Molly and Agnes and their late parents.

She tucked the letter in her apron pocket, not pulling it out until Roy was asleep in the living-room with the *St Elmo Gazette* spread across his chest, not until Clarence and Cordelia had gone off to the church young people's Mutual Improvement Association, not until the restless granddaughter fell asleep with oil of camphor on her teething gums. Even then Sarah took the letter into the bathroom, locked the door before continuing.

I have been relieved of my post as translator to the American colonel working in liaison with the French. I have been, in a word, sacked and under such circumstances as no decent woman should have to endure. The truth of it, Sarah darling, is that I cannot speak French. You cannot speak French. We cannot speak French. We never have. We never will. Miss Savage (O thou aptest of names) cruelly abused our innocence and the trust of our parents. In the guise of the French language she taught us merely a collection of nasal intonations, throaty-R's and strings of sounds correctly inflected, but signifying nothing. Would that that were the worst of it, my dear sister. Would that I could will my pen to halt here, but you must, you shall know everything.

Not everything she taught us was a jumbled lump of sounds. There were words. Words such as you and I, our sisters, our parents, would never have dreamed of speaking, not if devils sloshed our bodies with burning oil would we have uttered such phrases. But utter them we did. Utter them we have. Filthy beyond belief. In our dewy innocence we thought we were conducting polite intercourse. Nay. We referred unblushingly to the parts, the bodies of men and women and animals, those secret parts of women, the male member, that part common to men and women and animals for the use of defecation. Defecation itself. Excrement, Sarah, those lumps of ordure issued from the body. In the most vulgar parlance of all, Sarah, and described in French as *Lamaird*. Peace? Peace! We exhorted to Life, War, Love and Shit, Sarah. My pen cannot spare you further. Shit. *Lamaird* is the word for shit.

Sarah wept audibly, stuffing her apron into her mouth to stifle the sobs as she continued reading.

When I spoke French, as I knew it, the French officers at first paled and then blushed and then burst out at me with a volley of abuse recognizable as such in any tongue. I stood by, confused, appalled, asking, as best I could, to be informed of the problem, and with each word I spoke, their anger mounted and their arms flailed and their shouts deafened me till the American colonel demanded to know what I had said,

why the French were screaming at me, why they
ordered one of their own to come drag me from the
room, to lock me up, while I cried out at the injustice,
while I was marched, nay, dragged from the room
protesting my innocence, shouting, '*Lavee! Lagair!
Lamore! Lamaird!*'

The French locked me in a tiny room and not until
one of their own translators came in to question me
was I given full, brutal knowledge of my transgression. Our transgression. In our unspoilt innocence,
Sarah, we greeted people as the dirty rumps of dogs
and sheep. We said to men that they committed
unspeakable acts with animals. We said to women
that they committed unspeakable acts with everyone.
We asked not to be passed condiments of the table,
but the smelly effluvia of old women, the juice of
men. We believed we were expressing pleasure in
someone's company but in fact, we were commenting
approvingly on the length of the male [*scratched out*]
and when we believed we were complimenting someone on a job well done, we were telling them that they
had passed gas with fire. I cannot continue. This is
but a portion of the French that tripped daily from
our virginal lips under the instruction of that viper.
That serpent. That devil, Miss Savage. When the
French translator told me these things (ourselves and
a young private in the room) I endured as much as I
could before begging him to stop. Next the Americans questioned me. Satisfied finally that I was but
the victim of a cruel, cruel jest and not an agent of the
Hun, they released me from my incarceration and
ordered me to return home.

I refused. I cried, I begged, I demanded, I vowed
to do whatever was required of me, whatever the war
might ask. I volunteered to go into the trenches if

need be, but please, please do not send me home to St Elmo, to allow this story, the mockery of everything my parents believed in, this folly and disgrace to follow after me.

At last they relented. I have no training as a nurse, but need none to do the work they have assigned me. The lowest of the low. I carry bedpans of bloody urine and I wash bloody rags and burn bloodied bandages and boil bloodied scalpels. I beat down beds that men have died in. I throw disinfectant on the floors where they have vomited. I pull the soiled pants from their blasted legs.

Can you imagine how the story of my disgrace has spread all through the lines, the Americans, the French, the British all know of it and laugh at me. Perhaps the Hun is laughing too. Perhaps even heaven laughs at me. My dearest darling sister, I may tell you that I am mocked, yes, but I am not beaten. I shall redeem my honour. I shall keep my own counsel. But at night, Sarah dearest, in the privacy of sleep, the only privacy vouchsafed us, I toss on my pallet and dream of Miss Savage, though I see her in my dream only as I saw her that one terrible, terrible dawn, that fleeting glimpse of the woman sitting naked at the edge of the bed, her small white teeth bared in . . .

Sarah could read no further. She crumpled the letter tightly in her hand while her breath came hard and sharp, stabbing swiftly through her breast to remember that infamous dawn when their home was split asunder by screams and shrieks, blast after blast shooting through the house, resounding from the hall when her father had collided with Mabel standing face to face with the naked Mr Norby carrying his clothes, coming into the hall and visible across the expanse of kitchen, Miss Savage's door flung open and the woman herself seated, smiling, naked on the edge of the bed.

Sarah glanced once again at the cruel words peering up from the crumpled sheet, suffered yet another pang when she imagined Molly and Agnes's reaction to the hideous cruelty perpetrated against their innocence and the innocence of their parents. The blood descended rapidly from her head, leaving her faint and woozy and just then, Sarah collected herself, forcefully, physically commanded her body to obey while she sorted through her thoughts. Why should Molly and Agnes know? Why? She asked herself again and again, psychically shaking off the name Dumpling and all its implications. Why indeed?

Sarah acted in haste, took the fetid letter to the kitchen sink where she struck a lucifer and lit it afire, pushing open the kitchen window so the smoke should not waft into the living-room and disturb her sleeping husband. Trembling, but filled with the conviction of her own correctness, she watched the letter burn, hoping that the flame that consumed the paper would likewise consume the soul of Miss Savage for time and all eternity. And even at that, Sarah could not imagine her repentant.

The baleful task fell to Ephraim. Leona was bedridden. The catatonic Mabel was sentenced to the dining-room, not to come forth till Ephraim himself should open the door. The sobbing girls ordered to stay in the bedroom

[128]

until their father should release them. Mr Norby and
Mr Pilch (for he was implicated – somehow) had been
dispatched from the house by the dawn's early light,
ordered in anger, fear and loathing into the streets of
Leona, California.

Ephraim gulped as the two men stepped into the
desert dawn, walking towards the Golden Grotto,
knowing that word of their abrupt departure from his
roof would percolate from the Golden Grotto through
every Indian nook and Chinese cranny, amongst the
miners and the whores alike, before noon. Knowing too
that he had not the slightest chance of conferring with
Skaggs. But the door closed on their retreating backs
and it was done now. Worse lay in store. Much worse.
The terrible matter of the infamous Miss Savage.
Should he –

His dilemma was cut short by the appearance of Miss
Savage herself. Her hair done up, her collar neatly
bound about the neck, the jacket of her suit buttoned,
her movements brisk as ever, she strode into the kitchen
in complete possession of herself, in complete possession of the situation. At the very sight of her, the ghosts
of Ephraim Judd's Mormon ancestors rose up in fury,
screaming at him to assume the patriarchal stance, ac-
cost the evildoer with the full weight of her transgression against God, humanity and the family that had
taken her unto their very bosom. But Ephraim could
only glare at her.

'You shall have to do better than gawk at me, Mr
Judd,' she said lightly, placing her carpet-bag on the
floor and brushing the feather on her hat.

'You're no better than a common . . . a common . . .'

'Whore? I beg to differ. I am not a whore and I am
certainly not common. Oh contrare. You are common.
You and your family are insufferably common. Bour-

geois,' she added the stinging epithet remorselessly, 'vulgar and I despise you. I have always despised you. You and your common wife and your foolish virgin daughters –'

'Do not mention my daughters!' cried Ephraim. 'Get out of this house.'

'Oh, I am leaving, Mr Judd. But not in disgrace. Call it what you like, but not disgrace. I am a woman of the world. I have seen and done and endured what a man as common and limited as you cannot even guess at.'

'Of course you have! You . . . you bawd!' he shouted, retrieving the word from the long-ago days at Ma Grant's Saloon and Pleasure Palace.

'It was not a disgrace,' she maintained. 'It was a necessity.'

'Get out! Get out!'

She jabbed her hatpin through the crown of her hat. 'I have given your daughters the only moments of illumination their sorry lives will ever know.'

'Out! Out!'

'When they are married, when your daughters are drudges and chattels to drovers, farmers and nasty-minded little clerks and hulking railroad brutes, they will remember me! I have spent my life revenging myself on people like you, Mr Judd, on your smugness, and certainties, on your pretensions and your assumptions and your pious, untested values.'

'No decent woman –'

'Ha! I despise decency, Mr Judd. Loathe it. Decency and complacency and stupidity. I have nothing but contempt for those things. Nothing but contempt for you.' She laughed, baring her small, white teeth. '*Lavee, lagair, lamore, lamaird*! Good day, Mr Judd.'

And with that, she picked up her bag, the same bag she had come with more than two years before and marched through the kitchen and the hall to the foyer, took her coat from the hook and stepped out to the porch, into the pale, relentless glare of morning, leaving the door ajar behind her. She walked, looking neither right nor left, down the single yellow ribbon-road of Leona, California, to the dock to await the supply train due that morning.

From the window of the Golden Grotto Cafe, Mr Norby watched her tiny figure retreat, the sun brazenly lighting her red hair. 'What a woman,' he murmured.

'You must have been out of your god-damned mind,' said Abner Pilch (proving himself once and for all, unworthy of the Judd girls). 'You are a god-damned fool.'

'What a woman,' Mr Norby sighed and returned to his hash, grits, eggs and coffee.

June, 1918

My dear sister –

Mine eyes have seen the coming of the end. How can the world survive this? Passchendale. That is the name of this place. Were it not so hideous, I could laugh to think of that name given to this purgatory. They sing a song here, Sarah, 'The Bells of Hell Go Ting A Ling A Ling', but no hell created by Satan could equal this creation of man's. This mire of blood and squalor and *Lamaird*. Truly those words, *Lagair*, *Lamaird* were meant to be spoken in the same breath. Did Miss Savage know?

I have earned my way from the lowly tasks first given me, to the ranks of nurse. I wear a red cross emblem on my sleeve, but the emblem itself is splashed and splattered with blood. I cannot keep it clean. I have not slept in twenty-four hours. I dare not sleep now. If I did, I would sleep like the dead

and the near-dead need me. I have held down boys no
older than Clarence while their legs were amputated
to save their lives. I think of Clarence constantly,
though I must in all candour tell you I never much
liked him, but he is in my thoughts constantly when I
see fair-haired youngsters, their lips twisted in the
unmistakable grimace of death. Boys, all of them are
boys. The soldiers have all died. The French and
English and Germans alike are sending young boys to
be slaughtered. Boys like Clarence. The waves of the
dead are inexorable and still there is no peace. No life.
No love. Only blood and slaughter. *Lagair*, *Lamaird*. Only those obscenities and shelling and gas
and barbed wire and bombs and rockets. It is endless.
It never stops. Like the sound of the mill and the
mine that constant rumble and thump beaten into the
very furrows of your brain, that . . .

'Open up, Ma.' Cordelia rapped at the bathroom door.
'I need help with my costume, Ma. I can't find my
torch.'

Sarah flushed the toilet, turned on the taps in the sink
and quickly washed her face, bringing it, dripping, out
of her hands to meet her grey reflection. She opened the
door to behold Cordelia dressed as the Statue of Liberty
for the Liberty Bond Drive parade in downtown St
Elmo.

'Ma? You look awful, Ma. You seen a ghost? You
look –'

'Your torch is in the kitchen. I will get it.' Sarah
clenched her teeth and went into the kitchen for the
papier mâché torch where she found Clarence practising his salute in front of the tiny mirror at the back door.
'What are you doing?' she demanded.

'Practising,' he replied with a grin.

'What for?'

'For when I join up, Ma. Soon's I'm eighteen, I'm going to join up and hinky dinky parley voo, Ma.'

Sarah walked up to her son who towered over her. She stared into his youthful face, his empty blue eyes, his unfurrowed brow, unwillingly seeing the twisted grimace of death, the obscenity of his ignorance. Sarah took a deep breath and slapped his face.

Clarence winced; tears and shock struggled over his face. 'You shouldn'ta done that, Ma. I'm a man now. Shouldn'ta done that to a man, Ma.'

'Shut up, you little fool.'

Clarence bolted from the kitchen, the screen door squealing, slamming in protest. Chest heaving, Sarah stared out to the laundry flapping on the lines and from the centre of town she could hear the high school band futilely warming up to the opening accolades of 'The Battle Hymn of the Republic'.

'Close that piano this instant! I never want to hear that song again!' Leona barked as Mabel fingered out the tune. 'Never, never again.'

'Yes, Ma.'

'Are you packed?'

'Yes, Ma.'

'Then go get your coat. We're leaving.'

'Yes, Ma.'

'And don't walk like that!'

'Like what, Ma?'

'Like that. With your shoulders straight and as though . . . as though . . .'

'I'm never going to be a tall woman, Ma.'

'Just do as I say. I can't bear it.'

'Can't bear what?'

'And don't answer me with a question!'

Leona Judd adjusted her hat and looked around the home she was leaving forever. For once, it was quiet. The desert wind could be heard, its little yellow claws scratching at the windows, gnawing at the doorframe, snapping at the gold tassels festooning the room. No more thump and throttle of the mine and mill. The mine and mill were closed till further notice from Empire Mining and Milling. Abner Pilch had found what he was not supposed to have found, what a graduate of the Colorado School of Mines would probably have found even if Ephraim had briefed Mr Skaggs. And what Abner Pilch found rippled through Leona, California, even more quickly than (and right on the heels of) the story of Miss Savage, the (ha ha) governess and Mr Norby, the (ha ha) man from the eastern syndicate who had bought the gold mine at a fraction of what he'd originally been willing to pay. Indeed, the Judds saw only a penny of that pittance because aside from the shattering discoveries in the mine itself, there were equally shattering discoveries to be made in the books and ledgers, shrill demands for payments long, long overdue from far, faraway firms.

That day in 1889, the Judds closed the door of the white wedding cake of a house for the last time and walked down the gold-dusted single street carrying their few bags to the dock to await the supply train from St Elmo. Already, the town seemed forlorn, deserted, vanquished: the miners had been given drafts drawn on Empire Mining and Milling instead of their last month's pay and many of them, predictably, got drunk, and looted businesses, most of which had already been closed down anyway. Certainly the industrious Chinese seemed to have vanished overnight and as the Judds walked down the street, the doors on their empty shacks

squealed and banged in the wind. Broken windows of
the Golden Grotto, the Gold Camp Laundry and the
Dry Goods store gaped at them like open maws. A can
of peaches rolled lazily down the step of the looted Dry
Goods and seemed to shine and wink and beckon,
pawing at Mabel's skirt like a lost cur. Dust blew into
her eyes and she rubbed them against the gilded glare.
When they reached the dock, the wind picked up, sand
blew over the narrow gauge tracks and a hard knot of
fear congealed inside Mabel as she prayed for the train
to get there, soon, fast, now, before the sand swallowed
the track altogether and snatched their every hope of
escape.

The Judds limped back into St Elmo with their suitcases, a few hatboxes and a trunk of household goods,
with nothing to show for the glory days of their gold
mine grandeur. Empire Mining and Milling took over
their white house and stripped it and Indians moved
into the shell, some two dozen of them hunkering
together in the high, airy splendid rooms, the house
rendered all the more ghostly when a fire leveled the rest
of the town, the flames licking out, reaching for the lacy
balustrades just before the wind reversed and carried
the blaze in the other direction. After that, even Indians
left Leona, California.

Perhaps their resounding defeat, financial and social
disgrace ought to have destroyed Leona and Ephraim,
but it did not. Almost immediately Ephraim went to
work for the St Elmo Feed and Seed and spent the rest
of his days measuring out oats and alfalfa to leather-
palmed ranchers. He died in 1912. Bereft without him,
Leona died in 1913. She was a loyal wife first and
foremost, so the reversal of their fortunes did not funda-
mentally alter her intrinsic self. If she shed tears for

her daughters' shattered prospects, she did so privately and without a word to any of them.

The family stayed in St Elmo where the girls' ability to play 'The Battle Hymn of the Republic' went untested, where no one noticed or gave a damn that they could walk with books on their heads: chin up, back straight, mouth shut and eyes on Higher Things. That they were poor and plain did not stop Agnes, Molly or Sarah from marrying, from marrying young. Nothing stops a Mormon girl from marrying. Their husbands resembled Young Lochinvar only in so far as they came out of the west: Latter-day Saint men, farmers, and clerks and railroad men. Agnes and Molly and Sarah cursed their rudimentary math skills as they tried to balance narrow household budgets and saved the rag-ends of soap and bone and bits of gristle; they denounced their limited literacy when they struggled with recipes for eggless cake and red-eyed beans, as they skimmed grease off and saved it, as they covered up the holes in their stockings with boot blacking, as they burnt their fingers on hot, heavy irons and rose before dawn on inferno-summer days to build washday fires, to bake bread they would eat without butter. They cursed 'Ozymandias' that they could not sew a patch on a pair of workingman's pants, or dye a rusty skirt to make it look like new, or put up a jar of peaches without the rot seeping in. Between them they bore and nursed and reared, they sat by the sickbeds and buttoned the hand-me-down shoes and shirts and dresses of twenty-one children while they cursed King Lear and Sir Walter Scott and Shelley and Dickens and the Bröntes, while they cursed the French and Higher Things.

All except Mabel. The suitors came and went, but Mabel Judd kept her eyes on Higher Things, wore her specs to see those Higher Things more clearly, went to work at the library and kept her back straight and her chin up and her mouth shut. When she did open her mouth, she was blunt to a fault. Her sisters bore her presence at first with Christian forbearance and then, increasingly with wormwood and gall.

'Zeke swore if she told him not to eat with his knife again, he'd walk out and never come back,' Agnes complained to Molly and Sarah as the three gathered in Sarah's kitchen Christmas Day, 1907.

'Mabel means well,' said Sarah, flouring her rolling-pin.

'Oh, you always say that, Dumpling. She's out there right now with the men in the living-room and I heard her tell Roy he shouldn't say ain't. Roy don't think she means well, Dumpling, I can tell you that.' Agnes plunged another clove into the thick white rind of fat enveloping a scrawny ham. 'Why isn't she in here with us, helping? She eats, don't she? She can just get in here and help the women.'

'Mabel doesn't cook, Agnes. You know that.'

'That's cuz she lives with Ma and Pa. I told Ma, Christmas Day, Ma, you don't need to cook. We'll do it. I said it right in front of Mabel and she just stayed sitting where she was, looking at me like ... like ... looking right through me. Like I wasn't even there.'

'Just like Miss Savage,' said Molly, peeling parsnips into a newspaper spread across her lap. 'Mabel's getting more like Miss Savage every day.'

'Oh Molly, how can you even say that woman's name in the same breath with Mabel's?' Dumpling cried.

'Why not?' Agnes demanded. 'Mabel says it enough. And don't you think she doesn't. My oldest girl comes home t'other day and asks me about Miss Savage.

That's right! By name. The whore-of-Babylon's very name. My girl tells me a friend of hers is at the library, talking to Mabel and Mabel's going on and on about learning Shakespeare and poetry and French from our governess, Miss Savage, and how we had all these there wonderful refinements.' Agnes bit down hard on the last word, like the end of a line of thread. 'I set that girl straight. Right there. Right then. I can tell you that.'

'Well, maybe Mabel was just too young to understand what . . .' Molly frowned and parsnip skin flew from her fingers. 'Well you know what I mean. Maybe Mabel didn't understand what she saw that night. Maybe she still doesn't. She isn't married, you know.'

To her sisters' surprise, Dumpling laughed out loud. 'How can you *not* understand when you're face to face with a naked man? When your own Pa comes out and finds you screaming, face to face with a naked man?'

'I'm only saying . . .' Molly intervened.

'And on top of that –' Dumpling went on, a thread of contempt lacing her voice, 'Mabel looked across the kitchen and the door to Miss Savage's room was wide open and Miss Savage was sitting on the bed, stark naked too. Married or unmarried, you understand that! It don't take marriage to make you understand that!'

The parsnips fell from Molly's hand and Agnes dropped her clove. They said, more or less in unison (as they had recited more or less in unison), '*She saw that!*'

'Yes.' Dumpling deflated a bit; her sisters could always cow her.

'And even after *that*, Mabel went down to the dock to wait for the train with her?'

'Yes. She went to the dock to wait for the train with Miss Savage and Miss Savage just sat there without even speaking for a long time, without even looking at Mabel till she took her hand.'

[138]

'We never heard this, Dumpling! What happened then?'

'You want to know past that, you'll have to ask Mabel yourself.' Sarah wiped her hands fiercely on her apron. 'But I won't hear anything more said against Mabel. Not in my house. You do what you want in your house, but not here.'

'I hope I have not done you a great disservice.' Miss Savage clutched Mabel's hand, but kept her gaze riveted to the narrow-gauge track before her, the distant desert beyond. 'I came here never thinking I would grow to care for any of you. Thinking I was beyond caring for anyone. But you – you are different, Mabel.' She clutched the girl's hand tightly and then released it. 'You are special.'

'Thank you, Miss Savage.'

'The train should be here soon.'

'Yes, Miss Savage.'

'You have a mind, Mabel. That is more important than a gold mine. Twenty years ago I might not have said such a thing, but it is true. Gold, beauty, your very health, your ideals, your family and friends, they may all be snatched from you, but your mind is your own. If you have your mind and courage, you can do a great many things in this world. People will always tell you that you can't, but you mustn't heed them.'

'Just like I didn't heed Pa when he told me I couldn't come wait for the train with you?'

'Yes. Like that. You have courage, Mabel. Your father will no doubt punish you.'

'I s'pose, but ...' Mabel began to sniff, 'I just couldn't ...'

'Don't blubber, Mabel. Say what you have to say.'

[139]

'Oh Miss Savage – what will I do without you?'

'Exactly what you would have done with me. Grow up. All girls grow up. The graveyards are full of grown up girls. Ladies,' she added disdainfully, 'ladies are nothing but grown up girls.'

'And boys? Boys grow up too, don't they?'

'Yes.'

Mabel twisted her hands in her lap, bit her lip against the question she longed to ask, knowing if she did not ask it now, she would never have it answered. 'Do they grow up to do what you and Mr Norby were doing, Miss Savage?'

'If they're lucky.'

Together they looked down the track, molten and annealing in the inferno waves of heat. Mabel swallowed hard, longing to ask precisely what Mr Norby and Miss Savage were doing, but so paltry was her vocabulary, so devoid of anything but Lochinvarish gesture that she could not frame the question and it dissolved on her tongue for want of words. Instead, she asked, 'You want to move into the shade, Miss Savage?'

'No. It would look like retreat. Never retreat. Courage and carriage, Mabel.'

'Inflection and conviction?'

'Exactly. Inflection and conviction are everything. Strike your own path, Mabel. Use your mind and your courage and scorn piety and custom. They are nothing but fetters. Break those fetters and strike your own path. It is difficult. But rewarding. Sometimes.'

'Not always?'

'Nothing is always. Don't you remember 'Ozymandias'?'

'"Nothing beside remains/Round the decay,"' Mabel chanted, '"Of that colossal wreck, boundless and bare."'

[140]

'"The lone and level sands stretch far away,"' continued Miss Savage with a wistfulness altogether foreign to her voice. 'Just like this bloody desert.'

Mabel looked out across the boundless barrenness, out to the bruise-coloured mountains ashen in the early morning light and then to Miss Savage, equally ashen in the early morning light.

'I hope you will not have occasion to hate me, Mabel. I doubt the occasion will rise for you to – to know, the extent of what I have taught you, but if you do – no, don't interrupt, it's bourgeois to be ill-mannered – please remember that I never meant you personally any harm. I have great faith in you.' Awkwardly, Miss Savage put her arm around Mabel's shoulders as the train whistle shrilly split the distance. Mabel began to cry. 'Don't cry. I can't bear it. Run along home now.'

'But the train's not here.'

'All the better, I despise farewells. I shan't say goodbye.'

'Orv-wa, Miss Savage?'

'Yes, something like that. Now, off you go. Go, I tell you. Cry at home. Please, Mabel, I beg of you. Go.' She rose and as the tears spilled down her cheeks, she bustled Mabel off the dock as the supply train clacked and clattered forward on the narrow-gauge track.

June 1918

Dear Sarah –

In all this carnage, this colossal wreck of humanity, this boundless decay, amidst these rats, annihilations, daily death, a miracle has unfolded. The old persistent miracle rendered fresh each time. The old persistent miracle of the flesh. I have met a man.

Sarah stifled a little cry and flushed the toilet to further mask her reaction to these words. She always read Mabel's letters in the bathroom. She always collected the mail as soon as it arrived, before anyone else could see there was, or might be a letter from Mabel. This day there was a letter from Clarence as well, from Platts- burg, New York where he was training with the Army. That letter she tossed to Roy. Sarah knew well what Clarence's letter would say: the usual litany of woe, how he hated the food and sleeping quarters, the weather, and having to mix on equal terms with unconverted Jews and Catholics and people with accents. Nothing Clarence would say would surprise her, so she gave that letter to Roy and retreated to the bathroom with Ma- bel's letter.

'Dumpling!' Roy cried, banging on the bathroom door. 'Dumpling! What's Clarence mean?'

'What, dear?'

'What's Clarence mean, "Oh Ma, you were right to slap my face." When did you slap his face? Dumpling! Open up.'

'I can't just now dear, I'm on the toilet,' she lied cheerfully.

'Get out here where I can talk to you. What's this about your slapping Clarence? Dumpling!'

'Quit calling me that, Roy.'

'What? What! I'm talking about Clarence!'

'I'm talking about me, Roy. Quit calling me Dum- pling. My name is Sarah.'

'What's got into you? Get out of that bathroom.'

'Not till you quit calling me Dumpling, Roy. I'm never coming out till then.'

'What?'

'You heard me, dear. I mean it. I'm not coming out.' She heard his heavy footsteps stomping away from the bathroom door. She heard the screen door slam. From

[142]

the backyard she heard the ring of the axe; Roy always chopped wood when he was upset. She unravelled her sister's letter.

A man, English by birth, gentle by nature, who has lost his arm, but not his soul. Not his heart. He was my patient and now he is my lover. I write you this my dearest sister not to shock or horrify you, but so that you will know that if I die, I have lived. I have lived, Sarah, and loved and been loved. Love, Sarah, not all those vainglorious, Lochinvar gestures, not all that simpering, posturing piety. But love between a man and a woman. Bert and I have our love and we have this moment and it may be all we have and all we'll ever have. *Lagair* has taught me that much of *Lavee*. *Lagair* has taught me *Lamore* may flourish in the midst of *Lamaird*. I use the word without a blush. *Lamaird* is part of the price of being gifted with flesh, just as love is the reward for being cursed with flesh. Everything perishes. The body you are loving to-night may, on the morrow, be a blasted bit of black-ened flesh impaled on barbed wire. But love such as ours is not fragile as flesh. It is an expression of the flesh, but it transcends flesh and once your heart and spirit and flesh have been imbued with such love, you are never quite the same, are you?

'Are you?' Sarah wiped away her tears and listened to the steady thwack, thwack, thwack of the axe. She stepped to the bathroom window, parted the curtain and looked to Roy standing over the woodpile, his shirt off, the sun gleaming on the blade of the axe, his white shoulders, on the graying hair matting his chest. Could Roy ever be a blasted bit of blackened flesh? A surge of love, hard and visceral, shot through her compounded,

[143]

annealed with the fear of loss, the need to have her flesh imbued with love. She tucked her sister's letter in her pocket and went outside to her husband. Roy continued to thwack at the wood until he saw her. Then he put his axe down; a look of infinite sadness crossed his face. Sarah put her arms around him, her head against his chest, breathed in the warmth of his familiar scent.

The war ended before the Army could send Clarence Over There. Spared *Lagair*, Clarence had nonetheless seen something of *Lavee* beyond St Elmo, California, tasted the sweetness of salt-sweat lingering at the neck of a Plattsburg lass and this was closer than he'd ever come to *Lamore*. Certainly, he had broadened his acquaintance with *Lamaird* in its many guises, though he said nothing of any of this to the admiring girls in the bunting-draped St Elmo station who welcomed him home when he was demobbed. Greeting him as well were his Aunt Agnes and her feckless husband, his Aunt Molly and her dour husband, his cousins, his sister Cordelia, his married sisters and brother and their toddling broods and his parents. His Aunt Mabel was not there.

Mabel Judd never returned to St Elmo. Her name, however, was not listed on any sort of glorious plaque commemorating the supreme sacrifices of St Elmo youth in the Great War. Of course, she was not one of the St Elmo youth. She was forty-two, stout, bespectacled and wistful when she went to France to translate, when she discovered she possessed the vulgar tongue alone, when she sacrificed every scrap of piety and custom she'd been taught to reverence, cast all this off in the name of love.

Her lover, although one-armed, was a man of good

humour, good instincts and incredible luck. He was
amongst the first to join in August, 1914 and though he
had been badly wounded more than once, he survived:
of his original battalion, only seven other men could say
the same. After the war he returned to London where
his family owned a pub in a district much frequented by
rowdy music-hall types and even lacking his right arm,
he went back to work with the jocular observation that it
only took one arm to pull a tap or pinch a girl. He was a
married man, but his wife had left him early in the war.

All but this last bit of information, Sarah shared with
Molly and Agnes when she informed them that Mabel
was not coming home. (Sarah tidied up the pub, referring to it as a small family business.) Moreover,
Mabel had further good reason for not coming home; in
early 1919 she had been delivered of a daughter she had
named Sarah. *A child?* said Molly and Agnes more-or-
less in unison. *At her age?* to which Sarah replied that
she saw no reason to think that Mabel was lying. *Well, is
she married?* And Sarah, with appropriate carriage and
courage, inflection and conviction, said, *No, she is not*.
At that, Molly and Agnes concurred reflectively that the
family should declare Mabel Judd dead, dead in
France, a victim of the war. Sarah objected: *Say that
and I shall call you liars*, she told her sisters. *Mabel did
not die. Mabel lived*.

She lived till 1940 and died a victim of the Blitz. She
remained as loyal a wife to Bert as Leona had been to
Ephraim, though she was not able to marry him legally
till 1921 when Bert got word that his first wife had died
of the Spanish influenza which took up the task of global
death and destruction after Armistice ended the war.
With courage, carriage, inflection and conviction, Mabel survived it all; she forgave the aptly named Miss
Savage her cruel joke, even came to see it as a joke; she

made a funny story of it, delighting her regulars at the pub with her emulation of the French officer's face when she first offered her expertise. Perhaps it was the war itself that taught her forgiveness, forbearance; certainly it taught her not to put her faith in Higher Things. Mabel put her faith in love and was rewarded with a one-armed man who remained forever smitten with her and a daughter who adored her. Mabel's daughter was very likely the only child in England to be sung to sleep with 'The Battle Hymn of the Republic'. When she sang, behind the cadence of her own voice, Mabel invariably heard the counterpointing thump and throttle of the mill and mine, the clank and rattle of the supply train; she saw the neutral empty sands stretching far away, the indifferent bleached-blue sky blazing down, the boundless bare desert shrouding narrow-gauge tracks, the dust still blowing golden in a vanished street where the wind alone was left to rattle the broken panes of that colossal wreck of a house, to testify to its departed grandeur, to whistle and moan through that airy, aching splendour, those empty rooms, that antique land.

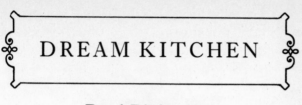

DREAM KITCHEN

Paul Pickering

Manfred whistled in the kitchen while his wife lay lard-white on their pink bed upstairs in the ridiculous green-tiled Italian-style house just off the Grunwald. Manfred would have liked to have a house which backed directly on to the park. He loved to see the children play. He liked to watch them on the swings and see their smiles in that flying moment, legs kicking with joy, before they fell back on the chain-held-arc to earth. He would have delighted to look straight out on the mysterious birch trees and spring-time daffodils. Instead, Manfred and Ulrike were a street away, a row of houses from paradise, and on one side was the bronchial rattle of the S-Bahn that roused him every morning as the dirty red and white trains wheezed their way out of East Berlin, to do their civic duty in the West, which these days was to transport senior citizens to the Grunwald, or to see fellow seventy-year-olds in the East. But the trains did not wake Ulrike.

The morning was bright. Manfred whistled louder. He whistled so loud the air caught in his moustache and made it fly up at the corners, like wings. In the old days he used to say those wings could take his thoughts where he wanted. Ulrike would laugh and brush the boyish, straight hair out of her eyes. She would tell him he was too young to have a moustache, even if it allowed him to dream. She would laugh and run away through the trees and he would catch her and hold her perfect face in his hands. He knew every curve and indentation. As the years passed Ulrike's face had ceased to be just beautiful. The face was part of him, as he whistled on that bright morning, and began to cry. Manfred's tears fell on the apple he was chopping.

When you are a child and hopeful you dream on the run. Lovers dream in bed. The dreams run ahead of them and up into the beckoning sky. But by a trick at twenty-seven Manfred was no longer young. His dreams no longer sprinted among the far clouds. Manfred came into his kitchen to dream, away from the world. He now dreamt to shut doors not open them. His only solace was behind the heavy wooden door of the kitchen. His dream kitchen.

The kitchen did have all the latest equipment of five years ago. Like every kitchen in the city it was a little shrine to the West and the free market. It was also a reminder of Manfred and Ulrike's wedding; laughing in his mother's garden in Wuppertal. They had gone away on a Caribbean honeymoon where it rained hot showers.

'I had no idea you liked cooking,' Ulrike had said three weeks after they returned. 'Let's skip dinner and go to bed. An accountant should cook the books ...' Manfred had looked away as she stood naked in the doorway. She had laughed and told him not to be a little boy. Why was he such a little innocent? Her strong hands had squeezed him tight between the legs.

Manfred cooked. But he never cooked the books.

Dreams bring a fierce innocence. An innocence which protects itself in panic ... In the distance a falcon circled over the Grunwald looking for a rustle of grey fur and the hint of a pink nose beneath the autumn leaves.

The knife was in Manfred's hands. He had bought the knife in the Kaufhaus des Westerns department store and was proud of it. The knife had been imported from France. The handle was black and heavy and felt like bone. The blade was so sharp you could splice a hair in two. Whenever he cooked he always took out the knife from its plastic and rubber sheath and put on his apron. The apron was blue and white and Manfred kept it starched and clean and it hung behind the heavy door. The door was of old oak and had come from Manfred's mother's farm. The rest of Manfred and Ulrike's house was styled in the hushed modernity of thick beige carpets and muted chrome. The door stood out like an innocent man at a political convention. Manfred examined his reflection in the kitchen window. On his hands he wore black rubber gloves. The gloves were thick and heavy and were the type fishermen used in the cold arctic seas to gut their catch. A friend had given him the gloves. Manfred loved to wear them in the kitchen.

'You look like a high priest in the temple. You look like you are about to sacrifice the poor little animals . . .' Ulrike said one night, as she came into the kitchen. The ends of her high heels had scraped against the black and white stone tiles of the kitchen floor. She had been out entertaining clients in a loud restaurant on the Kudamm. She worked for Mercedes and had begun to dress a little differently. She wore more make-up and eased sticky mascara onto her eyelashes before she went out at night. Once she would never have worn high heels; now she said the boys expected them. Her skirts were shorter. She wore stockings instead of tights.

'Where is the harm, if I can get some business? It's only for a little time, my dear. We can save money and start something on our own. You'll see. Don't worry, none of them ever lay a finger on me . . .' On those evenings she would kiss him and her breath would be sour with sweet Sekt.

[151]

Soon, Ulrike's heels became as high as her expectations. Her dresses became more expensive. She had, she said, an account with the firm. The labels in the smart black suits revealed they were from Paris. Often she had to stay overnight in Dusseldorf. Soon she began to bring her business partners home and it was Manfred who cooked while Ulrike made charming conversation and pouted her red lips over the candle-light. Once, as he brought in a dish of chicken with truffles – chicken in half-mourning was the literal translation from the French – Manfred did not recognize Ulrike. Only those cheek-bones and that boyish flop of hair, and, of course, the lilting energy in her voice, restored his faith that the woman, the slightly drunken woman in the black dress, was his wife.

'Oh, Manfred, you look so funny in your apron. Doesn't he look so funny in his apron? And that moustache ... A moustache on a ginger-haired man, I ask you ...' Her friends laughed, and Manfred retreated into his kitchen. His dream kitchen.

At first the dreams were so good. He would make blueberry flan and the juice would run on to his fingers. He would think of the blue of Ulrike's eyes. Her eyes were almost too blue. Her mother had been a doctor and had made the little girl wear masked glasses for the first thirty days of her life. That way, she said, the eyes did not change colour. They would not become dull brown, the colour of beggars' overcoats. Ulrike hated her mother and her father had died in prison. Her blue eyes reminded Ulrike of endless arguments with her mother. To Manfred the blue eyes would change into two blue-birds and he and Ulrike would go flying high over Berlin and away into the enchanted forest where all the houses were made of marzipan and kind old women toasted cheese on long forks and made chocolate drinks.

Everyone would be enchanted by the beauty of Ulrike.
Even the animals of the wild wood.

The knife cut into his finger. Manfred came back
from his dream.

'So what do you do, Manfred?' said one of the grey
suits that smelled of the same aftershave. 'You don't
cook all the time, do you? He doesn't cook all the time
does he, Ulrike? You don't keep the poor man chained
in the kitchen? Do you treat him rough, Ulrike?'

They laughed. The laughter was not gentle.
The sound was not the innocent merriment in the marzipan cottages of the enchanted forest. Manfred imagined the leaves of the giant trees as he chopped the
parsley.

'He's an accountant.'

'Where's he an accountant?'

'At the old chemical plant . . .'

'They make medical supplies,' said Manfred, defensively. He had just put down the dish on the table of
smoked glass. In his hands he held the knife. On his
hands were the thick rubber gloves.

'Perhaps you can help us, Manfred?'

'Perhaps he can be of some use?'

'I think so . . .?'

Ulrike looked at him beseechingly. She was about to
leave her job with the car company. She wanted to go
into business on her own. It was something to do with
these men in dark suits whose eyes twinkled when they
glanced at her. They never brought their wives.

Manfred and Ulrike had argued. She smashed a glass
and swore she did not want to spend the rest of her life in
that little house near the Grunwald and the rattle of the
S-Bahn line. The sound of decay. The song of the
miserable East.

He would do anything for her, he soothed. He would

cook for her. Manfred cooked most days. But he never cooked the books.

Her tongue would slowly wind round inside his mouth like the hand of a clock. Ulrike would be on tiptoe. She would be naked. He felt the hair between her legs against his hand. Her legs were so strong. He would do anything for her. She did not belong to the men in suits ... she belonged to him. What use was money to two blue-birds?

When they first met she had despised money. She had despised things. They had marched against the Americans, against corruption in local government and against nuclear power. She had touched his face and looked deep into his eyes.

'The future will be different, Manfred. You will see ...'

Now he saw. He watched her unclip a stocking from her suspender belt. The future was more different than ever he, her sweet Manfred, could have imagined.

Once they had been vegetarians. He had become a vegetarian a year before she had after a visit with a farmer friend to an abattoir. Manfred knew some vegetarian recipes and so he cooked all the time. Ulrike had let him.

'I love to be waited on,' she said. 'I love to be waited on by a caring and gentle man.' They had planned to live in the country. Now she did not come alive before midnight.

'I love you, Ulrike ...'

But lately, increasingly, he bought red meat. Manfred liked to cut the red meat with the sharp knife made specially for French chefs. He liked the cut against the grain. He liked to feel the unflinching steel slice through to the oak board beneath. He bought a rabbit and skinned it himself, dressed in his rubber gloves and apron when Ulrike was away in Dusseldorf on a business trip. The head peered at him from the draining-board. He felt the velvet of the creature's soft ears. He could smell the dawn in its nostrils and taste the grass on its sharp white teeth. Manfred wished he could dream the rabbit back to life.

'I love you, Ulrike. How I love you.'

When he cut the meat he was a pure white knight, riding out at the head of a fantastic grey army of marching men. The tramping of feet, perfectly in time, could be heard from one city to the next on the still air which hung over the German plain. The smell of blood and fire consumed him. Often he would pop a piece of the raw steak into his mouth like a bon-bon. The figures of Ulrike's suave companions would swarm before him like bees and then drop away; so many drops of blood. He had to ride out. He had to protect her. But when she stared at him, his dreams never got beyond the kitchen.

She licked his lips after he cooked steak for her that night.

'You would do anything for me, would you, Manfred?'

'Anything *liebling* . . .'

'Would you get me this? I know they make it at your firm. One of the people we are in business with . . . He has a clinic. He needs the chemical. It's an anaesthetic, I think. The government are very stuffy about these things. He is no longer on the medical register, you see . . .'

Manfred was a cook. But he had never cooked the books. He had never cooked the books until the day of the stocktaking.

He pointed at some black bottles on a shelf.

'What are these?'

'My God, Manfred. Do you realize you have asked a

question about my compounds? This is the first time in four years. We must have a celebration.'

Manfred and the chemist smiled. They had played together in a weekend football team before the chemist's wife had a baby. Manfred wanted Ulrike to have a child. He would take the toddler to the Grunwald; to play on the swings.

'No seriously, what is it?'

'No kidding?'

'Is it some kind of anaesthetic?'

The chemist laughed.

'Oh, you wouldn't feel anything if you took a dose of that. The effect is like an insulin overdose. You go into a coma. The body functions keep ticking over. The compound was devised from the poison a Larder Wasp uses to paralyse tarantula spiders so her young can feed on them . . . Really grisly.'

'But what do you use it for?'

'Well, believe it or not, they are experimenting with very small quantities in heart disease . . . The truth is, Manfred, I don't know . . .'

'You can't buy it?'

'Why would anyone one want to buy tarantula poison? Come on, Manfred. Let's get on . . .'

Manfred cooked, but he never cooked the books. At least not until that day he took down two of the stubby black bottles from the shelves and amended all the dockets and invoices and computer records accordingly. The poison vaults of the chemical plant were vast. They had been built in the last war. Here they had made the crystals for Zyclone B, the gas they had used on the Jews. Eight cases of the compound were at the other end of the vault. New workers were shown them as a curiosity.

The two bottles were in his pocket as he researched

the Larder Wasp in the American library. The truth
had made him shudder.

'Manfred . . . this is Paul. He is the head of our little
venture. I am sure you have much to talk about,' en-
thused Ulrike later that night. She was so beautiful. He
envied her.

Manfred took the small hand and almost immediately
wished he was wearing the thick black gloves he used in
the kitchen. The hand was limp and cold. The man had
a flabby white face and a completely bald head. But his
eyes shone with a steely enthusiasm. He was dressed
more conservatively than a bank manager. Yet, no one
could meet those eyes and deny that the man was a
leader. The eyes frightened Manfred.

Ulrike saw Manfred frown and kissed him lightly on
the cheek. She smelled of expensive perfume.

'I am in business with your wife . . .'

Paul's tone was firm. He held his Balkan Sobranie
cigarette like a dart.

'Thank you for the little favour you did for us.'

Ulrike put her arm around Manfred.

'What do you want it for?' he asked.

'Oh that's a secret,' said Paul. 'We doctors like to play
our cards close to our chests.'

'What sort of doctor is he?' Manfred asked Ulrike
later.

'Don't be boring, darling . . . Let's enjoy ourselves.
Darling, I may have to go on a business trip to France
with Paul. You don't mind, now, do you?'

While she was away in France Manfred read the
stories about the transplants. They were sensational
accounts in *Bild Zeitung* about gypsy children being
drugged so they were barely alive and then being
dumped at hospital doors minus a kidney. The kid-
nappers used a rare drug to subdue their prey. They

used a compound similar to the venom of certain insects.

Manfred cooked. But only once had he cooked the books. In his mind he was the innocent knight on horseback with a flashing sword. He was losing Ulrike. When she came back from France he knew she was slipping away. He could tell the way she touched Paul's tweed-jacketed elbow. He forgot all about his fears . . . about the article in *Bild Zeitung*. Paul was going away on a trip to Turkey.

'I want your lovely wife to change her hair. When I come back I am going to persuade her to have a perm. It would look so much better curly. Don't you think, Manfred . . .?'

In the kitchen he did nothing but think these days; think and dream. He could not dream of Ulrike any more. Her eyes no longer turned into two blue-birds. She had been taken by someone else.

'Oh, Manfred, everything is going so perfectly. Soon we will have enough money to move away from this miserable little house. We could even move to Dusseldorf . . .'

'I always wanted a house in the next street near the children's playground.'

'Oh no, darling. Why settle for innocence when we can afford any experience. I never thought we would be rich, darling. All it takes is a little courage. Darling, you are not eating your salmon. You took so much trouble . . .'

The next day she went into a coma.

He had called the family doctor and the man had taken her into the hospital. They had run tests and found nothing. They could not understand why she did not need to breathe on a machine. Manfred asked if she could come home and they allowed it. A nurse visited every day. Paul had rung and Manfred had not told him about the coma. Paul had not rung again. He was off on another trip.

After two weeks Ulrike began to haemorrhage under the skin.

They had been a glorious two weeks. Manfred had sat looking at her naked body, dreaming of the times they had had together. He could even hold her eyelids open and feast on those blue eyes. Manfred and Ulrike could be blue-birds again.

But it could not last forever. Manfred cooked but he only once cooked the books and there is a price to be paid for everything. Manfred's mother had told him that.

Ulrike was still breathing. The deep trusting breaths of a child asleep. And then he had the idea.

Once it was a tradition at carnival-time to make fake death-masks in sweet, shortcrust pastry. The masks formed the top of small fruit pies which were eaten by revellers when they came home from the parties. A lover would always eat the image of his loved one.

Manfred cooked. But this time he was not going to cook the books.

He mixed the sugar and the butter and the flour and rolled it out on a wooden board. Today he was not dreaming. Then, wearing his black gloves, he cut out the shape of a heart in the pastry with the sharp black-handled knife, made in Paris.

Manfred held the pastry out in front of him as he walked slowly upstairs.

For a last time he looked at the beautiful face. Here and there was a line where at the university everything had been smooth. But this way she would age no more. She had once begged him to kill her if ever she betrayed their ideals. She had given him a rosebud. He had offered her a lilac blossom. Gently, he covered the face with the pastry and a tear dripped down as he held the pastry tight over the nose and mouth.

He held the pastry tight until the breathing subsided.

Ulrike's eyelids flickered as she died. To Manfred it announced the blue-birds flying free. She would be no longer at the mercy of men who smoked Swiss cheroots and smelled of the same aftershave they bought duty free on international flights. She would be his again. They would be able to dream for all eternity.

Outside the window of the kitchen he saw a hawk hovering and then wheeling out over the Grunwald. White fleecy clouds were blowing up. He closed the comforting oak door behind him after he had placed the pastry mask carefully on the formica worktop. He had prepared the pastry-case two days ago and baked it blind in a hot oven, the pastry weighted with beans so it would not fluff up. Now, he stirred in the blueberries. They tasted so fresh. They reminded him of her eyes. They were as sweet as her lips. She was running ahead of him along the Kurfürstendamm, laughing. Theirs was the future.

Slowly he uncorked the bottle of poison.

A teaspoonful had produced paralysis.

He poured the rest of the bottle into the pie.

Manfred cooked. But this time he was not going to cook the books.

For a moment he was disturbed by the ugly business with gypsy children and then dismissed the shameful vision. He thought only of blue-birds.

The pie was in the oven. He calculated the minutes on the oven clock. He had time now to put their documents in order. He would leave both their organ donor cards for the police. Manfred had already posted a letter telling them what he was going to do. He felt so calm.

At last the pie was ready.

It had been a success.

He could see her features perfectly.

Manfred had been concerned the eyes would lack detail. But her cheekbones were there. All that was missing was the boyish shock of hair.

It was almost sacrilege to eat the pie. But eat he did. With every mouthful of sweetness he saw her face. He saw her face and tasted the bitterness beneath the berries. As he finished the last mouthful the 'phone rang.

'Ah Manfred, this is Paul . . .'

'I thought you were still away . . .'

Manfred felt a stiffness at the back of his hand. He put the heavy knife down on the telephone table and pulled off one of the black gloves, holding the receiver under his chin. His lips tingled, like when he was a child and first had a block of American ice-cream. Paul was excited.

'I thought I would be the first to tell you.'

'About the transplants?'

There was no point in pretending anymore.

'What transplants? No, I wanted to be the first one to tell Ulrike about our project's triumph. Is she there? The chemical you got. Don't you remember . . .? We've found a cure for baldness. Don't tell anyone but that poison is one of the ingredients. In very small and safe quantities, mind. It wouldn't matter anyway. The only person to have the full formula is Ulrike, and it's in her pretty little head. She is such a clever girl. My hair is growing! I have no need for hair transplants. It is really growing! We are all going to be rich . . . You can cook what you want now, Manfred . . . You can have things beyond your wildest dreams. We had an idea the formula was good but needed to do some trials in Turkey . . . We are going to be rich . . .'

At that moment Manfred realized he had only ever wanted Ulrike. She would forgive him. He knew she would forgive him. He had saved her.

He could no longer hear Paul talking as he hit the floor. Manfred and Ulrike were blue-birds flying high over Berlin, bound for the enchanted forest. For every recipe works in a dream kitchen.

OPEN TO
THE PUBLIC

Muriel Spark

Warily she moves from room to room, lingering over the mortal furniture which resembles in style, but has long since replaced, the lost originals. This is the house of the young Jean-Jacques Rousseau, Les Charmettes, on the outskirts of Chambéry in the Savoie district of France, where from 1736 to 1742 he vitally resided with clever Mme de Warens, his mature friend, thirteen years his senior, to whom he was official lover and whom he called 'Maman'. It was their summer residence.

It is early spring. There had been few visitors, the guardian told her when she bought her ticket and a brochure downstairs at the entrance. As in most of these out-of-the-way preserved houses of the famous, the good guardian was willing to unfold the history of the place down there in his lodge beside a stove, and not at all anxious about letting a well-behaved and quiet-looking visitor roam free among the chilly rooms, downstairs and up.

It is upstairs that she finds a fellow-visitor. She is not sure why she is surprised but possibly this is because she hasn't heard him moving about until she comes upon him staring into the little alcove where Jean-Jacques Rousseau's bed, or a replica of his bed, is fitted.

The man is tall and thin, somewhere about thirty, casually dressed in a black short coat and greenish-brown trousers. When he turns to look at her she sees his jersey is black with a rim of his white shirt showing at the neck, so that one might take him for a clergyman, but for the trousers. He has a long face, fairish hair, greyish eyes. His casual outfit is slightly outdated although in fact quite smart and expensive. And she has seen him before. He looks away and then he looks again in her direction. Why?

Because he has seen her before.

She continues her tour of the rooms, noticing details as is her way. Close details. The wallpaper in Mme de Warens' room is original 18th century, it is said, with small hand-painted flowers. This is the grandest room in the house. Two great windows look out on to the cold garden of early spring and beyond that, the valley and the mountains. Down there in the garden the enamoured young man Rousseau waited each morning, looking up for the shutters to open and 'it was day *chez maman*' –

She goes downstairs again, having another look at all there is to see. She sees the other visitor at the porter's vestibule, his back turned towards her. He is buying postcards. She leaves the museum and goes her way. Outside the gates a small cream-coloured Peugeot is parked.

You must have heard of Ben Donadieu, the biographer and son-in-law of Henry Castlemaine the novelist. He had married Dora Castlemaine in 1960, passionate about her ageing father's once-famous novels which were already falling into a phase of obscurity. About Dora herself he was not at all passionate and for this she was rather thankful. Sixteen years older than Ben, she was then forty-six, spinsterish. Her true object of love was her once-famous father. She married Ben, then about thirty, mainly because he had a job as a school-master, a means of livelihood to assist her father's dwindling income and to enable her to give up her job and devote herself to her father.

Henry Castlemaine loved his daughter dearly, and himself a little more. He accepted the basis of the marriage as he had in the long past accepted the adulation of his readers and the discipleship of young critics. Ben moved into the Castlemaine house and in the evenings and school holidays set about sorting the Castlemaine papers, and taking voluminous notes on his conversations with the ageing novelist. Castlemaine was now eighty-five.

It was about three years later, after the biography was published, that the Castlemaine revival set in. The Castlemaine novels were reprinted, they were filmed and televised. When Henry Castlemaine died he was once again at the height of his fame.

He left his house to his daughter, Dora. All his papers, all his literary estate, everything. Ben, however, had the royalties from his biography of Henry Castlemaine. They were fairly substantial.

In those last years of Castlemaine's life, their financial position had improved, largely through the initial efforts of Ben to revive his father-in-law's fame. They were able to employ a cook and a maid, leaving Dora free to be a real companion to her father and take him for drives in their new Volkswagen.

Nobody was surprised when, after Castlemaine's death, the marriage broke up. Its only real basis had been the couple's devotion to Dora's father. Ben, now still a young and sprightly thirty-five and Dora fifty-one, oldish for her age, had nothing in common except their memories of the old man. He had been authoritative and tiresome, but Dora hadn't minded. Ben had felt the personal weight of his famous father-in-law. He had put up with it, for the sake of the admired works, and his own efforts to promote them, day by day, in his study, docketing the archives, on the telephone to television and film producers.

In the early days of his marriage he had tried to make love to Dora, and succeeded fairly often out of sheer enthusiasm for her father. Dora herself couldn't keep it up. She was obsessed by her father, and Ben was no substitute. Now Ben was left with the proceeds of his biography. His work was done. Dora was immensely rich.

Henry Castlemaine was buried. A crowded memorial service, reporters, television; and the next week it was over. Henry Castlemaine lived on in his posthumous fame, but Dora and Ben were no longer a couple.

It was at this point that very little was publicly known. It was understood that Dora refused to leave the house of her childhood and her father's life. Ben took a flat in London and grumbled to his friends that Dora was stingy. She gave him an allowance. The proceeds from his biography could not last forever. He wrote a lot of Castlemaine essays, and was said to be thinking of some other subject, something fresh to write about.

Within a few months Dora suggested a divorce:

Dear Ben,
I intend to see my lawyer, Bassett. He will no doubt be in touch with you. I know Father would have wished us to stay together and to love each other as he wished from the start. It was Father's wish that I should never want for anything, indeed he hated to talk about the financial details of life in those old days when his books had started to fade out, and we met. I know that Father would have wished me to show my

appreciation, and express his acknowledgment of, the part you played in our life (even although I am of course convinced that the revival of Father's great reputation would have been inevitable in any case). That is why I have instructed Bassett to offer you a monthly allowance which you are free to accept or reject according to your conscience. The divorce should go through as quietly and smoothly as possible. Father would have wished that at least. Above all, Father, I think, would have wished for complete discretion on the fact that our union was a marriage in name only, even although the situation could be amply testified to by the domestics (who are of course always aware of everything, as Father always said). So I could have obtained a divorce quite easily on other grounds than mutual consent thus saving the allowance I am offering you in amicable settlement. I trust you have benefitted by your stay with us under our roof for these years past.

Father would wish me to enjoy the fruits of his labours, and soon I shall be taking a trip abroad, especially to those haunts so beloved of Father.

Yours, in good faith,
Dora Castlemaine

It was that 'in good faith', more than her formal signature, that chilled Ben's bones. He recalled a phrase from one of Henry Castlemaine's books: 'Beware the wickedness of the righteous'.

What is there to see in the austere and awesome birthplace of Joan of Arc at Domrémy-la-Pucelle in the Vosges? It is full of grey-walled emptiness, and there is no doubt someone has been here and has gone. It stands just off the road, in the shade of a large tree. Nearby is a bridge over the Meuse where a man hovers, looking down at the water. A small cream-coloured Peugeot is parked close by, waiting for him, with the driver's door open. He has got in once and got out again. He has looked round at the woman who has been watching him while he tours the simple birthplace, now open to the public. The woman watches him as he drives away, too fast, away and away, so that the guardian at the ticket entrance comes out to join her on the road, staring after him.

Ben and Dora were never divorced. He showed her letter round their friends. It had been the couple's boast that they had few friends, but, as always when 'a few friends' come to be counted up, they amounted to a surprising number. Most of them were indignant.

'That's a shabby way to treat you, Ben. First, you build up a fortune for her, and now she . . .'

'Ben, you must see a lawyer. You are entitled to . . .'

'What a cold, what a very frigid letter. But between you and me, she was always in love with her father. It was incestuous.'

'I won't go to a lawyer,' Ben said. 'I'll go to see Dora.'

He went to see her, unannounced. The door was opened by a tall, fat youth who beamed with delight when Ben gave his name and demanded his wife.

'Dora's in the kitchen.'

The father's smell had gone from the house. Ben glanced through the dining-room door on the way to the kitchen. There was new wallpaper, a new carpet. Dora was there in the kitchen, unhappy of face, beating up an omelette. The kitchen table was laid for a meal, which meal no one could guess, whether lunch or breakfast. It was four-fifteen in the afternoon. Anyway, Dora was unhappy. She clung to her unhappiness, Ben saw clearly. It was all she had.

The flaccid youth scraped a chair across the kitchen floor towards Ben. 'Make yourself at home,' he said.

Ben turned to leave.

'Stay, don't go,' said Dora. 'We should sit down and discuss the situation like three civilized people.'

'I've had enough of three civilized people,' Ben said. 'There was your father and you, so very civilized; and I was civilized enough to let myself be used and then thrown out when I was no more use.'

The flabby youth said, 'As I understand it you were never a husband to Dora. She let herself be used as a means to your relationship with her father.'

'Who is he?' Ben demanded, indicating the young man.

Dora brought an omelette to the table and set it before her friend. 'Eat it while it's hot. Don't wait for me.' She started breaking eggs into the bowl. The youth commenced to eat.

'Isn't there a drink in the house?' said Ben. 'This is sordid.' He got up and went into the living-room where the drinks were set out, as always, on a tray. When he got back with his whisky and soda, the young man's place was empty, part of his omelette still on his plate. Ben then saw through the kitchen window the ends of the young man's trousers and his shoes disappearing up the half-flight of steps which led to the garden and a door to the lane behind. Dora, with her omelette-turner still in her hand went to shut the kitchen door which had been left open.

'You can have this omelette,' said Dora. 'I'll make another for myself.'

'I couldn't eat it, thanks, at this hour. What happened to your friend?'

[171]

'I suppose he was embarrassed when he saw you,' said Dora.

'About what?'

'About his coming to live here and opening the house to the public. I owe it to Father. First I'll have a trip abroad and then, believe me, I'll arrange for a companion, an assistant, somebody, to help me turn the house into a museum. Father's rooms, his manuscripts.'

'Well, that was my idea,' Ben said. 'That's what we were always planning to do when Henry was dead.'

'You aren't the only Castlemaine enthusiast,' Dora said. 'I'm not too old to marry again and I could open the house to the public, only certain rooms, the important ones. I've had the house repainted and the floors mended. I could do it with a new partner.'

'Why on earth should you want to marry again?'

'The usual reasons,' Dora said. 'Love, sex, companionship. The Castlemaine idea wasn't enough, after all. You can't go to bed with an idea.'

'You used to,' he said, 'when Henry was alive'.

'Well, I don't now.'

'Do you mind if I look over the house before I go?' Ben said.

Dora studied her watch. She sighed. She put the dishes in the sink.

'I'll come with you,' she said. 'What exactly do you want?'

'To see for myself what it's like now.'

They went from room to room. The chairs were newly upholstered, the walls and woodwork freshly painted. In Henry Castlemaine's study his papers were piled on the floor on a plastic sheet, his desk had been replaced by a trestle-table on which more papers and manuscripts were piled. 'I'm working on the papers,'

[172]

said Dora. 'It'll take time. A lot of his books have been re-bound and some are still at the binders.'

Ben looked at the shelves. The books that Henry had used most, his shabby poetry, his worn reference books, were now done up in glittering gold and half-calf bindings.

'You'll never get through those papers yourself,' Ben said. 'It's an enormous job. The letters alone – '

'I'll have them in showcases,' Dora said, her voice monotonous and weary. 'I can get help, lots of help.'

'Look,' said Ben. 'I know you can get help. But it's a professional job. You need scholars, people with taste.'

'All right, I'll get scholars, people with taste.'

'Do you intend to marry that young man, what was his name?'

'I could marry him. I haven't decided,' she said.

'Do you mean he's a manuscript expert?'

'Oh, no,' she said. 'I wouldn't let a fellow like that touch Father's papers. But he'd be very good at the entrance-hall, giving out tickets, when I open the house to the public. Can't you see him in that role?'

'Yes, I can,' said Ben.

'The divorce should go through – '

'Look, Dora, I must tell you that I'm going to make a claim. I'm entitled to a share of what I've built up for you over the last seven years.'

'I expected you would. The lawyer expected it. We'll make a settlement.'

'Castlemaine was nowhere when I married you.'

'I said we'll make a settlement.'

'It's a sad end to our ambitions,' Ben said. 'We were always going to open the house to the public, Henry knew that. Now you'll make a mess of it, are making a mess of it. You'll never get through those archives.'

'Are you proposing to come back here and work on the papers?' she said.

'I might consider it. For Henry's sake.'

'But for my sake?'

'For Henry's sake. You didn't marry me for my sake. It was always Father, Father.'

'Yes,' she said, 'and now Father's dead. We have no more in common.'

'We still have our ambition for the Castlemaine museum in common, our dreams.'

'It's time for you to go. I want some sleep,' Dora said, her eyes fixed on her watch.

As she closed the study door there was the sound behind them in the study of a bundle of papers slithering to the floor, blown by the draught. Then, another thump of paper urged on by the displacement of the first lot. Dora took no notice.

The visitors, it seems to the young girl-student who is taking her turn at the entrance-desk, appear to be nervously aware of each other, although they have arrived separately. There is something old-fashioned about them both. It is not exactly the cut and style of their clothes that gives this impression; it is not exactly anything; it is something inexact. They are both English or perhaps American: the girl's ear is not attuned to the difference, especially as they have each said so few words when buying their ticket. 'How long has the museum been open?' and 'Is that really Freud's hat?' Freud's hat, a bourgeois light-brown felt hat, is hanging on the coat-stand with Freud's walking stick. The girl follows the visitors. The man is tall, good-looking, around thirty. The woman, prim with her hair combed back into a bun is older. They look studious, as do most

people who come to visit the house of Sigmund Freud at
19 Berggasse, Vienna. But the fact that they look at each
other from time to time anxiously, then anxiously look
away, makes the young guardian of the shrine feel
increasingly nervous. There are precious objects lying
about: a collection of primitive artefacts on the studio
table, manuscripts and letters in the glass-topped show-
tables. Could the visitors be accomplices in a projected
robbery?'

'That is the Couch,' says the girl-student. 'Yes, the
the original Couch.' The couch is large, floppy and soft.
One could go to sleep forever in it, sinking deeper and
deeper.

'And this is the waiting-room.'

'Ah, the waiting-room,' says the young man.

'Is it haunted?' says the woman, touching one of the
red plush chairs lined up against the wall, themselves
waiting for something.

'Hunted?' says the puzzled girl.

'No, haunted. Ghosts.'

'No,' says the young woman, looking behind her in
sharp surprise, for the man has left abruptly, and is
already outside the door of the flat. When she turns back
to the woman she is amazed to find nobody there.

At the family home of Louis Pasteur the bacteriologist
at Arbois, in the rainy Jura, she is there and so is he.
'This was the dining table. This is the board where he
carved. What rain! – will it never stop? You would like
to see the laboratory, Madame, Monsieur, this way.' It
is taken for granted they are a couple. The laboratory is
scrubbed but somehow dusty, and a few old books are
lying about realistically. '. . .his researches into organ-
isms and fermentations.'

[175]

'Few people,' says the young man, in lucid but for-eign French, 'realize that pasteurized milk comes from Pasteur.'

'True,' says the guide.

The couple leave together. Outside in the rain she says, 'It's time for you to stop following me.'

'I'm not following you,' he says, 'I'm following our ambition. It's for you to go back where you came from. It was you who broke away.'

'There is no contract,' she says. 'No pledge. It was you who provoked the rift. We never had a marriage that you could call a marriage. As I've told you, I have always intended to open Father's house to the public after Father's death.'

'You'll never do it,' he says. 'Not without me. I'm part of the ambition. I have to go on.'

'You're the ghost of an ambition,' she says.

'So are you, the ghost of a dream and a plan.'

He gets into his car and drives off leaving her in the wet, old street.

Dora opened the door of her father's study and closed it again. It was two years since he died. Her new young man was the third in the series and, like his two prede-cessors, his enthusiasm for helping to put the papers in order and setting up the house as a museum, had waned or perhaps was never there. But unlike the others he has had a good effect on Dora. This young man was in the wholesale fashion business; his attempts to smarten-up Dora's appearance had been successful. In her fifties Dora looked healthy for the first time in her life. His devotion to her, or rather, his quite eccentric passion, always did wonders for her morale, as she herself put it.

'Apart from being Henry Castlemaine's daughter,

what is there in me for you?' she once asked the new young man.

'You're fascinating by yourself.'

It was, in a way, all she wanted to hear or know from him. The very next day she had telephoned to Ben. A woman's voice answered the 'phone, a silly voice. 'Who's speaking?' – 'His wife.' – 'Oh, wife.' – 'Yes, wife.' (Voice off : 'Ben, it's for you. She says she's your wife.') – A pause and Ben is on the 'phone. 'Yes, Dora, what do you want?' – 'Lionel and I have to make a decision about Father's papers. I think you could be helpful.' – 'Who's Lionel?' – 'My friend.' – 'I thought he was Tim.' – 'No, Tim was last year. Anyway – ' – 'I'll come round one day.' – 'Better make it soon.' – 'Some time in the next couple of weeks, I can't manage sooner.'

She is appalled to see him at the Brontë's house of doom and dread, at Haworth in Yorkshire.

'This is where they walked up and down at night, after dinner, here in this dining-room, planning the future – '

Outside, in the graveyard among the tombstones, there by Emily Brontë's grave, she turns and says,

'Stop following me.'

A small group of American visitors are watching them. They see a neurotic-looking woman in her mid-forties apparently trying to shake off a bewildered man in his late twenties or early thirties, both slightly out-moded in their appearance.

'People are looking at us,' he says.

'It is my one hope,' she says, 'that we should open the house for Father. I've been round so many houses. They are all so bleak. Museums have no heart.'

'Stop haunting them,' he says. 'That's what I've come to tell you.'

[177]

'Then you'll be free, is that it?'

'Don't tell me,' he says, 'that you're free, wandering around in this timelessness, as you do.'

They walk away, he to his car and she to nowhere. The American group are already standing before the solemn Brontë graves, reading the inscriptions.

It is at Lamb House, Rye, in East Sussex that the ghosts of their ambition finally reach a decision.

'Would you like to sign the book?' says the curator. 'This is where James received his visitors; yes, it is rather small, quite poky; yes, indeed with his bulk he must have found it quite cramped. But upstairs – '

Out in the garden beside the graves of Henry James's dogs Ben says,

'I don't know how you could bear to open your old home to the public. It's so charming as it is.'

'If it wasn't for Father I would feel the same,' Dora says. 'But Father's ambition was always for his fame to be perpetuated, for ever and ever, it seems, elongated, on and on into the future.'

'The future has arrived,' he says, 'and you've done nothing about it but sit around drinking with your young men, thinking of your father.'

'And what have you been doing?'

'Sitting around drinking with my girls, thinking of your father.'

'To hell with Father,' she says.

Dora opened the door.

'Lionel was desolate,' she said. 'I was a bit sad myself, for he was the best of the lot. But he knew he had to go.'

'You've got a new haircut,' he said.

[178]

'Have you come for Father, his papers?'

'No, I've come for you.'

She led the way upstairs in the new freedom of her trousers, and opened the door to the hopeless study, with its piles of archives going back to 1890 or worse.

'I suppose we should give them to a university,' she said.

'We would never be free,' he said. 'Those ghosts, those ghosts, would never let us go. Letters from students, letters from scholars. It would be the same old industry.'

They lit a bonfire in the garden that night. It took them many hours to burn all the Castlemaine papers. But they sat around drinking in the back wash-house, watching the flames curl round the papers and going out every now and again to feed the fire with a new armful, until they were all consumed.

This story is a sequel to 'The Fathers' Daughters' from *The stories of Muriel Spark* (Bodley Head).

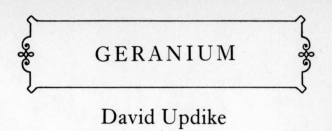

GERANIUM

David Updike

He would live, the woman told him, at the back of the house, in the two small rooms which, now that the children were away at college, they no longer used. As they went up the back staircase he followed a step or two behind her, so that his eyes fell on the ruffled, blue and white fabric of her seersucker shorts, and below, the smooth brown skin of the back of her knees, burnished brown by the late summer sun.

'And sometimes we use this room too,' she was saying, with a sweeping gesture of her hand gliding through the dusty beams of sunlight that fell through the window nearby, 'but you'll have this part of the house pretty much to yourself.' She was neither young nor old, fortyish he guessed, halfway between his parents' age and his: her hair was a frazzled, reddish-brown, and her eyes a pale, iridescent blue with a faint latticework of lines fanning out from the corners of her eyes, dissipating on the flushed bloom of her cheeks. The rooms were small, but had a beautiful view of the trees and the lawn and the river beyond, and he knew instinctively that he would take it, and live there, and through the windows he would see the seasons changing, leaves turning yellow, then brown, and then falling, only to be covered by a blanket of snow which, melting in the warm April sun, would give way to green grass and yellow flowers before the whole lovely cycle repeated itself again.

'And there is an apartment above you, where Hope Hilliard lives, and another below that Peter Veen rents

[183]

out as a studio – he's a painter. Have you met Peter? Well, he's very nice. We're having the gutters redone and the entire house painted this fall, so there might be some banging around for a while, but that should be over by Christmas.'

He moved after Labor Day, and true to her word he was woken each morning by the good-natured sounds of workmen going about their business – ladders clanging, buckets being dropped, their manly banter – as they stood around sipping coffee in the first liquid rays of the sun. It was a beautiful fall – soft days of sunlight, leaves tumbling past his window, and beyond, ships gliding back and forth on the smooth broad belly of the river. At dusk he would walk to the end of the lawn and watch the sun set, and on his way back to the house catch occasional glimpses of domestic life within – Mrs Charters gliding through the kitchen with an enormous salad bowl, her kindly husband washing dishes at the sink, their adolescent son procrastinating in the rooms above, pacing past the window like a caged animal.

He had always been attracted to families, drawn to the emanate warmth of domestic life, and was always cheered by the sounds that seeped under his door – someone thumping up the stairs, Mrs Charters' tinkly laughter, the gentle din of familial banter. He was, in a sense, between families himself – the one which produced him, and the one which, in theory, he would produce, and was also, for once, between girlfriends, a bachelor in fact as well as spirit, and perhaps as a consequence his thoughts sometimes drifted toward the figure of Mrs Charters – 'Lauren', as she suggested he call her – as she went about her daily routine: in jogging clothes when she returned, lightly sweating, from her morning run; in worn dungarees with a red kerchief wrapped around her head as she raked leaves on a

[184]

Sunday afternoon; with briefcase in hand when she returned home after a day of work. One morning he looked out the window and saw her at the end of the lawn in something like a bathrobe, her hair still wet, her head held high in a moment of contemplation so deep he could feel it a hundred yards away. And then her reverie was broken by the sound of a slamming door, and there was Mr Veen, hands in pockets, striding towards her across the lawn: she turned and smiled, as in a movie, speaking words which made Veen laugh but which Michael, though he tried, could not hear. And then they strolled up the lawn together and disappeared into their respective sides of the house.

Mr and Mrs Charters were about the same age Michael's parents had been when they were last married, a decade or so before: she was as beautiful as he was handsome, and both had reached the stage, a kind of epiphany of adulthood, when, though 'middle-aged', they were still capable of things spontaneous and athletic, possessed of a lingering spark of youth, a sense of themselves as vibrant, sexual beings. Mrs Charters had turned forty the previous spring, she told him one day on the driveway, but then added 'But I don't feel forty – not at all. I feel like I could do anything, still.' She said this with a certain wavering conviction, as if trying to stave off the ominous spectre of middle age.

Michael's downward neighbour, Veen, was a pleasant, cheerful man who would arrive each morning before seven, announced by the crackle of gravel on the driveway, and the slamming of his door which, unfortunately, was right beneath Michael's bed. He would stay until almost midnight, working, presumably on his meticulous canvases, or on someone's tax return by which, he had confessed, he earned his 'bread and butter'. He was a slight, kindly man with soft blue eyes and a beard on the verge of turning grey. And although he was friendly, and eager that he and Michael 'get to know each other' he always seemed to be walking backwards, away from him, as if anxious to get back inside, out of sight of the world. Another thing Michael didn't quite understand was why he never had paint on his hands.

'Well, gosh, I never really thought of it,' he said when he asked. 'You're not supposed to are you? I guess it's left over from my banking days – neatness. Beside, paint has lead in it. I need all the brain cells I have left!' He looked tired, as though he thought too much and slept too little, and was turning to go when, almost as an afterthought he said 'My gosh, Michael! Do you know how free you are? No kids, no house, no college loans to pay. You could pack up right now and move to China if you wanted.'

'And do what?'

'Whatever – live! But I couldn't do it – not without affecting the lives of other people – my wife, kids – defaulting on the house.' He seemed to be working his way towards some sort of confession, then retreated. 'But I guess the grass always looks greener, and all that stuff – every sword has two edges.' Too much philosophy for this early in the morning. 'It's nice to have you around,' he said with a faint smile, and walked slowly across the driveway and into his rooms.

A few nights later Michael returned to the house to find the driveway filled with cars and the house surrounded by loitering teenagers, and on his way to his room he ran into Mrs Charters as she hovered around upstairs, superintending from a distance this party thrown by her son.

'Do you think it's all right?' she said when she saw him. 'We told them they could drink, but they can't drive home. We have car pools – only the sober ones can drive.' She was wearing a black evening-dress, and her hair fell in whispy strands down around her neck, and she seemed slightly nervous, giddy, as she peered down the staircase onto a sea of noisy teenagers. 'Do you want a beer, Michael?' she asked, and before he could answer called down to an idle red-head, who seemed relieved to have something to do and soon bounded up the stairs with a beer.

'Thanks, Pete,' she said, rubbing the boy's auburn head. She was the kind of woman one loved doing favours for.

As Michael stood and sipped his beer she bummed a cigarette from a teenage girl and coolly, calmly smoked, and somehow started talking about marriage. 'I mean, in the sixties,' she said, 'it was wild. Tom and I were your age – younger, really – and we all had children – two, three, four. We would just bring them along to parties. It didn't matter. They would sleep right through it. And later,' she said, her voice lowered to a whisper as she glanced over her shoulder, 'we were all having affairs. We almost divorced – I left for a weekend but I couldn't stand being away from the children so I returned. And of course I still loved Tom. It was different back then. We were just kids.' She was interrupted by the sound of something crashing below, and suddenly clutched onto Michael's arm. 'I have to go down,' she said. Michael watched as she glided down the carpeted stairs and then, his beer finished, snuck back to his room.

That winter he worked at night and would return to his room after ten, stepping in through the side gate and crunching across the frozen snow, and would sometimes catch glimpses of Mr and Mrs Charters as they went about their ablutions upstairs. One breathless, moonlit night under a canopy of bluish stars he paused in the shadow of an enormous oak to watch as Mrs Charters, framed in a lit window, exchanged one garment for another, arms raised high above her as her dress fell away and a diaphanous nightgown collapsed down around her like a parachute. Michael was too far to really see, but from his shadowy lair was moved anyway, and shivered both with cold and with the pale intimation of nudity.

Spring finally came and, after a year of bachelorhood – the longest he had gone without a girlfriend since high school – he became friends with a pretty Indian woman named Sashi who taught bilingual education in a school in a nearby town. Their courtship was mercifully brief: they kissed on the second date and made love on the third, and soon thereafter she was spending weekends at the house, sleeping late, reading in the sun, taking long walks through the quiet, blooming streets of the town. Michael was overwhelmed by the lushness of the place – the deep green lawn, blooming forsythia bush, then lilacs, the flowers that sprouted from flower beds he had not even known existed. One morning when he returned from town with a carton of milk he saw someone working in the flower beds at the far end of the lawn and, when he got closer, recognized Mrs Charters.

'Isn't it beautiful!' she exclaimed when he reached her. 'It's such a beautiful spring.' She was wearing her gym clothes, and her small, pale hands had been stained the deep brown of loamy earth; her face was flushed, and beads of sweat clung to her skin like dew. 'We planted all this last fall, but we had no idea it would look like this. By the way, Sashi is wonderful! I talked to her the other morning – she's really very beautiful.'

Just then a door slammed, and Veen came bounding

out of his apartment wearing overalls and new work gloves.

'Good morning, Michael!' he all but shouted. 'What gets you up so early? Are you a gardener too?'

'Your door,' Michael wanted to say to the first question, but didn't, and instead said 'No, not really,' to the second, but Veen didn't seem to have heard him: he was already hard at work, nattering away to Mrs Charters, crouching among the weeds.

'Now why is Veen gardening with Mrs Charters?' Michael asked Sashi later, peering out the window to where the two had spent the better part of the morning. 'And where is Mr Charters?' Sashi was lying in bed, reading a week old copy of a New Delhi newspaper.

'Maybe he doesn't like gardening,' she proposed diplomatically.

'Maybe he doesn't like Veen – I wouldn't if she was my wife.'

'Luckily, she's not.'

'Unluckily. And what does he mean by "free, free"? A couple of months ago he gave me this big spiel about how free I was, and could do anything I wanted – fly off to China if I wanted. And do what there? Walk around eating breadcrumbs? And what is he so shackled for if he spends eighteen hours a day down here painting – I wonder what his wife thinks.'

'Oh, leave the poor man alone – he's probably having a mid-life crisis, or something.'

'And I'm going to have a pre-mid-life crisis if he keeps slamming the door every morning. Just because he can survive on two hours of sleep every night doesn't mean the rest of the world can.'

'He slams the door? I never hear it.'

'And then he stomps his feet, too, in case the slam didn't work.'

[189]

In response Michael had got into the habit of rolling over in bed and banging the floor with his fist, but never quite hard enough for Veen to actually hear him. It was on one of these mornings that, by chance, Michael looked out of his window in time to see a peculiar thing: Veen, at the far end of the lawn, crouching down into the flower bed, lightly plucking a rose from among the flowers and, holding it gently between his fingers, sprinting across the lawn with it, almost on tiptoe – but not, he noticed, to his own apartment, but rather to the other side of the house, towards the Charters' back door. Later that day he looked for the flower in Veen's, then the Charters' window, but it was nowhere to be seen.

'They're probably just friends,' Sashi said. 'You don't know if it was for her, anyway.'

'Yeah – the kind of friend you give roses to. And if it wasn't for her, why didn't he come back to his own place. And why was he running?'

'Hmm,' Sashi said, returning to her book. 'What do you care, anyway?' She was lying naked under a mountain of covers. 'I think you're just jealous, because you wanted Mrs Charters for yourself.'

'Perhaps, but that's no excuse for him – they're both married.'

'So? Maybe they're unhappy. You know, in India it is quite acceptable for a man to have an affair, as long as he's discreet about it.'

'Right – as long as it's not a married woman, it's acceptable. And he doesn't go around slamming doors about it, and sprinting across the yard for no reason.'

'Oh well, they're probably just friends,' she proposed again, climbing out of bed and stretching, her skin the colour of beaten copper in the first warm rays of the sun.

'Be careful,' Michael said. 'They'll see you.'

'Let them. I have nothing to hide.'

It was true – he had no real case against them: only the rose, and the morning in the garden, and Veen's own rambling speech about freedom. But Michael was, unfortunately, finely attuned to the signs and signals of infidelity, having observed through the tinted glass of childhood the symptoms of his own parents transgressions, and witnessed, after his father had taken up with another woman, the evolution of his mother's 'friendship' with Mr Thorn – the spontaneous visits to borrow a ladder or return a saw, the hurried cup of tea, the flushed cheeks and whispered words as they sat together at the kitchen table, the hurried walk back across the yard and the cloud of dust his car left in parting, the distant growl of its little engine settling down through the trees. In Veen in particular he thought he caught the fragrance of emotional duress.

Spring faded slowly and summer swelled up from the south, the high arching oaks filled with leaves that made soft lowing sounds in the wind on sultry summer nights, and thunder storms that rolled up the river and violently broke over the house, cracking and thundering and drenching all in sheets of rain before moving on, leaving the house and the garden a sodden, sparkling paradise, glistening in the morning sun. For a month they had gone away, to his parent's house in the country, and when they returned the lush green lawn had turned brown, and the leaves had begun to fade and fall under an amber August sun.

From his window Michael thought Veen looked invigorated, happy, and his suspicions were confirmed when he met him one afternoon in the drive. 'I like the fall – get back to work, paint a few pictures; no taxes.

Cool nights, warm days.' Mrs Charter's beauty had turned up a notch, heightened by a tan, and perhaps by the new job she had taken in a neighbouring town. As for their friendship, imagined or real, Michael had abandoned his mean-spirited snooping, sickened by his own morbid curiosity, and was busy thinking of other things: his relationship with Sashi had continued on its own inexorable course, and to his private amazement they spoke of marriage as something natural and inevitable, even for him. For, although he had long since lost his appetite for bachelorhood and his capacity to absorb those lonely nights at home, oscillating between the telephone and the television and long, solitary walks through dim-lit streets, he was reluctant to part with the sense of himself as a roving, predatory being, and could not quite imagine that Sashi would be the last woman he would ever 'be' with. It was the thought of himself domesticated, at the end of his sexual rope that frightened him, and perhaps triggered his interest in goings-on elsewhere around the house and garden. He even shared his anxieties with Sashi, but it didn't seem to faze her. 'I mean, it's not ideal, is it?' she had said. 'But people are people. It doesn't mean you have to destroy a marriage. Americans are so silly that way – one affair and it's all over. In India, we do not understand this. Here, everyone is so willing to give everything up. You know, women might want to have an affair too,' she said with a little laugh, sauntering out of the room.

And so he slowly adjusted to the sight of her belongings intermingling themselves with his – a bra suspended from a bathroom hook beside his pyjamas, a pair of red high heels next to his muddy boots, bottles of perfume, and things for the hair and skin and other agents of beautification that had taken over the bathroom window sill. He took these as harbingers of change

– the end of something and the beginning of something else – and tried to prove himself in small, domestic ways – cooking the dinner, doing the laundry, taking her out to dinner and paying the bill himself – concessions to 'commitment' he had always resisted with his previous, American girlfriends. He sometimes hypothesized that being with Sashi, with someone from another country, was liberating for both of them – released them from the patterns and expectations of their own cultures and allowed them to live in a world of their own choosing.

He had almost entirely forgotten about Veen when, one morning while scrubbing out the coffee pot at the sink, he happened to glance out of the window as Mrs Charters, dressed for work, walked out onto the driveway to her car, and as she opened the door there was a bang, a door slamming, and there came Veen, hands in pockets, striding out to speak with her. There was something in the way they stood, in the way she kept stalling getting into the car and in the way, when she finally did, that she rolled down her window, exchanged a few smiling remarks before, with a little wave, she drove off and Veen, beaming, skulked back to his rooms, that reactivated his obsession; thereafter, each morning at twenty-to-eight or so he would glance out the window, or listen for the tell-tale slam and, once heard, go to the window and watch through the wilting leaves of an unwatered geranium, as they exchanged their morning pleasantries before he pulled himself away, and Mrs Charters drove off with a surreptitious little wave.

Michael had continued his habit of rolling over each morning, after Veen arrived, and banging the floor with his fist, but Veen apparently never heard him, nor got the message. For his part, Veen claimed he could hear

Michael walking around in his 'hob-nailed' boots, and half complained. 'Geez, Mike, what's going on up there. It sounds like Sherman's Army is going through! It must be those hob-nailed boots you wear.'

'I just do it to keep you awake – I know you fall asleep over those tax returns, all those late nights you keep.'

'I see you have your eye on me,' Veen said and laughed. 'We'd love to have you and Sashi over for dinner sometime, as soon as the quarter's over, and thing's let up a bit.'

'Great, we'd love to. We'll be there,' Michael said, heading up to his window. And although he felt chastened by the invitation, he could not help noticing that, on Thursdays – the day Mrs Charters had once told him was her day off, neither her nor Mr Veen's car was ever in the driveway.

'You're like an old lady!' Sashi said to his revelation. 'Why do you even care?'

'I can't stand to think of him ruining a beautiful marriage. You know, I was their son's age when my parents split up.'

'So, you lived, didn't you?'

'Yes, but I'm emotionally imbalanced.'

'That's true. But why do you always blame him for it? For all you know, *Mr* Charters and *Mrs* Veen are involved, and they're just trying to figure it out. And besides, you *like* both of them, so why don't you give them the benefit of the doubt. Maybe you should have your head examined, so you can leave them alone?'

'Actually, I think he's just in love with her, and she needs the attention. That's why . . .'

'Please!' Sashi said. 'Let them be.'

It was a few mornings later, while sleepily consuming a bowl of cornflakes, the milk so cold it made his teeth ache, he heard Veen's car on the drive and, a moment later, heard the door closing so hard it made the windows rattle. He waited for a moment, then stood up, jumped a few inches into the air and came down hard on the heels of his hob-nail boots – and made the windows tingle again.

'What happened?' Sashi sleepily asked from the bed.

'Counter-terrorism.' He was back eating his corn-flakes when the phone ran: it was Veen. 'Everything all right up there?' he asked. 'I thought you might have fallen out of bed or something.' Michael flushed, and made up a lie about dropping a box of books, but he could tell that Veen had called out of genuine concern and felt, upon hanging up, chastened.

'Who was that?' Sashi asked.

'Wrong number,' he said – his second lie within a minute. It was not Veen's fault, perhaps, if he didn't know what sound the door made, and not his fault either, perhaps, that he had fallen in love with Mrs Charters; Michael would have himself, maybe, if Sashi had not appeared in his life, and things been slightly different – if, for example, that time she had come to retrieve the rent cheque and for a moment they had stood together in his room, beside the bed, talking . . . What would he have done then, Sashi or not, had the opportunity arose, say, to kiss her? Although he had never been adept at 'picking up' women, never possessed of that careless spark of indifference that women are attracted to, and allows them to collapse into one's arms an hour after meeting, he had always prided himself on being an opportunist, willing and able, if not obliged, when a rare and precious gift was offered up from the Gods of romance and desire. What did one do with such gifts, he wondered, when one was married? How would he respond to such moments, with the double weight of church and state bearing down upon

him? 'Husband', 'Wife', 'Marriage', strange and heavy
words he never thought, somehow, would apply to him.
They planned to go to India for the summer, and their
trip, it seemed, would be greatly simplified if they were,
at least, 'engaged'.

'And you will have to write to my family,' Sashi said
matter of factly, 'and make clear your intentions.'

'What intensions?'

'Well, you figure that out,' she said with a self-satis-
fied smile. 'Or don't write them – and I'll just stay in
India after our visit, and you can come back here.' He
felt like a man in a small boat in the middle of a fast-
moving river without a pair of oars. In the distance, he
could hear the gathering rumble of the falls.

Such were his preoccupations in those brief, lightless
days before Christmas, after the thump, that he almost
entirely forgot, or forced himself not to think about
Veen, until he called one morning and invited them
both to a Christmas party at his house. 'Just an annual
thing,' he had said, 'eggnog, smoked ham – the whole
ball of wax. I wasn't going to have it at all but my friends
kept calling up and asking why they hadn't had any
invitations so I had to have it after all. See what happens
– you get roped in by expectation: the world wants you
to be who they think you are. Well, it will be fun. I hope
you both can make it.'

'What should I wear?' Sashi asked desperately on the
afternoon of the party, pacing the apartment in a slip
and bra and knee-socks, occasionally diving into the
closet now filled with her dresses. She had moved out of
her own apartment, and into his, the week before.

'Something festive,' he suggested, and she responded
by putting on a long black dress and a string of plastic
pearls in which she looked, he could not deny, beautiful. He put on a tie under his plaid, V-neck sweater, a

pair of grey, seldom worn trousers, and together they walked the half mile to Veen's, out into the clear, cold stillness of a winter night. The sky was wonderfully clear, the air cold, and through the leafless trees they could see a dome of bluish stars that seemed, as they walked, to slowly turn on its axis. From a block away they could hear the din of the party, and then see the house, giving off a cheerful holiday glow, and as they walked arm in arm under a procession of street lights, he imagined the street as the aisle, and Veen's house, at the end of it, the altar.

Veen greeted them at the door, shook Michael's hand, bent over to kiss Sashi, and then introduced them to his wife, a short, older-looking woman who shook Michael's hand vigorously and then said, rather loudly, 'Well, it's about time! I've heard so much about you.'

'No wonder,' Michael muttered to Sashi as they pushed off into the party, wading through a sea of married people to the drinks where he poured an eggnog for Sashi and then one for himself. When he turned around she was being cross-examined by an eager-looking couple barraging her with the usual questions about India, what she was doing in America, where she learned such excellent English. Her usual answers to such questions were terse, if not rude, and Michael, not wanting to witness the exchange, drifted off into a corner of the room where a group of children were watching *How the Grinch Stole Christmas*, then over to the food table where he picked at a delicious, salty ham and had a brief, bantering conversation with a woman with soft, greenish eyes and, it seemed, no bra; they were soon joined by her nervous, vigilant husband, a business-type nursing a ginger ale who started asking Michael the usual questions about who, and what, he was, and he escaped back to the eggnog and then to the TV where the children were laughing and the Grinch, perched high on a sleigh laden with stolen presents, was teetering on the top of an enormous snowdrift which, Michael knew, would soon collapse, sending the Grinch on a long, wonderful ride down the mountain, into a moonlit village filled with sleeping children.

Sashi was sitting on the couch with an ardent young fellow who had not, apparently, learned of her boyfriend, or else did not care; he was listing hopefully toward her, legs crossed, hand on chin, nodding attentively as he listened in rapt, empathetic attention and Sashi babbled on about something, basking in the emanant warmth of male hopefulness. Michael did not want to meet him, nor watch the Grinch on his long, precarious slide, and so moved away and found himself on an unavoidable, collision course with Mr Veen who, like him, could not seem to quite find his niche at the party and moved furtively on the fringes of conversations.

'Well, well,' he said when he saw him, 'you look festive – I always wanted to see what you'd look like in a neck-tie. It looks good – it suits you. I'm glad you both could make it. You must find these old folks a little dull, but that's the way it is when you get to be my age – can't be helped.' He looked relieved, happy to have someone to talk to, and lightly pulled at his beard as they talked. 'Most of these people I've known for ten or twenty years – but now I see them only once or twice a year, at parties like this, so I guess it's not such a bad idea – gets us all out of the house for a few hours. Anyway, it's great to see you both. We don't see nearly enough of each other – though I hear you a lot – must be those hob-nail boots.' Here Veen smiled and then laughed, and laid his hand on Michael's shoulder. 'No, seriously, just kidding.' Michael recognized this as the perfect chance of mentioning the slam, but then didn't: he had begun to sleep through it anyway, and as they talked on – first about his work then about Veen's painting, and former career as a banker, his eyes fell on the pale, freckled back of a woman who stood nearby. The back, and the low-cut black dress looked familiar, but it was not until she turned and smiled and came towards them that he realized it was Mrs Charters.

'There you are!' she said, to both of them. 'Merry Christmas, Michael,' she added and, leaning forward, let herself be kissed. 'I didn't see you here. Where is your lovely girlfriend?'

'On the couch, talking to someone.'

Whether from the eggnog, or the winter cold, or just from her own happiness her cheeks were flushed a rosy shade of pink, and her hair fell in frazzled wisps down across the nape of her neck. She wore no necklace.

'She's quite a woman,' Veen said.

'Sashi?'

'She's lovely. Do you think you two will ever get married?' Mrs Charters asked, leaning slightly forward, glancing over her shoulder towards the couch.

'Married?' Michael said, in semi-feigned alarm. 'Possibly ... well, probably, really. We're going to India this summer, so maybe when we come back, in the fall.'

'Really?' said Veen, slowly. 'I didn't know you were the type?'

'I'm not, but sometimes you have to do things anyway – isn't that the way adults are supposed to think?'

'Hey, that's a good line,' Veen said. 'I'll have to remember that.'

'You know,' Mrs Charters said thoughtfully, looking at Veen and then at Michael, 'you two are really very much alike.'

'Well, gee . . . I consider that a compliment,' Veen said.

Michael could tell that he meant it, and softly added, 'Likewise.'

Mrs Charters bummed a cigarette from someone named 'Ginny', Veen refilled his eggnog and then Michael's, and as they talked, laughing and drinking and feeling, for once, at ease, some other part of him looked out through the texture of the moment – the swirling smoke, the fragrance of pine from a nearby tree, the strains of a Christmas carol some jolly soul was beginning to sing – and in some deep and silent space before him he saw them standing together in the amber light, each looking healthy and happy, vulnerable and hopeful, somehow, younger than he had always thought of them. And then there was a moment when the conversation paused, when there was nothing more to be said but they continued to stand there anyway, smiling, and for an instant it seemed they were offering themselves up to him, shyly and silently confessing, revealing to him their love and asking for his blessing. He knew; they knew he knew; and in the sharing of this secret he could see that they were relieved of a great and unseen burden. Something then left him, and he could feel himself smiling back, all three smiling, and for once he saw the beauty and sadness of their love, the loneliness of circumstance, the hardship of things to come. He could see, too, that they had wanted him to know all along: all love needs an audience, and through the leaves of a wilting geranium, he had become theirs. Without his ever knowing they had adopted him their son.

THE
AMERICAN DREAM

Georgina Hammick

Blow the whistle and get on the track
Of Campbells' Pork 'n' Beans!
Once you're on it you'll never go back
To ordinary beans!
Campbells' are best, so buy 'em today!
Once you've tried 'em, you will say:
Goodbye to the rest – I'm buyin' the best –
Campbells' Pork 'n' Beans!

They sing a lot, now they're in America. They sing the songs everyone is singing and whistling this year – 'Cruising down the River' and 'Put another Nickel in' are two – and they sing the commercial jingles that interrupt wireless programmes over here. *Radio* programmes. They sing about jello and shampoo, about soup and soap. One of the jingles they like best, that appeals to them most, because so far-fetched, is a duet. A male voice starts off:

Here comes the Camay Bride –
Oh! What a lucky groom
To have a girl with a complexion
Just like roses in bloom –

and a female, a girlish voice intercepts to explain:

It's the Camay mild soap di-et,
Give up careless care and try et –
With your vurry vurry first cake of Camay
Your skin grows softer, smoother, right away-ay-

[203]

They are singing this today as they run down the stairs. They run out of the house and into the street with their ball, and begin kicking it about on the pavement (or on the sidewalk. The words they choose, the words they use, depend on their mood; depend on whether they feel, at a given moment, pro- or anti-America and Americans, loyal or disloyal to home). They are identically dressed in red and white striped T-shirts, cotton dungarees and sandals.

It's a hot day, and after a bit they're fed up with kicking the ball, and head towards Meakin's store for a popsicle. While the boy jogs and dribbles the ball, dodging the shoppers, his twin sister runs along the tops of low brick walls. She runs like a tightropist, in jerky bursts, her outstretched arms seesawing for balance. When the walls give up she jumps down and trots beside him.

A woman, in a mauve poplin dress and with a little mauve hat tipped over one eye, and with her arms full of shopping, stops in front of them.

'Say, are you two twins?' this woman asks. 'Aren't you perfectly darling?'

The girl nods vigorously. The boy shakes his head.,

'No. No relation at all,' he says.

The woman seems amused. She laughs. She shifts her shopping from one arm to the other. She shades her free eye with her free hand.

'You're British,' she says. 'Why, that's wonderful! I just love your accent. It's the cutest – '

'We're English. We haven't got an accent.' The boy frowns. He bounces his ball twice. 'You're the ones with the accent, not us.'

'Well well well,' the woman says. 'My my.' She does not stop smiling, but her smile now has a fixed, stuck on quality. If I tug at the corner of that smile, the boy decides, it will rip off in one go, like Elastoplast, and afterwards there'll be a black hole in her face.

The woman stares at them for a moment, still smiling; and then steps backwards and then sideways, and then walks on.

This is not the first time they've been stopped by a stranger. They've been accosted, in one way or another, ever since they arrived in Washington. It even happened on the *Queen Mary* coming over. They might be film stars, the amount of attention they're getting. They might be *movie* stars.

They walk on down the street. The street, Q Street, is empty of school-age children because it's a Tuesday afternoon in term time, and school-age children are at school. They're not at school because when their mother went to the nearest suitable one to enrol them, she was told by the principal: Yes, sure, it'd be a real pleasure to have Robert and Josephine in school while their father was in Washington; they were nine years old, weren't they, they'd go into the fourth grade. Their mother argued with the principal about this. She'd been round the classrooms, she'd cast an eye over the maps and nature posters on the wall, she'd glanced at the exercise books of people in the fourth grade. People in the fourth grade were just about learning to read and write, their mother deduced. Robert and Josephine had been reading and writing for *years*, she told the principal, they were *extremely* articulate, they had an *unusually* wide vocabulary, they'd been learning French for a whole year *at least*, Robert was due to start *Latin* in the Autumn. They'd be wasting their time in the fourth grade. The Principal, so their mother told them afterwards, shrugged and spread his hands at this, and

said he was sorry, you couldn't skip grades. Not in his
school. That was how the education system was geared
to work in the United States of America, and it worked
just fine.

'But we can't have you bimbling about all morning,
getting under Carrie's feet,' their mother said, 'we can't
have you getting in Celestine's hair.' And so, when
there's time, she takes them on sightseeing tours and
educational outings, and she sets them work to do at
home.

They do this work, which their mother calls their
assignments, in a little room at the top of the house that
looks over the thin houses, and thin trees, opposite. At a
table in the window they sit side by side and write essays
on 'My Favourite Painting in the Mellon Gallery', 'Our
Day in Williamsburg', 'The Visit to Chesapeake Bay'.
'A Walk in Rock Creek Park'. They draw portraits and
self-portraits, they paint imaginative compositions and
still lives. They design posters and book jackets. They
learn poems – from *The Oxford Book of English Verse* –
by heart, and write them out in their best writing. When
they know the poem, when they're both word perfect
(Josephine invariably the first to reach this state, Josephine 'the literary one, the *chiel amang us*,' their
mother tells visitors – 'we think, we hope, she's going to
be a writer one day') they take the book to their mother
so that she can test them. Their mother will be in the
kitchen, showing Celestine how to cook the lunch; or
she'll be seated on her dressing-table stool, waving her
hands up and down to dry the polish on her nails; or
she'll be at her desk, writing letters home. (Or she'll be
lying on the sofa with her eyes closed, listening to *The
Story of Helen Trent* on the portable.) Wherever she is,
whatever she's doing, she'll say: 'Well done, good children, but I haven't time now, I'll hear your poem later.'

[206]

Their mother, like all mothers probably, leads a busy life. She doesn't always have time to hear their poem later.

No arithmetic, no maths, is done in the room at the top of the house because their mother is no good at it. It doesn't matter. They're only in America for six months. They aren't missing anything they won't be able to catch up on when they get back to school.

The only thing they might be said to be missing is the company of children their own age, but they have each other. And there is America, new and shiny, loud and colourful, a land of plenty where sweets are not, where candy is not, rationed. It was the Land of the Dream, their father told them once, the place where if you bought the product, you got the girl; the country where even a bellhop could, in theory anyway, make it to President. It is the Land of the Free – a term they understand through their being allowed, for the first time in their lives, to roam the streets – of Georgetown – unaccompanied and at will. Not least, it is the land of advertising jingles and peanut butter.

At Meakin's store, they buy double popsicles and tubes of Lifesavers, rum-butter and Wild Cherry. The store is empty except for Mr Meakin and a negro. The negro is sitting on an upturned orange box; he holds a bottle of Pepsi in one hand and a bag of salted peanuts in the other. Every so often he shakes a few nuts from the bag into the bottle, and then he tilts back his head and swigs, chewing the nuts and swallowing the Pepsi at one and the same time. How is this done? They drop their popsicle wrappers in the trash can, and stand in the doorway and watch. The negro is wearing a wide straw hat, tipped back off his face. Sweat, like tears, streams down his cheek and his neck, trickles over a sharp and painful-looking Adam's apple. I will never forget this,

Robert tells himself. I will always remember this negro
on this orange box, swallowing and chewing.

Robert discovered this remembering, storing trick
two years ago, when he was seven. He was hiding under
the grand piano in the Music Room at school, during
the Hobbies Period they have there on wet Saturdays.
He was homesick, or perhaps it would be more true to
say, mothersick; and while all around him boys and
girls (the girls included Josephine: their parents chose a
co-educational school so the twins should not be separated) buzzed among the scratched tables and swapped
cigarette cards and stamps; or sat at the tables and
impressed sheet after sheet of cheap drawing paper with
pencil Spitfires and Messerschmitts (and bullets and
flames and smoke), he stayed under the piano, sniffing
his knees and staring at rain, hosing the windows in
squally bursts. A climbing rose had broken loose in the
wind, and it flailed and whipped the window nearest
him. Black rosehips, thrown at the glass one minute,
were torn away the next, and the sound they made – a
rattle, a sawing scrape, a relentless tapping, like someone desperate to get in – was the most desolate sound
he'd heard. I shall remember this afternoon, he told
himself then. I shall remember that sound, and the rain,
and the way my knees smell. Now, in America, if he
chooses to, he can recall every detail.

When the negro has finished his Pepsi and the nuts,
Robert and Josphine leave the store.

'Pepsi Cola hits the spot!
Two whole glasses, that's a lot!
Twice more flavour, twice more pep –
Why take less when Pepsi's best?'

It's Josephine who sings this. 'Shall we go to the drugstore?' she suggests. She's taken the popsicle from her mouth and is examining it. The tip is bleached now, drained of sweetness and of orange juice.

'No point. The new comics won't be in yet.'

And there is no point, for they go to the drugstore for the purpose of reading the comics. Occasionally they may sit at the high stools at the counter, and have a banana split before reading the comics, but mostly they don't bother, they just read the comics. The comics are kept in a low rack on the left of the entrance. They'll go in and kneel on the lino tiles and read *Batman* and *Superman* from front page to back, and then replace them in the rack. Mike, the drugstore manager, never objects. Perhaps because they're twins, perhaps because they're British, he never suggests they buy a comic.

On the way home Robert dribbles his football through the shoppers and the hurrying business men, and Josephine dances beside him, counting her steps in sevens. She starts with the right foot: 'One, two, three, four, five, six, seven,' then shifts to the left: 'One, two, three, four, five, six, seven,' then returns to the right. Nearly everything she does has to be done in sevens. She has to climb stairs in this way, she has to brush her teeth twenty-one times (seven goes at the right side of her jaw, seven at the left, etc.). Robert cannot stop her, although he, and everyone in her orbit, has tried. Josephine has had rituals before. Until the age of four she was a headbanger, unable to sleep without first thumping her head against the pillow, at the same time emitting a monotonous moaning hum. She could keep this up for hours. After the headbanging, there was a period of touching things – railings, or lamp posts, or pillar boxes – on walks, of having to go back and touch any she'd left out. And when that blew over, or lost its power? Something to do with neatness, and shoes, and joins in the carpet. Josephine never chooses to explain, or perhaps is unable to, what her rituals are about; will not disclose what consequences must result from a failure to carry out her 'orders'.

Eight doors from home, the toe of Robert's sandal lifts the ball over a low wall and into a front yard. A fat girl in a frilled cotton dress is standing in the yard. She picks up the ball and holds it against her chest.

'You lost your ball?' She hugs it to her. She looks about the same age as they are, except that she has bosoms already, they wobble through the thin cotton. She has mousey hair, parted in the middle and held at the sides with pink plastic bows. The hair is quite short, and it sticks straight out from her face, perhaps because the ends are frizzed.

'It's dumb to play ball on the street,' the fat girl says. 'Dumb and dangerous. I'm not permitted to play ball on the street.'

Without consulting each other, they jump onto the wall at the same moment, and jump off it again into the fat girl's yard.

'I saw you two before today. You're twins,' she informs them.

'You don't say,' Josephine says.

'You talk real strange. You foreign or something?'

'Yep yep yep.'

'Why aren't you in school?' Without warning, the fat girl throws the ball at Robert, a dud throw that manages to be both short and wide. He retrieves the ball; then he asks her why she isn't at school anyway? For example?

'I'm sick,' the girl says. 'I've had a fever, I've been sick four days now.'

They stare at her with interest. She does not look sick, particularly, merely fat and pale.

[210]

'My name's Yvonne,' the sick girl says. 'It's French. My second name's Claybeau. That's French too. My ancestors were French on my Daddy's side. My Daddy's an admiral. What does your Daddy do? Is he French?'

Their father is a diplomat, and English. Robert tells Yvonne this.

'Uh-huh.' She does not seem impressed. 'Uh-huh.' She turns to Josephine. 'What's your name?'

'Josephine,' Josephine says. 'It's a French name, I believe, although I myself am not French.'

There is silence after this. Robert bounces his ball twice in the admiral's flowerless yard. He turns to go, and so does Josephine.

'Hey! Do you two twins have skates?' Yvonne Claybeau calls. 'Come back Saturday. Come lunchtime Saturday and meet my Mommy and my best friend Bobby Jane. If I'm not sick by then we'll skate the block. Come a quarter after twelve.'

Yvonne Claybeau is a blancmange. It's impossible to envisage her on skates. It's impossible to imagine her wearing anything other than a pink frilly dress.

'Be tactful,' their mother says as they lace their skates on Saturday morning. 'Come home straight away if you're not expected,' says their mother, who like most mothers, probably, does not believe in the validity of invitations issued by nine-year-olds, especially when the parents of the parties concerned are not acquainted.

The Claybeaus are expecting them, however. Admiral and Mrs Claybeau are very old, more like grandparents than parents. Mrs Claybeau's hair is blue-white, and she wears it in a fancy roll down the back of her head. Her large corsetted body is draped in a

[211]

clinging lilac dress. There's a lot of lilac about this year, and mauve. Their mother wears it, and it suits her, but it does not suit Mrs Claybeau, Robert decides. It makes her skin look grey.

The Admiral is large also, and unhealthy-looking, and he has a snub nose. He is a tall, old, masculine version of his daughter Yvonne.

Then there is Bobby Jane.

'This is my vurry best friend Roberta Jane Dyson,' says Yvonne. (She is wearing Bermudas today, pink ones, so tight across her bottom the line of her under pants shows through.)

'Hi,' Roberta Jane says. She shakes hands. She is skinny and tall, taller than Robert, he is displeased to see, skinnier than Josephine, who is not skinny. (Josephine is not fat, either. Not fat. 'Well covered' visitors to the house sometimes remark. 'Bonny'. 'What a bonny girl Josephine has become!')

Bobby Jane has an interesting face. She has blue eyes that have a black ring round the iris. She is pretty, she may even be beautiful. Josephine's plaits are short pigtails, the texture of horsehair, always escaping their ribbons, but Bobby Jane's plaits hang down her back in two neat silken cords. She has on old blue pedal pushers that don't fit, they are too big for her, a red tee shirt, white gym shoes. White sneakers. There is something about her, an air, a look, that isn't young, that's not like a child. She is ten and two months, they will learn later that day, but she could be twenty. She is the Camay Bride, it comes to Robert. O what a lucky groom.

Lunch is peanut butter and jelly and lettuce and mayonnaise sandwiches, and strawberry milkshakes. They eat it in awkward silence in the kitchen, standing up, leaning against the mushroom-coloured work tops.

When they've finished, Yvonne Claybeau dabs at her mouth with a pink paper napkin.

'You guys wanna come see my boudoir now?' It is more of a command than an invitation, but they are curious, and they follow her through the thick carpeted hall, up thick carpeted stairs, along a thick carpeted landing. Yvonne chooses a door and holds it open.

'No, not you,' she tells Robert, who's waited till last, 'you wait here. Boys can't go into little girls' boudoirs.'

He's seen it though. Pink walls. A pink silky bed, covered with cushions and dolls. Above the bed, a crucifix, its crossbar strangely looped with a string of beads. A plaster Virgin on the windowsill. A picture of Jesus wearing a nightdress and a crown of thorns. Wearing an enormous, ornate halo.

> 'Halo everybody, Halo!
> Halo is the shampoo
> That glorifies your hair, so
> Halo everybody, Halo!'

Robert sings this on the landing, kneeling outside Yvonne Claybeau's closed boudoir door.

From now on they meet Bobby Jane and Yvonne after school on weekdays, and in any spare time they have at weekends. The meeting place is always the Claybeaus' house, and arrangements are made by a telephone call to Yvonne. They imagine she must sit by the telephone all day, it is always she who answers it. 'Admiral Claybeau's residence. Spea-*king*?' she always says.

At the Claybeaus' house they sit at the kitchen table and test each other on general knowledge, and they swap travellers' tales. The Americans have the advantage when it comes to knowing the population of Arkansas, and they can argue between them about how long it takes to get to Baltimore on the pullman; but neither of them has a clue as to what Big Ben might be, and neither has been abroad. Neither of them has seen an ocean-going liner. When Robert and Josephine, in order to explain the size of the *Queen Mary*, describe her staterooms and shops, her swimming pools and ballrooms and dining rooms (stopping here to elaborate on the amazing Cabin Class menus, and on the decorated menu cards – a different design for each meal of the five-day crossing); when they rave about the mechanical horses they rode every day in the Cabin Class gymnasium, the Americans have nothing to counter with except silence. Silence and raised eyebrows. And exchanged, secret, disbelieving smiles.

At the Claybeaus' house they play Kick the Can in the back yard; they watch *The Lone Ranger* and the *Howdy Doody Show* on TV. Occasionally Mrs Claybeau takes them to the cinema. On these expeditions she chauffers the Admiral's Lincoln convertible, and they ride in the back on stiffly upholstered, sickly green seats which smell horrible (but she won't allow them to have the windows open). Once in the ticket queue, she'll turn suddenly, and extend a fat gloved palm, as though offering sugar lumps to a horse, and this is the signal for them to produce their money. The first time this happened, they hadn't any money on them. (It was their mother's fault; they'd asked her for some, and she'd said 'Mrs Claybeau won't expect you to pay, sillies, you're her *guests*!' Their mother had laughed at the very idea.) Mrs Claybeau tapped her handbag as they went through their pockets. Josephine eventually came up with a nickel. 'Bring it round tomorrow,' Mrs Claybeau said. 'You two twins had better shape up.'

The Camay Bride never comes on the cinema outings, a blow to Robert because he thinks about her all
the time, and hopes, and fears, to sit next to her in the
dark. When the visits are planned she always seems to
have something else to do. '*Red River* was wizard,' he
told her, 'you really missed something there.' It was the
best film he'd seen, he told her, 'better than *Yellow Sky*'
(but she hadn't seen that one, either). She listened
politely as he recounted the plot. 'Movies are no big
deal, I guess,' she said.

'They don't like boys,' is Josephine's explanation
when he complains about the huddles the girls get into,
the conversations he's excluded from, after tea, in
Yvonne's pink boudoir. 'They haven't got brothers,'
Josephine reminds him. 'The boys at their school are
mean. They call Yvonne a fat pig, and they swing on
Bobby Jane's plaits. They have no reason to like boys.
They put up with you because you're my brother.'

Nonetheless, Josephine's facts do not square with
Yvonne's continual boasts: 'We'll be dating boys soon,
Bobby Jane and me. We'll be dating boys when we're
eleven. I'll be permitted to wear make-up next year, and
then I'm gonna date Irving Wentworth. He's the best-
looking boy in our class.'

Robert wants Bobby Jane to deny these promises,
made on her behalf by Yvonne, but she never does,
although she won't confirm them, either. When Yvonne
goes on and on about boys and dating, she stares down
at her hands, spread out on the kitchen table (her nails
are oval, and clean, and have little white half moons at
the base). Like a sheepdog separating a ewe from the
flock, he tries, sometimes, to nudge her away from the
others and get her on her own, but she will not be
nudged. His efforts at conversation she blocks, politely
evades, slides round.

'Do you like reading?' he asked her once (for despite their mother's lack of faith in the American educational system, it's clear that the two fourth graders they know can read, and better than haltingly). They were standing in the Claybeaus' kitchen, drinking banana milkshakes that tasted of Kolynos.

'Sure I like to read.' Bobby Jane removed the flattened straw from her tumbler, pinched it to make it cylindrical, blew through it. 'Everybody does, I guess.'

The offhand putdown was a lie – everybody did not like reading – but he plugged on: 'What books then? What d'you like best? Adventure? Murder? Ghost stories?'

'Oh, all kinds.' She smiled, but she didn't look at him. She tipped her glass; she guided her straw into the remaining bubbles, where it stuttered and sputtered like a motor bike. She turned her face and her attention away from him to Josephine.

'I like your plaits,' he said another time, the words coming out in a rush of breath as he caught up with her in Pennsylvania Avenue. 'Your plaits are ... swell.'

She stared at him. She rolled upright, in perfect control, back and forth on her skates. Back and forth. He pointed. He didn't dare touch her plaits.

'Oh. My *braids*. Oh. Thanks.' She flipped one over her shoulder, then locked her hands behind her back and swooped off, neatly zigzagging.

What Robert knows about Bobby Jane, he learns from his sister – information imparted voluntarily, without his having to probe, but released only slowly, in short bursts – when they are doing their assignments, when they are cleaning their teeth, when Josphine feels like it. When she feels generous. Or is it mischievous?

'Her father's dead, you know,' Josephine remarks as

they sit over their Quaker Oats (*delicious! nutritious! makes you feel ambitious!*) at suppertime, waiting for *The Shadow* to frighten them out of their wits. 'Perhaps I told you? He was a bomber pilot, stationed in Suffolk. He died at the very end of the war. Bobby Jane doesn't remember him, hardly. Hey, it's time.' Josephine stretches a hand to their mother's portable, and fiddles with the knob. 'Who knows what evil lurks in the hearts of men?' Orson Welles enquires menacingly. 'The Shadow knows.'

'Her mother's a cripple,' Josephine announces casually, 'she caught polio when Bobby Jane was six. That's my rubber you've got there, I need it,' Josephine says. (They are not enjoying their assignment, which is: 'Give a brief history and, where applicable, explain the functions, of the following: a) The White House; b) the Capitol; c) The Lincoln Memorial; d) the Pentagon; e) the Washington Monument. Illustrate in pencil, if you can, from memory.')

'She's a writer,' Josephine says, 'she writes poetry. She's a famous poet, Bobby Jane says. *Quis?*'

'*Ego decent.*'

But it's not decent; it's only Josephine's postcard view of 'The Capitol Under Snow', which she wants to swap for Robert's 'The White House in Cherry Blossom Time'. They got the postcards from the drugstore. They were hoping for an aerial shot of the Pentagon – how could you make sense of its five sides otherwise? – but the postcard stand hadn't held any views of the Pentagon at all. 'Well well well,' Mike said when they told him why they needed it, 'that's a kinda serious request. Let's see now what we can do for our friends the twins.' He went through a drawer first, then a cardboard box of old, black and white, bargain price postcards, but no luck. He seemed as disappointed as they were, and perhaps because of this, wouldn't let them pay for the cards they did find.

'Bobby Jane is a sort of housekeeper,' Josephine confides. They are in the drugstore again, squatting on the lino tiles in their dungarees, reading *Batman* and *Superman*, cover to cover. 'She does the shopping and the cooking, and the washing. They haven't got a maid or anything.'

What must it be like not to have a maid or anything? There was always someone in London. In Washington there are two: Celestine, an eighteen-year-old Jamaican, who lives in and whom their mother is teaching to cook ('but it's hopeless,' their mother sighs, 'quite hopeless. She's incapable of retaining the simplest instruction'), and Carrie Hawthorn, an American, a negress, a grandmother, who comes in daily to do the laundry.

Celestine is sad and giggly by turn. When not in the kitchen, trying to make sense of their mother's instructions, she shambles about the house with a feather duster. She stares out of windows a lot. They worry about her. They ask her: 'Are you homesick, Celestine?' (They are homesick sometimes, for England, for English voices on the wireless.) She giggles or weeps, but she won't say.

Carrie Hawthorn does the laundry in the basement. The basement has a concrete floor, perfect for roller skates, and while Carrie transforms the jumble in the laundry basket into uniform flat parcels on the ironing board, they skate round her. Carrie doesn't mind this. 'You go right ahead, honey', she says, 'you don't bother me one bit.' While Carrie irons she sings – old sad negro songs about cabins and cornmeal and cotton fields and deep rivers. About Lindy Lou.

'Lindy, did you hear that hummin' bird singin' las' night?' Carrie will sing, pressing both hands and all her birdlike weight on the iron to remove a stubborn crease, lifting the iron to her cheek as though she's listening to it. 'Honey, it was singin' so sweet in the moonlight.' Every so often she'll place a finger on her tongue, and then touch the flat of the iron to test it. This produces a hiss, and a little puff of steam. It shows off the softness and pinkness of Carrie's tongue in contrast with the dark cracked leather of her lips. 'Lindy, I'd lay me right down and die, and die, if I could sing as that bird sang to you-oo, my little Lindy-lou-oo.'

Robert feels sorry for Bobby Jane that there is no Carrie Hawthorn at her place. He knows where her place is – a depressing apartment block, a few doors down from Meakin's store. A couple of times after school he's skated there on his own and loitered, but she's never appeared and asked him in. And there've been no invitations to tea there, not even for Josephine.

'She doesn't ask us because of that supper, I bet,' Josephine says. 'I know I wouldn't if I was her.'

By 'that supper' Josephine means the one they invited Boby Jane and Yvonne Claybeau to, at their house.

They asked if they could eat in the kitchen, the way the Claybeaus did; if they could cook it themselves, if they could have a proper American menu.

'You know, Ma, hamburgers, hot dogs, fries, ketch-up; ice-cream n'chocolate sauce. Coke. You know, things they're used to, things they like.'

Their mother was writing letters when they petitioned her. They stood either side of her desk, right up close, as close as they dared, and watched her blue fountain pen etch the blue air mail paper. She wrote in firm bursts, the pen hovering above the page when not pressed to it, her beautiful mouth folded into a concentrated line, the line twitching a little at the corners.

[219]

'OK, Ma?' Robert picked up a heavy glass dome and turned it over and studied the green baize on its bottom.

'Don't say OK.' She didn't look up. 'Don't fiddle, there's a good child.'

He put the paperweight down.

'Can we though? Is it *all right*, Mother darling?'

'Don't be cheeky.'

The pen reached the end of the page. Their mother read through what she'd written, and blotted it, and plucked another sheet from a tooled leather paper holder. He made a face at Josephine. She was sometimes able to suceed where he failed. If he had the advantage of being a boy and the first born (by twenty minutes), she had the advantage of being a girl and the 'baby'.

Josephine shunted sideways, to within an inch of their mother's elbow.

'May we, Mummy, please? Please.'

Their mother removed the hornrims she wears for close work and laid them on the empty sheet of paper. She leant back in her chair. Then she picked up the hornrims and put them on again. Then she picked up her pen and continued with her letter.

'We'll see,' she murmured, folding her lips together. The pen gathered speed. 'If you're good children. We'll see.'

On the night they didn't have supper in the kitchen – of course not, it was impossible, they never did – they had it in the hall, which in Washington has to double as dining-room. To its formality was added Celestine's gloom as she shambled in and out with plates and dishes. They sat in silence while she made her sad entrances and exits, just the four of them at the too large dining-room (the moment their visitors arrived, their parents went out, dressed to the nines, to some do at the French Embassy).

'Hey, what kinda soup is this?' Yvonne peered into her bowl and sniffed. Robert looked at Josephine; Josephine looked at Robert. They recognised the brew, they knew what it was – their worst, their mother's favourite – a boiling up of chicken carcase and insides, and onions and celery and pearl barley, the concoction masked by parsley and a shiny, wrinkling skin of fat. Blistering fat. ('Yum yum chicky broth,' their mother enthuses whenever it appears, taking no notice at all as they gag and moan and slide off their chairs and hide their heads under the tablecloth 'full of nourishing goodness'.) How could she do it to them this evening? How could she? How?

'It's chicken,' Josephine said. 'More palatable with salt, in my experience.'

'You call this chicken?'

Impossible to blame Yvonne, for once. Nothing less like Campbells' Cream of Chicken could be imagined; could have been devised.

They picked up their spoons.

Immediately, at the first sip – in their anxiety they'd failed to warn the Americans to blow on their soup – Bobby Jane burnt her mouth. She cried 'Ow!' she spluttered, her face went red. Robert looked away, to the portrait of their mother in an emerald evening dress above the door; but Josephine jumped up, and ran to the sideboard, and grabbed the water jug (where was the Coke they'd ordered?) and filled Bobby Jane's glass.

'It's OK. I'm OK now.' Bobby Jane put out a fending-off hand. 'No, really Josephine.' Josephine slunk back to her chair.

They picked up their spoons again in silence. They lifted and sifted the contents of their bowls.

'Uh-oh. Uh-oh.' In Yvonne's spoon, held out for them across the table, lay a grey something with little

[221]

holes in it, a rubbery something with whiskers sprout-
ing out of it. Yum yum chicky skin. Yum yum yum.
Uh-oh.

'I can't eat this stuff,' Yvonne said.

'Neither can I, I guess. I'm sorry,' Bobby Jane said.
They put down their spoons.

Hardboiled eggs in cheese sauce, with bullet rice and
spinach-in-a-pool, came next – and left again, re-
arranged but otherwise almost untouched, minutes
after. The twins had been brought up ('There's a war
on, remember') to eat everything that was put in front of
them, no matter how unappetizing; even when the war
was over there were the 'starving Russians' to 'think of'.
To feel guilty about. Robert felt guilty now. Not so
much about the Russians, who hadn't been invoked
recently, but about Celestine's hurt feelings – she shook
her head as she removed the plates – over her rejected,
wasted cooking. If the visitors weren't prepared to eat
it, though, if they weren't prepared to *try* it, how could
he and Josephine?

When Celestine had taken away the plates, she set
about clearing the table. She did it very very slowly.
Egg dish, rice dish, spinach dish; salt cellar, pepper
grinder, serving-spoons. Four punishing journeys,
made without a tray. (She refused to let them help her.)
Meanwhile nobody spoke. Bobby Jane crumbled a
piece of bread and examined the ceiling. Yvonne
giggled behind her hand. By this time the twins were in
despair at their failure, and their guests ravenous.

'Ice cream, please Celestine! Ice-cream! Ice-cream!
Ice-cream!'

Celestine turned at the door. She looked perplexed.
She looked bruised.

'Yo' mother say nothin' 'bout no ice-cream. There'm
no ice-cream.' And she brought them the fruit bowl. In

[222]

it were five bright red, tough skinned, sleepy apples. The one Robert had tried at breakfast still had his teeth marks in it, upper and lower jaw, not a bad print, dark brown now where the skin was broken.

It's not surprising there've been no invitations from Bobby Jane. But if she doesn't ask them soon, it will be too late: they sail for England, for football and netball and new brown walking shoes and new grey knee socks, in three weeks' time.

She asks them one day when they're taking off their skates in the doorway of the Claybeaus' kitchen. (Mrs Claybeau does not permit skates in her kitchen. They make black marks on the linoleum, she says.)

'You guys wanna come round my place Wednesday?' Bobby Jane's head is bent over her laces, her face hidden by her braids. 'It's OK with my mother if you do.'

The question comes as such a surprise, is so out of the blue, no one answers.

'We can watch the *Howdy Doody Show* and *The Last of the Mohicans.*' Bobby Jane sounds casual. She doesn't care one way or the other. 'Let me know Monday. I have to go now. I have to fetch the groceries from the store.'

'It's too bad I can't go to Bobby Jane's place,' Yvonne Claybeau says sweetly, when Bobby Jane's gone. It's clear she's longing to be asked why not, and so, eventually, reluctantly, they allow curiosity to get the better of them.

'Why can't you go?'

'Well. We-ell.' Yvonne stops, and puts a small fat finger to her lips. 'My Mommy doesn't like me to.' She simpers and stops again, then says in a fake whisper, 'Bobby Jane and her mother aren't Catholics.'

[223]

'But we're not Catholics!' Robert is incensed. 'And you came to *our* house, I seem to remember.'

'I know, I know,' – Yvonne's tone is sweet and pitying – 'but you do go to the episcopalian church Sundays. You and your folks are kind of friends of Jesus, I guess.'

Friends of Jesus? Is that what they are? It does not describe their feelings on Sunday mornings in the Episcopalian church. The dreary hymns, the dull sermon, their tidy, uncomfortable clothes. The only service they've enjoyed in America is the one Carrie Hawthorn took them to, at her church. They were the only white people in the congregation. On arrival they were handed painted cardboard fans, shaped like palm leaves, and throughout the service they swayed and fanned themselves, as the others did. The preacher struck his chest from time to time, and called out: 'We're all sinners, Lord!' and from all parts of the church, men and women, and even one boy not much older than themselves, leapt up to agree: 'So right! Yes, Lord!' Having to return their fans when it was over was a blow, but afterwards they went back with Carrie Hawthorn to her place for Sunday dinner: fried chicken and sweet corn and sweet potatoes. Sweet apple pie and ice-cream.

'Bobby Jane's mother isn't able to go to church,' Josephine says. 'She can't walk. She's paralysed. So how could they get to church?'

'She could go in a wheelchair. Or the priest could visit her, maybe. If she wanted. The problem is,' Yvonne whispers, 'Roberta's mother doesn't believe in Jesus. She's taught Roberta Our Lady was just an ordinary woman, Our Lord was just an ordinary man. She's raised her that way. Isn't that terrible? Anyways, that's not all. The Dysons aren't our class. They're poor. Real poor. Their home is just a two room apartment, ground floor. They have to share a bathroom with two other families across the hall. The bath tub isn't clean, either.' She shudders. 'I saw it once. There's a green stain all over the bottom of the tub. The faucets have gotten mould on them. The living room's real shabby too. They don't have a machine to wash the clothes, they don't have a maid in to do the laundry –'

'Seeing is believing,' Robert says. 'See an Oxydol wash. See how Oxydol washes whiter than any other soap product.'

'Bobby Jane's always very clean,' Josephine says, 'and her hair shines. She's much cleaner and tidier than me. She has white teeth,' Josphine continues, 'as white as Celestine's. And her breath doesn't pong, except of peppermints.'

'Pep pep Pepsodent toothpaste [Robert sings],
Beats film on teeth and cleans breath too –
Pep pep Pepsodent toothpaste
Beats film on teeth – the old schedule.'

Yvonne Claybeau ignores these interruptions.

'Bobby Jane does the laundry in the sink,' she tells them, 'the same sink where she washes the dishes. They don't have a kitchen, it's just a railed off corner of the living-room. The living-room smells bad. It smells of fries and beans. Ugh. It's awful.' She leans back in her chair, she puts her hand over her mouth and speaks through her fingers: 'Awful.'

'Gee whiz. Golly gee. Jeepers creepers. Holy smoke.' (But irony is always lost on Yvonne.) 'I thought Bobby Jane was supposed to be your best friend. Your very best friend, you're always telling us.'

'She is too, she is so, Robert Partridge. She can come round my home anytime. My Mommy's always pleased to see Bobby Jane. It's not Bobby Jane's fault she doesn't believe in Jesus, my Mommy says. It's just that I'm not permitted to visit with her any more. That's all. But it's OK. I'm never gonna tell her why I can't go to her place, I always think up excuses, so she won't ever know.'

On the way home Josephine has to circle every seventh lamp post seven times, difficult to do on skates. She makes three tours clockwise, three tours anti-clockwise, one tour clockwise.

'The drapes in the living-room aren't clean,' Josephine lisps. (She is having a breather, between lamp posts.) 'The whatsits have gotten mould on them. Ugh' – she wrinkles her nose – 'it's awful, awful dirty.'

'You haven't quite got it, if you don't mind my saying. You don't sound *sweet* enough. Listen. Admir-al Clay-beau's resi-dence. Spea-king?'

'Anyhow, I can't wait till Wednesday,' Josephine says in her own, nettled, English voice.

But on Tuesday Josephine catches a feverish cold, and on Wednesday she's kept in bed, where she wheezes and streams and coughs and blows.

'Poor me, I'm so disappointed.' Little moans from Josephine into a wet handkerchief. 'Poor me, poor Bobby Jane.'

Robert wants to go to Bobby Jane's place. He does not want Josephine's cold. He stands in the doorway, leaning back, trying not to breathe.

'I could go by myself I suppose,' he says, pinching his nose.

'She won't want you without me.'

'She'll have made cookies and cakes though. Someone ought to go. Someone ought to eat them.'

[226]

'No, Yvonne told me they only had cinnamon toast when she went there. It tasted real bad, she said. But you could go along and tell her why I can't come.'

Josephine buries her nose in the wet handkerchief. She's having to blow seven times with the right nostril, seven with the left, etc. It's very tiring, she tells Robert, and it makes her nose and lip sorer than ever, but what can you do?

On the way to Bobby Jane's place, Robert sees his father's old black Chevrolet parked on the opposite side of the street. The windows are down, and there is his father in the driving seat, one shirtsleeved arm hooked out of the window, fingers tapping the car roof. He is listening to the baseball game, a substitute for the cricket he misses, and something he often does if he comes home early. He chooses the car radio, he says, so he can listen in peace without fear of children. (It is true he does fear children, and avoids them as much as possible.) Once though, when he saw Robert with the football, and caught his eye, he called him over and let him sit and listen to the game. Robert enjoyed this occasion – the smell of his father's cigarette smoke, the humbugs he produced from the glove compartment, his comments on the commentator of the game; but he doesn't want to catch his father's eye today. He puts his head down, and skates on.

Outside Meakin's store, he brakes, and goes through his pockets and counts the change he finds there.

'A jar of sourballs, please.'

Mr Meakin has his back turned. He is replenishing a shelf with large tins, large cans, of cling peaches, with smaller ones of fruit cocktail.

'Libby's fruit cocktail, a great selection,
Look for Libby's for perfection'

When you go to the store, look in Libby's direction –
Look to Libby's for perfection!
Luscious peaches, juicy pear-ares –'

'You're a crazy boy.' Mr Meakin shakes his head. He has a thin face, all lines and wrinkles, and his grey hair, closely shaved at the sides, grows like a brush on top of his head. A bristly brush. The brush Celestine uses – wafts – on the stairs. Mr Meakin wraps the sourballs in striped paper. The skin of his hands is shiny and loose; it resembles the rubber gloves he stocks, Large, Extra Large and Ladies, in a cardboard box on the counter.

'How's your mother?' Mr Meakin asks. 'Your mother's a real English lady.' Mr Meakin always says this, or something like it. 'Where's your prettier half?' he says. 'I don't believe I ever saw you two folks apart.'

His mother is well, Robert tells him. She's gone to Garfinkles for a new dress, or it might be a hat. His sister Josephine is in bed with a cold. 'How much are those, Mr Meakin?' He points to some bunches of red roses flopping out of a bucket by the door.

'They're past their best this time of day, I guess,' Mr Meakin says. 'They should be a quarter, but I could let you have them for fifteen cents. Aw, go on. A dime.'

Outside on the sidewalk, he sniffs the roses. They are scentless. Some are still in bud, but the buds are too heavy for their stems, and turning black. It is obvious they will never open. This is the first time he's bought flowers for anyone, and he feels foolish, holding them out in front of him as he skates along, while simultaneously trying to keep the sourball jar wedged under the other arm.

'Where are they?' Bobby Jane peers all round him.

She holds the door half open, or half shut. She is wearing an embroidered blouse with tucks in the front. She is wearing the blue skirt with red cherries on the pocket that she often wears and that he particularly admires. He wants to flee. He speaks very fast, to get his explanations and embarrassment, her disappointment, over with. When he's finished, Bobby Jane says:

'Oh. I see.' But he can tell she doesn't believe a word of his story about Josephine.

'Even if she had been allowed out of bed, we didn't think you'd want the germs.'

'No,' Bobby Jane says flatly, 'Mother mustn't catch cold. She gets real sick if she catches cold. She had pleurisy and pneumonia once, that way.'

'Josephine sent her love.'

Silence. She is waiting for something. What is she waiting for?

'Oh, and I have a message from Yvonne. She rang just before I left. She said to tell you they've got visitors, so she's got to stay in.'

'Uh-huh. Strange. She was in school today. We talked in recess. How come she never told me then?'

Silence.

'The visitors must have arrived unexpectedly.' But it sounds lame, even to him.

Silence.

'I can go home now, if you like.' Then he remembers the flowers. 'These are for your mother.' He shoves them at her. He pulls the jar of sourballs from under his arm. 'These are for you.'

Bobby Jane says thanks. She says she guesses he'd better come in, her mother is expecting them all. She says her mother hasn't been too well lately, that she doesn't have too many visitors right now.

[229]

He takes off his skates. He follows her through a dingy hallway. Behind them, the heavy street door clangs to, shutting out the sweltering afternoon, and locks itself.

The Dysons' living-room is shabby and untidy, at first impression much as Yvonne Claybeau described it. Yet within seconds he feels at home in it, and this feeling – of recognition, of belonging – is new; he's never felt quite 'at home' at home. (He's wanted to, he's expected to, but each time at the beginning of the school holidays when they've returned to South Kensington, and run from room to room to re-establish themselves, he's met with disappointment, solid as a wall. The organised flat, the glossy furniture, arouse no response in him except disappointment and a vague unease.) Now, standing in a strange room, taking in the untidy comfort, and the books, he perceives that there will be places he can belong to, and feel at ease in, that this might be achieved without Josephine.

Yvonne made no mention of books. They are every-where: on shelves and tables and chairs, on the floor, on the windowsill, on the divan at the far side of the room where Bobby Jane's mother lies, propped against cush-ions, under a tartan rug, her back to the wall.

'That's too bad,' Mrs Dyson says when Bobby Jane has explained why Robert is on his own. 'Never mind, honey, we'll get along fine without those girls. Won't we Robert?'

He nods. Bobby Jane says, 'Mother, Robert brought these flowers for you.' She holds out his roses. They looked crushed and sad. They are almost quite dead, he fears.

'Why, aren't I the lucky one! I haven't been bunched by a young man in years.' She touches the leaves with thin fingers, she sniffs the black buds of his scentless roses. 'Wonderful! You'd best put them in water, honey.'

He is now alone with Bobby Jane's mother.

'Pull up a chair,' she says, 'any old chair. Shove the books on the floor.'

He chooses a chair, he removes the books. Mrs Dyson reaches for the packet of Philip Morris on the table beside her. She shakes a cigarette from the pack. Her hands tremble, the matches rattle in their box, she lights up.

'Camels are milder,' he says out of nerves, by way of conversation. It's what the Camel adverts are telling everyone this year.

'Which may be why they're no use to me.' Mrs Dyson inhales and then coughs. She stares intently at him. 'Tell me what it's like to be a twin,' she says. 'Tell me the good and the bad, all of it. How does it feel to have someone around who looks like you, and talks like you, and maybe even thinks like you? I haven't met Josephine, of course, but Roberta tells me you're very alike. I imagine you must get compared all the time. Are you able to have any kind of separate life and identity?'

No one has asked these questions before. The questions he and Josephine do get asked are usually no more than social, and incurious, and jokey enquiries ('Are you the Heavenly Twins we've heard so much about?') requiring no more than a shrug in reply. Mrs Dyson's questions, he senses, are real, but he hasn't any answers. Being a twin is just a fact of his life. He's known nothing else, so how can he say? He takes refuge in the medical dictionary he and Josephine looked up once, when they were meant to be doing their assignment.

'We're not identical twins, we're not the same sex. We

[231]

came from separate eggs. We're fraternal twins. It's only by chance, by coincidence, we look alike.'

'OK, OK, so you're not identical. But you did spend nine months together, just the two of you, in a confined space, before you were born. That must count for something.'

He is thinking about this when Bobby Jane comes back into the room. She walks slowly to the window, bearing his roses in a green glass vase. She places the vase on the windowsill. The neck of the vase is too wide for so few roses, the stems will not stay down in the water, they float to the surface. The dark red flower heads and the black buds lean out over the rim of the vase; they look desperate to get away. They look mean. Why didn't he buy two bunches?

'Thanks, honey,' Mrs Dyson says, 'that's pretty. How are you doing out there?'

'I'm doing OK.' Bobby Jane crosses the room without looking in Robert's direction, and goes out through the curtain.

'I have the impression you're not too happy to discuss the twin question,' Mrs Dyson says, 'so maybe we should talk about something else. I'd be interested to know,' she says, taking a cigarette from the pack, laying it on the tartan rug, 'what you plan to do or be when you're through college. When you're grown.'

He doesn't know; he hasn't thought about it. (The future, the very idea of looking forward, frightens him. 'This time last week' is something he says quite often. 'This time next week' is not a phrase you'd associate with him; if he uses it, or something like it, it's usually in a semi-negative way: 'This time next week the exams will be over.' 'This time tomorrow, where shall I be? Not in this academy.') But an answer is expected from him, and he searches the room for clues, and his eye lights on the terrifying wheelchair (why had he not noticed it before?) – on its canvas, and leather straps and chrome. No, not a doctor. What else is there in the room? Books.

'I'm going to be a reader.'

'A reader? An academic, you mean? A publisher's reader? A proof reader?'

'I meant a writer.'

'Oh. Like your sister Josephine! Roberta told me. Two writers in the family – that's really something. Roberta doesn't plan to be a writer, I've put her off, I think. She can't abide poetry. As you know, as she'll have told you, she's hoping to be a gymnast, to teach gymnastics.'

He nods. But she hasn't told him, and Josephine hasn't told him, and he doesn't know.

You get to meet people as a teacher (Mrs Dyson continues), but it's a lonely life being a writer. Does he know that? Also, he has to have something to write about. Ideas, experiences. Does he keep a diary?

He doesn't. Josephine does. He shakes his head.

But he can make himself remember things (he suddenly tells her); and he's quite observant and imaginative, so his mother says.

Mrs Dyson blows a long funnel of smoke at the ceiling. He should keep a diary, even so, she tells him, it's good discipline. Memory, she'd like to remind him, is only fiction. We invent our own version of the past, of history, to suit ourselves; we improve on it as time goes by. Isn't that true? Doesn't he agree?

No. No, he doesn't, it's rubbish – and he's about to say so, when Mrs Dyson starts off again. She's being unfair on him, she says, he hasn't lived long enough yet to find out. 'Why don't you go give Roberta a hand,' she

[233]

says, 'she's baked a cake and some cookies. There are only three of us, so we can have a feast.'

On the other side of the curtain, in the tiny railed off kitchen, Bobby Jane is putting plates and knives on a trolley.

'Tea's all fixed,' she says, 'I baked a cake.'

'More women use Swansdown cake flou-errr than any other package cake flou-errr in Americaaaar,' he informs her.

'It's Betty Crocker,' Bobby Jane says.

'Just add water, mix and bake
Betty Crocker angel cake!'

'Oh sure. I made devil though. The devil mix tastes better.'

'We haven't got adverts on the wireless at home.' Something in her tone makes him think it wise to explain this.

'Wireless. Adverts. You slay me. Anyway, I know you don't. Josephine already told me, ages back.' Bobby Jane takes two glasses from a shelf and puts them on the trolley. 'Milk OK with you?'

Tea is over, the *Howdy Doody Show* is over, episode six of *The Last of the Mohicans* is over. He and Bobby Jane are sitting side by side, tailor fashion, in front of the TV set. Their elbows are almost touching. They are so close he can smell Bobby Jane. It is a fresh, sweet smell. (Of Halo shampoo, perhaps; of the Camay mild soap diet; of pep pep Pepsodent toothpaste.) Bobby Jane springs up suddenly and switches off the set.

'I'd better go home now,' he says, 'I'd better get back to Josephine.'

'OK. You can help me do the dishes first.'

They guide the trolley between them, over the

bumps and ruckles of the carpet, through the curtain. He does not tell her he has never dried a plate in his life; that at home in England, that at home in America, he is not welcome in the kitchen, and goes there only briefly: to get a drink of water, to steal a jam tart, to take a message from his mother to the cook. It would not be tactful to tell Bobby Jane any of this, he decides. But the silence now is not the comfortable one they shared minutes ago in front of the television set, sitting cross-legged with only inches between them, cramming their mouths with popcorn, passing the paper bag until it was empty. He must say something.

'I like your mother,' he says. 'I'm sorry she can't walk, Perhaps she will one day.'

'No,' Bobby Jane says, 'Mother's paralysed from the waist. She won't ever walk. But you don't have to worry about it. I look after her, and the nurse comes, Tuesdays and Fridays.'

Nurse? The matron at their school is called Nurse, it's the name they have to call her by. Nurse wears a flowing white headress like a nun's, she has a chalky creased face, she wears glinty spectacles and she blinks all the time. (Her eyelids are encrusted with warts.) After breakfast, Nurse waits outside the bogs with a notebook and red pencil, her eyes blinking and watering. You are not allowed to pull the plug until she's inspected what you have, or haven't, done. A red tick beside your name if you've 'been', a cross if you haven't. Two crosses in a row, and she comes at you with the castor oil. While they've been in America, he's forgotten about Nurse. Nurse has ceased to exist. Next time he comes out of the bogs, and finds her hovering and blinking, he will, he is certain, remember today. He will see Bobby Jane's arms in the sink, the dark splashes on her skirt, this sunlight on this windowsill. He will see himself standing here beside Bobby Jane, drying blue plates, thinking about Nurse.

'Why don't you like boys?' It's not the question he meant, he has no idea why he asked it. He knows at once that it's dangerous.

'I never said I don't like boys. I don't know too many boys, not that well. Those dishes don't go there, they go there.'

'Why do you like Josephine better than me then?'

'What kind of question is that?' Bobby Jane is drying her hands on the roller towel. She examines the palms, then she turns her hands over and inspects the backs. 'How should I know? Maybe Josephine is more my kind of person than you are. Is there a law that says I have to like you both the same? Just because you're *twins*?'

But she says this in a light way, a teasing way, that takes some of the unkindness out of the words themselves.

'Come again real soon. I enjoyed your visit.'

Bobby Jane's mother sounds tired. She is no longer propped up, she is lying flat, with one cushion under her head. The cigarette packet on the table beside her is empty now, the ashtray full.

'I like to meet Roberta's friends,' she says to the ceiling. 'Come back another day, and bring your sister Josephine.' (Has she forgotten they leave for England on Monday?) She turns her head towards him. She lifts a hand from the tartan rug. The fingers hang limply; he is afraid to take her hand.

'Thank you for having me.'

'Thank you for the tea,' he says to Bobby Jane in the hall. He puts on his skates. 'Thank you for the chocolate cake and *The Howdy Doody Show* and *The Last of the Mohicans*.'

'You're welcome.' Bobby Jane unlocks the street door, and holds it open. The evening sunshine, still hot, rushes in.

'We had fun, I guess, Robert, even without your sister and Yvonne.' He is thinking about this, he is down the steps and in the street, when she says something else, something he can't catch.

'What?'

'I said I can't make Yvonne out. She always accepts Mother's invitations, she always says she'll be glad to come to my place, and then she doesn't show. I don't get it.'

Bobby Jane confiding in him! How extraordinary! How amazing!

'It isn't Yvonne's fault.' (For although he can't bear Yvonne, although he and Josephine have never understood how Bobby Jane can be friends with her, it isn't, strictly, her fault.) 'She isn't allowed to go to your place.'

'How come?' She frowns. She seems quite nonplussed by this.

He hasn't planned to tell her anything. He doesn't think he has. Now, having embarked, he sees that here is a way of getting back at Yvonne. But he's not sure. He wants Bobby Jane to know, and does not want her to know. He wants both.

'Well?'

It is the 'well', the way she says it, the way she puts her hands on her hips that decides him, that makes him explain that Yvonne isn't allowed to go to her house because they're not Catholics, and because they're poor, and because they're not the same class as the Claybeaus. He says he knows all this because Yvonne told him. She told him and Josephine. 'So it isn't Yvonne's fault, exactly.'

[237]

After this there is a silence, during which he under-
stands that he's made a devastating and irreparable
mistake.

Bobby Jane lets go of the street door. She tucks her
skirt underneath her, and sits down on the step. She
rests her head on her knees. With the first finger of her
right hand she begins drawing slow circles on the step.
Big circles and bigger circles, smaller circles, figures of
eight.

'You shouldn't have told me that. I didn't want to
know that. I never wanted to know any of that.' She
doesn't look at him. She is talking to her finger, the one
that is making loops and circles on the step. He keeps his
eye on the finger.

'What you just told me hurts. I never did anything to
hurt you, Robert Partridge.' The finger slows, then
stops. 'Yvonne would never tell me what you just did.
Josephine would never tell me those things. Josephine
may be crazy in some ways, she may be some kind of nut
with all that counting, but she'd never want to hurt me.'

He keeps his eye on Bobby Jane's finger. The finger is
important. It's important to keep his eye on it. The
finger is drawing zigzags now, or mountain ranges. The
Alps, the Rockies, the Pennine Chain. Ziggerzagger.
Ziggerzagger. Zigzagzig.

'How would you like it if I told you the roses you
brought my mother were just dead old roses, ready for
the garbage? How would you like it if I told you I don't
eat hard candy? You wouldn't. But I wouldn't say those
things.'

But she just has. She's just said them.

'It's an odd feeling,' Bobby Jane says slowly, 'Yvonne
is my best friend, and I can't see her anymore. Mother'll
want to know why I don't go round her place, and I
won't be able to tell her. I'll have to lie.' She pauses.

'I've been friends with Yvonne since we started grade school. We're in the same class. There's no one else in our class lives on this block. There's no one else my age, even. There's no one else at all.'

She gets up from the step. He's aware that she's staring at him – or is it through him? She says, she shouts, 'I want to forget those things you said. I don't want to *know* them. How'm I supposed to forget them? Can you tell me that?'

He shakes his head. He can't tell her anything. What can he tell her? All of a sudden he wants his sister, he wants Josephine. If Josephine were here –

(Josephine? Josephine is in bed, sneezing and blowing. Waiting. Waiting for the moment he'll come round the door, so she can pat the bedclothes and say. 'Tell me all about it. Every single detail.')

'I have to go now,' Bobby Jane says. She takes the door key from her pocket. 'I have to get back to Mother.'

And she's gone. She's gone inside without saying goodbye, without saying another word.

They are on the boat going home. (The SS *Parthia* is a let-down after the *Queen Mary*, a slow small tub that takes seven days to make the crossing, whose menus and menu cards and gymnasium leave a lot to be desired.) On the boat, Robert invents a new ending for his visit to Bobby Jane's place.

In this new ending, Bobby Jane does not confide in him about Yvonne. Yvonne isn't mentioned, she simply doesn't come up. He and Bobby Jane say goodbye, in a friendly way, on the step. She smiles and thanks him for the sourballs – her favourite candy, she says. At the last minute, he bends down (bends down? No, he can't do that, she's taller than him), he leans forward and kisses her cheek.

[239]

Later on, sitting under the grand piano in the Music Room during the Hobbies Period they have at that school on wet Saturdays, he will remove the kiss as being unlikely, as being not something he would do. (As being not something Bobby Jane would accept. She would probably have ducked, he will realize, or pushed him off: 'Hey, what's with all this kissing stuff?' She would have giggled. Or slapped his face.) The kiss is too much at odds with what actually happened; so far from the truth, all it manages to do is point the truth up. So he will get rid of it. Eventually, for the same reason, he will reject the bit about sourballs being Bobby Jane's favourite candy.

But the new story won't stick, it won't stay down (in the way that a badly gummed label on a used envelope won't, but keeps curling back to reveal an earlier, and more substantial, life).

When Mrs Dyson suggested we reinvent the past to suit ourselves, she must have meant the process, largely unconscious, whereby subtle, gradual shifts and repositionings and blurrings occur deep in the mind. Shifts and repositionings of events, blurrings of motive, that will be transmuted, in the course of time, into real distortions. That will emerge, eventually, as full-blown fictions. As downright lies. As the truth.

Mrs Dyson must have been talking about self-deception.

She could not have meant that facts can be altered at will, or by an act of will; and the mind, the conscience, the alter ego, accept them.

Robert's invented version, polished and improved on, will not be the one that returns to him in dreams. It will remain, at most, an alternative, somewhere alongside, but not supplanting, the truth.

The truth? In middle age, Josephine will say that

what happened with Bobby Jane, happened 'in fact, if you want to know, Rob' to her. That it was he who was stuck in bed with a cold. That he never set foot in the Dysons' flat the whole time they were in Washington. (He only remembers it, he only *thinks* he remembers it, Josephine will say – stubbing out her umpteenth cigarette, lighting another – because she confessed it at the time. Because she gave him a blow by blow.) It's her story, Josephine will insist. Hers. It was never his.

BEYOND
GOOD AND EVIL

Jorge Luis Borges and Adolfo
Bioy-Casares

Translated from the Spanish by
Norman Thomas di Giovanni

Dear Avelino,

Please ignore that I'm not penning this on official paper – but – the undersigned is now a fully-fledged consul representing his country in this truly forward-looking city – a real Mecca of thermal baths!

The same as there's no regulation paper or envelopes at my disposal they haven't got around to finding me an office either – so I'm still unable to unfurl the beloved Blue-and-White banner of our Homeland. Never mind – I'm making do as best I can here at the Hôtel des Eaux which has turned out nothing short of a disaster. Three stars according to last year's guide – but it's actually miles behind places that are more conspicuous than reliable and that thanks to clever ads bill themselves as *palaces!*

The human element – and I won't beat around the bush – just doesn't hold all that much allure – at least not to this Argie swordsman. And when it comes to responding to the demands of a discriminating palate the chambermaid department isn't great shakes either. As for the clientele – forget it. Anyway I'll spare you the guest list and just say that the only thing around that seems to be in endless supply is little old ladies flocking to the fata morgana of the sulphur springs. Hold on a sec – there's more!

Monsieur L. Durtain the proprietor is – again no

point in beating around the bush – practically the world's leading authority on the history of this hotel of his and believe you me he doesn't let a chance slip through his fingers to let you know it. Take the private life of Clementine the housekeeper which he touches on from time to time. There are nights I swear I don't get a wink what with the stuff he tells me swimming round non-stop in my head. Then no sooner do I put Clementine out of mind when what happens? A visitation of rats no less – the bane of foreign accommodation if you ask me!

Better move on to something less provoking. To put you on the map about this locale I'll paint you a picture with – as they say – fairly broad strokes. Shut your eyes and imagine a long valley between two rows of mountains that compared to our Andes aren't really such great shakes. Take the much-vaunted Dent du Chat for instance. Put it next to our Aconcagua and you'd need a microscope to find it!

The traffic around town is livened up to some extent by the little hotel buses full of sick people – gout-sufferers a fair number of them – on their way back and forth to the baths. As for the baths themselves – the buildings – even a blind man can see they're exact replicas of our Constitution Station – only reduced in size and less imposing. I kid you not.

On the edge of town there's a tiny lake – but with fishermen and all. In the blue sky wandering clouds sometimes hang about for days spreading curtains of rain. Thanks to the mountains there's no wind to speak of.

One melancholy feature that I point out with a great deal of trepidation is the total absence – this season anyway – of a single Argentine – arthritic or not! But mum's the word lest this get back to the Ministry –

please!! If they found out they'd padlock the consulate and God knows where I'd be dispatched to next.

Having no fellow Argies to let off steam with there's hardly any way to kill time. How am I possibly going to run into someone for a game of *truco* – though of all card games two-handed *truco* never was my cup of maté? Hopeless. The gulf widens – there's none of what's commonly called 'food for conversation' and with disuse dialogue decays. The foreigner is a spoiled-rotten selfish beast who shows interest in nothing beyond his own nose. People here haven't a thing to talk about other than the imminent arrival of a certain Lagrange family. Let me tell you frankly – I couldn't care less. A big embrace to the whole gang back at the Molino –

> Yours –
>
> Félix Ubalde, the same Indian Scout of old

Dear Avelino,

What a welcome whiff of the human warmth of Buenos Aires your postcard brings! You can rest assured – and tell the boys this too – that old Scout Ubalde will never abandon his dearest hope of someday being back in the bosom of the good old gang.

Around here everything moves at the same pace. My stomach has not got over its intolerance of maté yet – but in spite of all the inconveniences – which are only too obvious – I won't give up trying. Didn't I swear that as long as I was abroad I'd make a point of drinking maté every blessed day?

Big news? None really. Except that the night before last there was this mountain of suitcases and trunks cluttering up the hall. Poyarré himself – a grumbling Frog if ever there was one – kicked up an unholy storm but he calmed down as he found out that the pile of saddlery belonged to none other than the Lagranges – or to give them their due – the Grandvilliers-Lagranges! Rumour has it they're real nobs. Poyarré leaked it to me that these Grandvilliers are one of the oldest families in France – only that around the end of the seventeen-hundreds due to circumstances beyond my understanding they changed their name a bit. Well – as they say – you can't make an old monkey climb a rotten pole. No one pulls the wool over my eyes that easily either. If it took two porters to move this family into the hotel are they real gentry is the question I asked myself or only descendants of immigrants who struck it rich??? In the vineyard of the Lord there's a little of everything.

A certain episode – on the face of it probably trivial – put me at rest. At my usual table in the dining-room – one hand squeezing the serving-spoon – the other deep in the bread basket – doesn't He who wears the Waiter's suit suggest I move to a makeshift table by the swinging doors that the staff – laden down with trays – are forever opening with a kick? I nearly hit the roof but – as the whole world is only too aware – a diplomat has to control his impulses and I opted to display my better nature and obey an order that was doubtless unauthorized by the mâitre d'. From my retreat I could see a phalanx of waiters joining my table to a larger one and the upper echelon of dining-room staff bowing and scraping before the entrance of the Lagranges. Word of honour – this Lagrange clan is a long way from being treated like trash!

What was the very first thing not to escape the attention of this old Argie swordsman but two girls who – owing to identical looks – had to be sisters. (Except the elder's a sort of red-head and has freckles while the other has the same features but is a brunette and pale.) Now and again a fairly well-built ogre I took to be their father shot an angry glance my way – as though I was ogling his daughters. Naturally I ignored him and went on giving the rest of the group the once-over. As soon as I have spare time I'll describe the whole cast in detail. But right now the old bed calls – and the day's last smoke.

An embrace from –
The Indian

Dear Avelino,

By this time you've probably read with avid interest my accounts *re* the Lagranges. Well – now I can say more! *Inter nos* the nicest of them is the grandfather. Everyone around here calls him Monsieur le Baron. He's an amazing character though you wouldn't give five cents for him – toothpick-thin, the size of a puppet, the colour of an olive but – sporting a malacca cane and snappy blue overcoat! I have it from the horse's mouth that he's a widower and his first name is Alexis. What a lark!!

In age he's followed by his son Gaston and G.'s wife. Gaston is pushing fifty-odd and looks a lot like a red-faced butcher on permanent watch over the wife and daughters. I can't quite figure out why he keeps such an eye on the Mme. But the daughters – they're something else! Chantal's the blonde and the one I'd never tire of looking at if it weren't for Jacqueline who shades her by a whisker. The girls are a couple of regular live wires – and that let me tell you lifts the old spirits – while the grandad's a museum piece. By which I mean at one and the same time he amuses you and is instructive.

What nags at me is a gnawing suspicion that they may not be nobs at all. Please understand – I personally have nothing against parvenus but likewise how can I forget I'm a consul and as such have a duty to keep up appear-

ances at least?? One false step and I've had it! In Buenos
Aires you simply don't run this sort of risk – someone
who's at all distinguished can be smelled half a block
away. Here on a foreign patch it gets confusing. I'd like
to see you try telling a dustman from a gent simply by
the way he speaks.

An embrace from –
The Indian

Dear Avelino,
The dark cloud has lifted! Friday I nonchalantly sidled
up to the hall porter's desk and taking advantage of the
same's deep snooze I read this memo: '9 a.m. Baron
G-L – coffee and croissants with butter.' A baron – just
think of it!!

I know that this news (which may not be devastating
but is nevertheless juicy) will be of interest to your sister
who's dying for any and everything that relates to the
Great Wide World! Promise her in my name a lot more.

Embraces from –
Ole Injun

Dear Avelino,
To the Argentine observer rubbing elbows with musty
aristocracy is really interesting. But word of honour – I
made my way into this delicate terrain strictly by the
front door. I was in the winter garden introducing
Poyarré – without much luck as it were – to the con-
sumption of maté when who should suddenly turn up
but the clan Grandvilliers!

With all the naturalness in the world they gathered
around the table – which was quite a sizeable affair.
Gaston – just about to light up a Havana – starts rum-
maging in his pockets only to find he has no light on

[250]

him. Count on Poyarré to try to beat me to it – but
wielding an old-fashioned wooden match this old Argie
got the upper hand. That's when I learned my first
lesson. Did the doddering aristocrat even bother to
extend his thanks? Fear not! He proceeded to puff away
with absolute indifference and – as if we were a pack of
nobodys – slipped his cigar case with the Hoyos de
Monterrey into his overcoat pocket. This gesture –
which many others would confirm – came as a complete
revelation to me. At once I realized I was face to face
with a being of another species – what's commonly
called a high-flyer! How was I going to engineer myself
into such a top-flight world??

It's impossible in a letter to detail the hardship and
unavoidable stumbling blocks I met with in the ensuing
campaign that I mapped out both skilfully and with
resolve. The fact of the matter is that two and a half
hours later there I was with the family – eyeball to
eyeball!

That's not all. As I conversed away just as polite and
witty as can be and yessed everything right and left like
an echo my rearguard action was up to something quite
different. I couldn't come straight out with the kind of
eyes or expressions that in my heart of hearts I was
burning to make. Instead I limited myself to the odd
enigmatic smile and a lowering of the eyes – meant of
course for the freckled face of Chantal but given the
placement of those around us it was Jacqueline (she who
enjoyed the less protuberant bosom) who became the
target of my drift. Poyarré with that servility so in-
credibly typical of him made us accept a round of
anisette. Holding up my end I surprised myself shouting out – 'Champagne all around!' Luckily the waiter
took this for a joke until a single word from Gaston put
him in his place.

[251]

Each bottle uncorked was like a volley aimed straight at my heart and as I slipped out on to the terrace hoping the air would revive me I saw my face in the mirror. Believe me it was even whiter than the bill. But when duty calls – the Argentine civil servant etc.! So a minute or two later I rejoined the company relatively recomposed.

All for now –
The Injun

Dear Avelino,
Great excitement all up and down the hotel! A case in fact that would test even a bloodhound's perspicacity. According to Clementine and other authorities last night there was – or had been – on the middle shelf of the knick-knack stand in the pâtisserie a medium-sized bottle with a skull and crossbones indicating it contained rat poison. This morning at 10 a.m. the bottle vanished into thin air. Monsieur Durtain lost no time in taking whatever precautions the situation called for. On a sudden impulse of trust that I shall never forget he sent me trotting to the railway station to fetch a policeman. Which I did of course – down to the last detail! The minute we reached the hotel the gendarme proceeded to question a good half the clientele which went on well into the wee hours – all without a single positive result. He even spent some time grilling me and without a hint of prompting from anyone I answered pretty near everything he asked.

Not a room was left unsearched. Mine was gone over with a fine-toothed comb that left it full of cigarette stubs. Only that damn idiot Poyarré who obviously has a connection or two and – you guessed it – the Grandvilliers were left untroubled. Nor did they question Clementine who had reported the theft.

That was *the* topic of conversation all day – 'The Disappearance of the Poison' (as one newspaper is calling the affair). In fear that some of the toxic substance might have infiltrated the menu not a few of the clientele forswore their dinner. I for my part limited myself to rejecting the mayonnaise, the omelette, and the zabaglione as they were all the same yellow colour as the rat poison. This or that spokesman hinted at the possibility of a suicide attempt but to date this ominous prognostication has gone unfulfilled. I'm keeping a close eye on events and will let you in on the latest in my next.

Until then –
The Injun

Dear Avelino,
Yesterday was a real cliffhanger – no exaggeration – and the hero of it (three guesses who that may be!) had his mettle tested with quite an unexpected ending!! I began by making a pass. At breakfast the girls came out with something about an excursion. Making the most of the timely hissing of the coffee machine I slipped in – whispering of course – 'Jacqueline, how about a stroll down to the lake later on?' You'll say I'm lying but her answer was – 'Make it twelve o'clock in the hotel tea shop.'

I need hardly tell you I got there ten minutes early – nibbling at my black moustaches and dreaming of the rosy prospect. At long last Jacqueline turned up. Not losing a second we slipped outdoors where I noticed that instead of the echo of our own steps you could hear those of the whole family – including Poyarré who crashed the party and was gaily treading on our heels.

We all caught the hotel bus which turned out a bit of a

money saver. Had I known there was a restaurant on the lake shore – and what was worse a first-class restaurant! – I'd have swallowed my tongue before suggesting such an outing. But by then it was too late. Elbows on the table – the cutlery clenched in their fists – and emptying the bread basket the aristocracy clamoured for the menu. In an ear-splitting whisper Poyarré said to me – 'Congratulations, my poor friend. Only by the skin of your teeth have you got out of having to buy an aperitif.' But the chance remark did not fall on deaf ears. Jacqueline herself was the first to ask for a round of Bitter des Basques for everyone – nor was it to end there!

It was time for solids next – and oh the parade of fois gras and pheasant to say nothing of the fricandeau and fillet which was duly rounded out with caramel custard!! All this abundance was liberally washed down with an uncorking of Burgundy and Beaujolais. Coffee, Armagnac and Havana cigars finished the banquet with a flourish. Even Gaston who's as stuck up as they come did not shy away from showing deference to me – and when the baron in person passed me the vinegar cruet with his own hand (mind you it turned out to be empty) I wished I had engaged a photographer so as to have been able to enclose a snapshot with this for all of you back at the Molino. I can picture it there in the window even now.

I had Jacqueline giggling over the one about the nun and the parrot. Then – with the sinking feeling of a lady-killer running low on patter – I came out with the first thing that occurred to me – 'Jacqueline, how about a stroll down to the lake later on?' 'Later?' she says and left me gaping – 'Why not beat it right now!'

This time nobody followed. After a meal like that – you have only to imagine! – the rest just sat around like Buddhas. The two of us alone, Jacqueline and I steered a course between banter and flirting – all of course strictly within the limits proper to my companion's social standing. The sun's rays pirouetted their fugitive fleeting scrawl over the aniline waters and the whole of nature rose up in response to the moment. From a sheepfold came the baa of a ewe, from the mountainside came the moo of a cow, and from a nearby church in like fashion came a prayer of bells. Nevertheless the order of the day was decorous behaviour – I bore up like a stoic and back we went. A bracing surprise lay in store for us. In our absence the proprietors of the restaurant – on the pretext of having to close early – had somehow or other managed to get Poyarré who kept repeating the word 'Extortion!' like a broken record to cough up for the entire bill which by throwing in his watch he just managed to do. A day like this – I'm sure you'll agree – makes one so glad to be alive!

Till next time –
Félix Ubalde

Dear Avelino,
My time here is turning into a veritable junior-year abroad. With hardly any effort at all I've plunged into an in-depth study of a layer of society that is – I might add – on the brink of extinction. To the keen observer these last scions of feudalism constitute a spectacle that cries out for our interest. Yesterday – to stray no farther afield – Chantal appeared at teatime with a trayful of crêpes stuffed with raspberries that owing to the pastry-cook's deference she herself had prepared in the very hotel kitchens.

Jacqueline poured them all five o'clock tea and I was slipped a cup as well. Without the slightest forewarning the baron pounced on the delicacies – snatching as many

[255]

as two to a hand – all the while creasing us with laughter over a succession of off-colour stories and anecdotes along with a series of jokes about Chantal's crêpes which he pronounced uneatable. He said that when it came to preparing food Chantal was incompetent – to which Jacqueline remarked that he was hardly the one to talk about food preparation after what happened in Marra-kesh where the government had done its best to save him by repatriating him to France in the diplomatic pouch.

Gaston stopped her dead in her tracks, pontificating that there's no family without its share of skeletons in the closet and that it's in the worst possible taste to air such matters before perfect strangers – among whom there happened to be lurking one of foreign nationality.

Jacqueline countered that if the dog hadn't stuck its nose into the baron's offering and keeled over Abdul Melek wouldn't have lived to tell the tale. In turn Gaston would only remark that autopsies were luckily not performed in Marrakesh and that according to the diagnosis of the vet who attended the governor the accident was brought on by an attack of over-exertion which is so common on journeys.

I kept nodding my head in turn to what each of them was saying – watching out of the corner of my eye how the old man lost no time annexing more and more crêpes. I'm no cripple either and nonchalant as can be I managed to lay my paws on the very last one.

À l'avantage –
Félix Ubalde

My Dear Avelino,
Hold tight – I'm about to fire off a scene reminiscent of those that used to curdle our blood at the old Majestic.

This morning as I was sleuthing my way down the red-carpeted corridor that leads to the elevator I couldn't help noticing that the door to Jacqueline's room stood open a crack. Well – seeing same and slipping in was all one! The room was empty. On a breakfast trolley I spied untouched food. Just then I heard male footsteps. Phew!! Quick as I could I inserted myself among some overcoats hanging from a hanger. The man with the footsteps was the baron. On the sly he sidles up to the little table. I pretty near gave myself away with a chuckle imagining the baron was about to gobble up the food on the tray. Except he didn't. He took out the bottle with the skull and crossbones on it and before my very eyes – which by this time were the picture of fear – he sprinkled the coffee with a greenish powder. Mission accomplished he left just as he had come in – without being tempted in the slightest by the croissants which he had also given a dusting. It didn't take me very long to figure out what he was up to – to wit: nothing less than doing in his own granddaughter before her time!!

How could I be sure it wasn't all just a dream? In a family as close and respectable as the Grandvilliers such things didn't often happen. Conquering my fear I inched up to the table like a sleepwalker. An objective test confirmed the evidence of my senses – there lay the coffee still dyed green and there the noxious croissants. In an instant I weighed up the alternatives. To speak out could easily expose me to a faux pas – to wit: what if appearances had betrayed me and I fell into disgrace as a slanderer and an alarmist? Yet to keep silent might spell the death of innocent Jacqueline – in which case the long arm of the law might reach out for me.

It was this last consideration that made me scream out in a silent cry (so the baron wouldn't overhear me).

Jacqueline came in wrapped in a bathrobe. I started out – as the situation demanded – by stammering. Then I said that it was my duty to inform her of something so monstrous that the words would not form in my mouth. Begging her pardon for my forwardness I shut the door tight and said that her distinguished grandfather . . . her distinguished grand . . . and before I knew it I was tongue-tied. She burst out laughing at the croissants and cup and said – 'I'll have to ask for another breakfast and see that this one Grandaddy poisoned is served to the rats.' I was utterly dumbfounded. In a bare wisp of a voice I asked her how she knew. She answered that everyone knew. 'Grandad has a thing about poisoning people – only he's so inept he hardly ever meets with success.'

Only then did I understand. Her statement was conclusive and these Argentine eyes suddenly beheld that vast terra incognita – that garden forbidden to the Johnny-come-lately. *The aristocracy simply have no prejudices.*

I was quick to notice that feminine charm apart Jacqueline's response was exactly what every other member of her family's – young or old – would have been. It was as if the lot of them in unison and without a trace of unkindness had said – 'Well, well, who's the clever boy then!' You won't believe this but the baron himself goodnaturedly accepted the failure of the plan he'd taken so much trouble over and told me – pipe in hand – that he bore no grudge against us. During lunch the jokes flew thick and fast and in the glow of such conviviality – I confided to them that tomorrow is my birthday!

Did the gang at the Molino drink to my health?

Yours –
The Indian

Dear Avelino,

It's been a great great day. Right now it's ten o'clock in the evening – which in this country means late – but unable to put the brakes on my impatience I'm going to treat you to a blow by blow account. The Grandvilliers – via Jacqueline – invited me to a dinner in my honour in the restaurant by the lake! In a local supermarket owned by an Algerian I hired a black-tie outfit with a matching pair of spats. Word of mouth had it we'd meet in the hotel bar at seven. Just after seven-thirty the baron was in audience and putting a hand on my shoulder in a joking but tasteless way he comes out with – 'You're under arrest!' He turned up without the remainder of his family but they were all out on the stairs and we went straight to the bus.

At the restaurant where more than one person knows me by sight and I am greeted with deference we ate and conversed in royal splendour. The dinner included all the trimmings and not one *single* blemish! Time and again the baron himself slipped out to the kitchen to supervise the cooking. I sat between Jacqueline and Chantal. The wine flowed like water and I felt as relaxed as if I was back on Pozos Street – and I didn't even hold back crooning the old tango 'Rag-and-Bone Man'. Having to translate it on the spot, I discovered that the tongue of the Gauls lacks the spark of our own Buenos Aires lunfardo and also that I had eaten too much. Our Argentine stomachs – made as they are for the traditional barbecue and tripe stew – are just not built for all the voulez-vousing your classical French cuisine demands. When the hour struck for the toast I had all I could do to get up on my hind legs to extend my gratitude – not so much in my own name as in the name of my distant country – for their homage to my birthday. With the last drop of sweet champagne we beat a retreat. Outside I breathed the air in deeply and felt a bit of relief. Jacqueline gave me a kiss in the dark.

An embrace from –
The Indian

P.S. – 1 a.m. The cramps have returned. I have no strength to drag myself to the bell. The room keeps going up and down, up and down and I'm in a cold sweat. I can't imagine what they put in the Tartar sauce but the strange taste won't go away. I'm thinking of you all – I'm thinking of the old gang at the Molino – I'm thinking of the Sunday soccer matches and ...*

*We call the reader's attention to the fact that the three suspensive points closing this letter were added by the Estate of Félix Ubalde, who is making public these *Savoy Letters*. As for the true cause of the *fait divers*, as they say in France, the veil of mystery still shrouds it. [Footnote by courtesy of Mr Avelino Alessandri.]

CHAMELEON

Lawrence Scott

Monty was born in a large old, colonial house in the town of Villahermosa near Merida, through which the Magdalena seeped, muddy and clogged with water-lilies. It was a town inhabited by tall men, renowned for its generals and young men who were trained to be generals because their fathers wanted it to be so. Monty's father had wanted to be a general. He admired Sir Winston Churchill in England and he had wanted Monty to be a general one day too.

But he himself never became a general, but continued all his life to dream of becoming one. When Monty was born he was named after General Montgomery at his baptism – Monty, the desert rat – for which a special dispensation had to be granted by the Pope in Rome through the Apostolic Nuncio in Caracas. His mother would liked to have christened him Jesus.

The little boy grew, but he was pale.

His legs were thin and cold like a lizard's which made him seek the naked stones in the sun to warm his cold reptilian skin. 'Come, Monty, sit in the sun,' his mother Emelda called, 'sit by the geraniums.' The boy turned and smiled at his mother as he sat next to the pot of red geraniums.

But when his father saw him he said, 'Straighten your back.' This was something that his father would often say. Monty got up and stood like a little Napoleon with his hands behind his back and looked out over the plain below the walled town of Villahermosa towards the

Magdalena whose source was in the Andean foothills. 'Now, walk like a man,' his father said.

In the end his father relented. The thin-legged lizard showed no signs of becoming the kind of boy who one day would be the kind of man who would become a general, though each day his father told him to straighten his back and to walk like a man.

Monty learnt to play the harp at Señor Figuera's, an old man who at the time of the civil war had not wanted to be a soldier or become a general, but prefered to sew and to be a tailor. Playing the harp had been passed down in Señor Figuera's family and he decided to pass it on to Monty because he had never married and had no sons. 'Send him after school,' he told Emelda, 'I will teach him to pluck the harp.' Monty learnt to play the harp well because it was a serious business for Señor Figuera. He also learnt to play the *cuatro* and could play a *joropo* and an *aguanaldo* and he even learnt to play the rumba and samba which came up the rivers on the barges with the travelling black musicians and circus people from Brazil and Colombia.

Monty, with his long fingers for plucking the harp, grew to have long legs; thin long legs which he still used to lay out in the sun on the naked stones near the pots of red geraniums even though he was now sixteen and his father's impatience with his undeveloping physique was now complete. Instead, he was turning his attention to his young nephew to see if he would fulfil his dream of becoming a general.

But, it was some years before this final impatience and turning away, that there had been an occasion of much greater disappointment for Monty's father.

At one end of the patio of the large old colonial house there was a trellis of white lattice-work, through whose filigree, lacy shadows played on the stone floor. This was particularly true at siesta-time when the house was completely silent and the heat sizzled outside and there was a scherzo of lizards among the dry almond leaves. If you were standing on the veranda, looking out over the plain of Villahermosa you would not have been able to see the Magdalena because of the blinding glare. The only sound was the cry of the *cigale* crying for rain, and the lizards, 'In this vale of tears, this *lacrimarum valle*,' as Emelda was accustomed to repeat.

Monty had kept the secret since before his first communion which took place when he was seven years old and the parish priest Father Rosario thought that he had truly arrived at the age of reason and could distinguish between good and evil.

When he was six Emelda allowed him to take his siesta on the patio in the hammock which hung between two banyan trees. He had been afraid of the dark in the shuttered room in the day and of the web of the mosquito-net. Monty never muttered a word, not even to his nurse Ernestina who together with Emelda looked after the boy and would leave him alone to sleep when she had seen him dozing safely in the hammock. 'Now, sleep my Montyquito,' she whispered as she tiptoed into the house.

When it first happened it seemed like a dream, partly caused by the strange unreality created by the peculiar silence of the siesta-time, the heat which turned the head and the glare which mesmerized the eyes. The day Monty first told me his tale he told me that it had been the sound of splashing water which had first alerted him; splashing as it were into the basin of a fountain over and over again with the same force and regularity (like the fountain in the middle of the square at the centre of Villahermosa), but he admitted that these associations must have most certainly been created by the

[265]

madness of the siesta. I remember now that when he first told me the tale we had been sitting in the botanical gardens and there had indeed been a fountain playing in the dip near the bougainvillaea arbour, and he had pointed to it in recognition at the time. Also, it had been siesta-time, but we were not asleep because it was now a different culture in a different place. This was the island of La Trinidad off the mainland where the British had ruled for so long bringing their cold habits.

While I wonder about these things now, I didn't at the time.

He was awakened from his six-year-old slumber by the sound of splashing water over and over again, so that hardly had it awakened him, that it seemed to be hushing him back to sleep again. This was how he had begun his tale. What seemed to be a kind of regularity stopped and it was this sudden change which eventually startled him and made him sit up in the hammock more alert than usual. He then slipped out of the hammock and walked stumblingly in his cotton chemise towards the sound of splashing water which seemed to be coming from behind the trellis of white lattice-work. He walked over the lacy shadows which fell from the filigree on to the stone floor.

The trellis of white lattice-work was an unusual feature of the old colonial house which had been in the Monagas family since fifty years before emancipation. It was unusual because it was a break in the quadrangle of the patio and was in effect a window into the patio of the neighbouring old family house.

Monty pulled himself up onto the edge of the geranium pots and tried to peep through the diamond-shaped lattice. His small fingers gripped where the old paint crumbled. Monty held fast and stared at the little girl Bernadetta who was sitting in a metal bath-tub and

[266]

pouring water over her head and over her naked body with a calabash. Then he got embarrassed and got down off his perch and went back to the hammock and tried to keep his eyes shut.

He said that it happened like this for years. It happened every day for six years and then it stopped abruptly on Bernadetta's twelfth birthday. Every day for six years he would pretend to sleep at siesta-time when Ernestina thought that he was dozing safely in the hammock, but instead he would climb up on to the geranium pots and peep through the lattice-work at Bernadetta.

Bernadetta was no stranger to Monty. Indeed, they had grown up together and had been taken for walks along the walls of the town by their nurses after siesta-time when the sun had gone down. They had played as small children do, innocently. But, now, some new sensation (he called it that when he first told me the story), some new feeling stirred in him because of the clandestine nature of the experience, peeping through the lattice-work, standing on the edge of the geranium pot. Yet, on the other hand, his peeping had been an act of innocence. He felt it to be so at the time and still now many years later, though he could see the possibility of an alternative interpretation. He was only six years old at the time, and when it stopped, twelve or fourteen. He could never quite remember how much older he was than Bernadetta. He could have called to her, but he did not and he never told her and kept it a secret always.

At the end of our first meeting Monty insinuated that the naked Bernadetta was only part of the secret and that if he felt eventually he could trust me, he would tell me the rest of the tale.

Clearly, there had been the initial curiosity of the small boy in the naked body of the little girl, but in the end it was not the young girl's nakedness which continued to fascinate the young Monty.

As she grew older, Bernadetta, thinking that she was entirely on her own would spend time dressing slowly after bathing: towelling, powdering and massaging her body with eucalyptus oil. She used to hang her petticoat and dress over a small bush which was in the sun. Monty would lie in the hammock until he heard the splashing of the water stop and then he knew that she would soon begin dressing. He stared in wonder as she slipped on her silk petticoat and pulled on her crinoline which had been lying on the grass ruffled like the petals of a wild white hibiscus. Then she would pull her dress over her head, her arms into the sleeves and then fluff the skirt out making it stick out like a star. He loved it when she would then twirl around, laugh to herself, throwing back her head and looking up into the frangipani tree blossoming over her, golden and white. Monty ducked at this moment, in case, looking up, her eyes might fall on him peeping through the lattice.

This was all there was to it, he insisted. I did not press him any further, but I did not at the time believe him and felt that there was some other denouement to the tale of the little boy whom they called Lizard and whose father had wanted him to be a general. I believed that with time and trust he would tell me the rest of the story.

This was all there was to it: the meditational trance each siesta as he viewed Bernadetta Montero dress herself after bathing in the silence of the siesta.

We had taken to strolling opposite 'Mille Fleurs', the house of a thousand flowers, where there was an avenue of yellow poui and where the coconut-sellers and oyster-vendors set up their stalls at night under the flickering flambeaux.

It was the day for Bernadetta's twelfth birthday and it was an unusually hot day for Villahermosa, and instead of the bedroom shutters being closed, they had been thrown open in frustration by the would-be sleepers who could not rest because of the interminable heat. Monty could have stayed in his room that day, because originally it had been the closed shutters at daytime which had made him go on to the patio for the siesta because he was frightened. But the habit was now so well-established that no one thought he should change after all these years because of the heatwave.

So as usual Monty lay in his hammock trying to read Cervantes which his mother thought would be good for him. He lay as usual until he heard the splashing of Bernadetta's bath cease and then he crept as usual to the pot of red geraniums, and because now he was quite tall he didn't have to stand on the edge of the pots, but could look over the trellis quite easily. And, today, he noticed particularly the shadow of the filigree which played with his own shadow on the terrazzo floor of the patio.

Because it was her birthday Bernadetta had a new dress, a birthday dress spread out over the hibiscus hedge. It was white broderie anglaise and the hem and edges of the puffed sleeves were trimmed with red ribbon. He longed to reach out and touch it and pass the satin ribbons through his fingers. He remained silent, as silent as at the moment of consecration during mass, during the towelling and powdering of Bernadetta's body: bit his lip in concentration as she played with the dress pressed against her naked body and twirled, pretending to dance and Monty ducked as she threw her eyes up to the canopy of frangipani bush as she had done every day since she was a little girl and he had first seen her at that very first siesta when she was six or five, when he was frightened and could not sleep behind the closed shutters in the dark and Ernestina had brought him to the hammock and told him to sleep and he had been awakened by the splashing of water as if it were from a fountain. He turned at the sudden crack behind him which he thought was a locust falling from the roof. At that moment, he told me, he remembered that he could hear the distant cry of the *cigale*, and he thought how good it was that the rain was coming. His father was standing directly behind him. In his concentration he had not felt the older man's presence. In his meditational trance he had not heard him. The crack was not the crack of a locust falling from the roof, but the crack of his father's boot stepping on to the back of a black bettle and breaking its back.

The man who would himself have liked to have been a general and who had long given up hope that this lizard of a son would ever be a general and had pinned his hopes on his younger nephew because he had no other sons, looked past Monty and stared at Bernadetta dancing under the frangipani bush with her white birthday dress pressed against her naked body. He turned away and went to the edge of the patio and looked out over the plain of Villahermosa and strained his eyes to see the Magdalena, but instead had to shade his eyes from the glare.

That evening, as we came to this point in the story, Monty broke off abruptly and said that he would have to go as he had an urgent appointment with a student to whom he was teaching English and that they were reading *The History of the English Speaking Peoples, Volume 2: The New World*, by Sir Winston Churchill.

Later, as I watched him disappear round the corner of Cipriani Boulevard, I smiled as I mused on his reading and felt the oyster from the oyster cocktail slip down my throat.

It was with a certain urgency that I met Monty the following week having had the chance to speculate to where his story might lead. I tried to push Freud to the back of my mind, indeed, to banish him altogether. I did not feel that the doctor of Vienna had a place in the New World and could explain the psychic mythology of a young boy whose dreams were the screams of conquistadorial genocide and whose demons were the lizards of the Galapagos: whose fantasies were in the romantic adornment of a young girl.

Quite unexpectedly Monty invited me back to his small apartment in an old part of the old town behind the walls of Lapeyrouse cemetery. On the way there we talked about the changing town and how some of the old balconies still existed at the front of the old town houses which reminded him of Villahermosa and Cartagena where he had been taken every year by his parents for a holiday.

We sat in a small room off the small veranda which was at the top of the low steps just off the pavement and the green moss-furred drain. The old woman from whom he rented the room kept plants and they grew in cut-down kerosene tins painted red and green and stood on the ledge of the wooden veranda. The plants were mostly anthuriums, seed ferns and asparagus fern which climbed the lattice and fell over the front, tangled where it could get a hold. The room was bare. In one corner was a harp with a stool next to it and on one wall a fairly large family portrait in sepia of a man and a woman sitting on the low wall of the veranda of an old colonial house. The woman had a baby in her arms and standing in the background was a black servant, the baby's nurse. Monty saw my preoccupation with the portrait and identified the man and woman as his

[271]

mother and father and the black nurse as Ernestina. The baby was himself.

We sipped rum with cubes of ice and talked. Or rather, Monty talked and I listened. Often he would pick up his *cuatro* and strum a chord.

I had left with the vivid image of his father's boot crushing the back of the black bettle on the patio of the house in Villahermosa overlooking the plain and in the hazy distance the River Magdalena. On the other side of the trellis Bernadetta was putting on her birthday dress trimmed with red ribbon. Monty's father continued to strain his eyes in the glare towards the Magdalena. Then without turning he said, 'Go to the tamerind tree at the back of the house and pick me a switch.' Monty did not look at his father but went down the steps and round the back of the house to the backyard where the tamerind tree grew and in whose branches he had played as a smaller boy. He broke off a thick switch from one of the lower branches and on his way back to the patio cleaned off the twigs and leaves with his penknife. He signalled to me with two fingers joined together to indicate the thickness of the switch.

He told the story methodically now. There were no embellishments. He did not digress to tell me of the *cigale*, of the River Magdalena, or of the trellis or how the water falling from Bernadetta's calabash reminded him of the fountain in the middle of Villahermosa. He stood behind his father and waited. He told me that when he recalled this moment, as he had done on many occasions and in many dreams which had found their own metaphors, he remembered that his mind was a black hole of nothing. Again I tried to banish the doctor of Vienna, Thebes, the crossroads, the murder, the plague. This was a new world. Occasionally, he said, there was a ripple of white and red. This tender image was fleeting and did not bring much solace at that precise moment, though it did, subsequently. His father then said, 'Take off your trousers and bend over.' He pulled down the boy's pants and whipped him sixteen times and then told him to pull up his pants and trousers and go to his room.

At that point I got up and went out on to the little adjoining veranda with the old lady's anthuriums and seed ferns. I looked out into the silent and empty street. I heard behind me in the room, the harp, plucked twice. I was holding my glass with rum and ice and I brought the glass to my lips to wet my lips, but I did not swallow the alcohol. My throat was tight and I found it difficult to swallow. When I re-entered the room Monty had his back to me: a small back of a slight man caught in the act of plucking the harp for the third time. I sat behind him. He turned and smiled.

He then got up and came towards me and took my hand. 'Come,' he said, 'come and see. I think I want to show you. I think I can show you. I think I can trust you.' He led me into his bedroom, knelt next to an old chest and lifted the lid, resting the back gently against the concrete wall. 'Look,' he said. From the chest he lifted a white broderie anglaise dress, the hem and puffed sleeves trimmed with red ribbon. He handed it to me and began laying out on the floor lingerie, satin scarves, lace handkerchiefs and a white mantilla. 'Look,' he said, 'my treasure, my solace.' I smiled.

'He whipped me, but he cannot take them away from me,' he said.

A FAIRLY CLOSE ENCOUNTER

A. L. Barker

The flight was delayed. Novalis, a reasonable man, reasoned with himself about airspace. One would not wish to rise and find it fully occupied, one would prefer to remain on the ground. Indefinitely, if need be. He sighed. He was too often disadvantaged by his habit of seeing through to the logical conclusion.

If Miranda and her aunt had travelled overland the journey must have taken a couple of days instead of hours. Was he prepared to sacrifice any of her time, to say nothing of his own – of which he had everything to say? It was now three months since he had seen her. We are to be married in the Spring, he had taken to explaining, she is a patriot, it is her wish that we be married in the centenary year. Asked about her, he would say she is dark, petite, and wears her hair long. Sometimes he volunteered the information without being asked, in order to speak of her. She was in no danger of becoming a formula while he so vividly recalled how her hair clustered about her neck but fell clear of her shoulders and her small exquisite bosom. It was the contrast between secrecy and boldness which enchanted him.

He had now to resign himself to losing one and possibly two hours of their precious time together, but reasoned that safety is not guaranteed, even on the ground. Railways are not infallible and boats even less so.

He was occupying one of the airport chairs, the two bouquets positioned across his knees; red roses for Miranda, freesias and nemesia for her aunt. The flowers

[277]

were tastefully presented in trumpets of regency-striped paper twined with silver gilt lace. He had gone to the best florist in town, Gucchi's, an establishment of the utmost sensibility. Serene white colonnades, a lily pool, a Cupid fountain, love-seats, pergolas, surrounded but did not overwhelm flawless blooms of all denominations, from orchids to anemones. Recalled in the noise and heat of the airport it seemed the nearest approach to Paradise available to metropolitan man. Miranda, he thought, would make a perfect Eve.

As a huge woman went by pushing a trolley laden with pigskin cases, he was reminded of air and the treachery of it. A casual wind could send Miranda's plane off course, a pocket could drop it into the sea. He worried about her, suspended above the earth.

He worried about their separation – how to resolve those three months without a kiss or a whisper between them? In Gucchi's, among the lilies and roses, it could have been pure artistry. The flowers he had brought were a fragile link, a promise which Miranda might not perceive. Here among crying children and sweating pigskin, how was he to promise her anything?

It seemed to be a matter of quality of promise rather than inhibition, for seemingly it was possible to deliver something, even among the children and pigskin. Opposite him, two people were implementing their promise to each other. Indeed, it looked as if it would be fulfilled, here and now, on the airport chairs.

Novalis turned his head away. He mistrusted demonstrations, even scientific ones. There was in this one some of the ancient science of love-making.

The indicator-board signalling 'Rome – delayed', revived his angst. He became concerned about the condition of the bouquets. How long could they remain fresh and presentable in this overheated, overtaxed atmosphere? Inside the cones of paper the roses still sustained beads of water on their velvet petals. But the freesias had darkened slightly and the nemesia let fall a dry floret. To this least of his worries he might apply reason. And did so, to occupy his mind, other thoughts being unproductive and defeatist.

If the plane were delayed a further hour, the roses would be presentable, the freesias less so. Another two hours and the aunt's bouquet would have suffered visibly but the roses, if not subjected to close scrutiny, might still pass muster. He reasoned that in the fuss following a delayed landing, Miranda would not be looking intently at her flowers, or at anything – with the exception of himself. The aunt's flowers he must be prepared to abandon in the waste-bin, Miranda's look he could not prepare for. It might happen at the moment of encounter or just before, or at some time or times afterwards. It must be expected when he least expected it.

Nothing was due to the aunt in the way of propitiation or *douceur*. The bouquet had simply been a nice idea. Hyper-anxious, he now foresaw that Miranda and her aunt would have their hands already full with the sundry items ladies carry on journeys. Added to handbags, hats, scarves, magazines, the bouquets would be unnecessary encumbrances. Any look he received from Miranda would surely contain an element of disapproval.

The couple opposite claimed his attention – not that they had any use for it, they were engrossed in each other. It was the engrossment which drew his eye.

In their late teens, neither children nor adults, they were currently coping with the problem of sex, and doing so with the rashness of children, which was preferable to the lewdness of adults. Novalis wondered at their indifference to their surroundings. In a limited sense it was sublime.

The boy was long-armed and something of a contortionist. He had his arms about the girl, his legs knotted knee over knee, ankle over ankle. His face was hidden in her neck. Like that, faceless and entwined, he was her setting. She spilled over him, lavish rather than large: she had more than enough of herself and could afford to be generous. Novalis registered her, without blame, as a slut. His had been a strict East European upbringing and he expected little or nothing from the West.

This girl was wearing a sun-top with the word 'Happiness' blazoned across her bosom, a form of advertising carried by all consumer goods. Her skin had become a bright crude pink with injudicious exposure to the sun. She might well be suffering from first degree burns. The boy's caresses were puppyish and rough and caused Novalis to wince for her.

It was announced that the flight from Amsterdam was landing, the provisional time of arrival of the flight from Rome was unchanged. A man with a rucksack on his back blocked Novalis's view of the couple and he fell to thinking about Miranda's aunt who disapproved of him on the grounds that he had no sense of humour. He believed that gravity was a virtue, but as the aunt was rich and childless and Miranda was her only niece, he was prepared to make an effort. He would present the bouquets with gallantry and some light-hearted remark such as 'Flowers for the fair'. Not that the aunt was fair, but he hoped she would take it in the spirit intended.

The man with the rucksack moved away in time for Novalis to see the boy taking the girl's neck in his hands. His thumbs met over her windpipe. Novalis experienced a sudden strong desire to see them sink deep into her flesh, and to see it change from pink to scarlet to dark purple under pressure. He was of course having a conditioned reflex: just as the sight of a gun provoked thoughts of its lethal possibilities, so must the sight of hands about a throat.

It was questionable whether these two were serious – the question must be what constituted seriousness for them. One did not know if horseplay was their nature or a protective cover. Protecting what?

The girl was watching Novalis. Her senses were no doubt permanently male-alarmed, but he got a mild shock when he realized that she was displaying for his benefit. Somehow she was contriving to relate her movements to him without his co-operation or approval. Certainly without his approval. He considered that she was vulgarizing the essentially private and delicate exchange between man and woman.

With distaste he observed how she wallowed about on the airport chair, her knees in black fishnet tights spread wide and mocking, her breasts rolling under the scanty sun-top, her neck arching so that the colour was strained out of it. Her eyes glittered at Novalis from under their lids, her lips parted to reveal the darting tip of her tongue. She pulled the boy's head down and bit his ear, said something which caused him to look round at Novalis and laugh.

Novalis turned away. The flight-indicator now estimated the Rome arrival time as 1500 hours. There was time for a cognac which might disperse thoughts which had become expendable. But what to do with the bouquets whilst he struggled through to the crowded bar?

He vacated his chair, positioned the bouquets across it and crossed to the bookstall. He made a quick classification of the publications on offer: travel and leisure guides by the score, women's interest pulps by the dozen, juvenilia for all ages, girlie art, political cartoons, horoscopes, language dictionaries, handbooks on health, antiques, bonsai gardening, hatha yoga. Nothing to command his interest. The display provoked thoughts on the sin of profligacy which had always seemed to him the most insidious vice.

Abstemious by nature and nurture, he deplored the current tendency to over-production. In his opinion too much of even a good thing resulted in loss of virtue and benefit and detracted from the quality of life. If small was beautiful, less was mandatory. He remembered his old professor in Prague asserting that world government could best be achieved by simple equations, one for each hemisphere.

Before going to the bar he glanced back in the direction of his chair, and saw the girl in the act of taking up one of the bouquets. She held it to her face, elevated her shoulders, swelled her bosom, clowning a mighty inhalation. Novalis envisaged the flowers shrinking, devitalized. Then she laid the bouquet along her arm and walked towards the exit, kissing her fingers to the air as she went. The boy laughed, men halted their luggage trolleys and stared.

Novalis hurried after her. 'Excuse me, I think you have my flowers.' She looked round. At close quarters hers was a soft spreading face, lacking East European bone structure, a florid English rose, unlike Gucchi's shapely blooms.

'Yours are over there, on that chair.'

'I have two bouquets, and plans for both of them.'

She put her head on one side, quizzed him with uncalled-for familiarity. 'Are you going to a funeral?'

'These aren't the sort of flowers for dead people.'

She had of course taken the roses, Miranda's roses. It disturbed him to see her with them. This girl was overpowering, she overpowered his thoughts, includ-

ing his thoughts of Miranda. Facing her, he was unable
to be aware of anything else, was compelled to remark
the consistency of her skin, as thick as cream, and as
moist. The sun had coloured but not dehydrated it. Her
lipstick was smudged by the boy's kisses. Her eyelashes,
spiked with mascara, signalled inanely – her eyes were
as bright and empty as an infant's.

'Findings keepings.'

'You did not find, you purloined and I shall be
obliged if you will return my property.'

'If I don't?'

'I shall call the police.'

He found it impossible to guess what she was thinking, if she was thinking at all. She seemed entirely
blameless, probably because she was mentally unreach-
able. Physically, of course, she was reaching for him.
Hastily he dropped his hand which he had extended to
take the flowers.

'What's going on?'

The boy had come to her side. A head taller than
Novalis, he had the lean and hungry look mentioned by
William Shakespeare: these two might indeed be de-
scribed as English bumpkins.

'He says he's going to call the cops.'

'If I have to.'

'Who says you have to?'

'This young lady has appropriated my flowers and is
unwilling to return them.'

'It's just a game she plays, to see how much she can
get away with. She doesn't want your flowers.'

'I do. They're lovely.'

There was tenderness in her voice. The boy winked
at Novalis. 'They only die.'

'You never bought me flowers.'

'I didn't know you wanted any.'

'They don't only die.' She was staring at Novalis, and
something quite independent of their surroundings and
circumstance, and of themselves, passed between them.
It threatened to engage them at an unplumbed depth.
Novalis had no wish to plumb it, or to be engaged. It
was unwelcome and quite unjustified by this chance
encounter.

The indicator-board was scheduling the Rome flight
as landing and at once his anxieties returned. Everyone
knew that an aircraft was most at risk during take-off
and landing. The flaps could refuse to open, the wheels
might lock, the brakes might fail, the plane overshoot,
hit airport buildings and catch fire. Miranda could be
snatched from him in the very moment of her coming
down to earth.

And there was the question of his own sufficiency at a
time when he would be expected to have enough for
them both. It was reasonable to expect that after they
were married their relationship would be such that each
would supply what the other lacked. But it was un-
reasonable to expect Miranda to supply all that he
lacked at this moment.

'My flight is landing. Please be so good as to give me
my flowers.'

'I only wanted to hold them.'

'You just did,' said the boy. 'Now give them back.'

She pouted, which did not become her. Novalis, who
had seen Miranda wrinkle her pretty nose and purse her
lips and look utterly charming, marvelled at the malice
of Nature which could provoke the same impulse with
such different results.

'I'll give you a flower,' said the boy, 'one you won't
buy in the shops.'

Novalis turned away and moved towards the arrival
barrier. She would arrive, Miranda and her jocular aunt

who considered him a stick. Miranda was minutes away and here he was, undeniably sticklike, empty of emotion.

'Hi, you forgetting these?'

He looked round. The boy was attempting to wrest the flowers from the girl. She held them on high, teasing, using them to beat him about the head.

'Keep them,' Novalis said bitterly.

Laughing, the boy parried her blows. 'I don't let my girl accept presents from strange men.'

'I have no further use for the flowers.'

'I'll pay you for them.'

'That will not be necessary.'

The girl said, 'I was going to give them back anyway.' She was unbecomingly damp from her horseplay. Sweat shone in the creases of her arms, in the cleft between her breasts.

The boy held up a coin. 'If you paid more you were done.'

'I don't require payment.'

The boy bent down and dropped the coin into the side of Novalis's shoe. Entwined, they went, the girl cradling the flowers on her arm. She turned and blew Novalis a kiss.

Miranda saw him at once. For him she had a seeing eye which dispelled the obtrusive people between them.

They moved towards each other, she with serene assurance, he stiffly, his heart risen into his throat. They met, she took his hands, her ungloved fingers warm on his. She kissed his cheek. 'How cold you are.'

'I have been waiting.' An absurd comment when the airport lounge was stiflingly hot.

'I know – we were late taking off and when we arrived

[285]

there was nowhere for us to put down. Darling, you are so pale!'

'The excitement of seeing you.'

'I hope you aren't going to faint,' said Miranda's aunt. 'It's really not necessary.'

'I'm quite well, thank you.'

He was glad that he had left her flowers on the chair. It would have been improvident to present them. She was a tall, well-structured woman, carrying a well-structured handbag, an umbrella, and a carrier-bag containing duty-free purchases.

'Allow me – '

'Save your strength for the luggage. Let us go and find the carousel.'

'Darling,' Miranda took his arm, 'has it been awful – waiting?'

He knew that she was referring not merely to the airport delay, but to the time they had been parted. They looked into each other's eyes. Then and there he should have said yes, oh yes! It was the moment: if he could have found the voice, the warmth and closeness must have come as surely as day must follow night. 'I have been watching people.'

'How dull!' cried the aunt. 'People are so predictable.'

'Things happen.'

'What things?'

The prospect of describing the incident of the girl and the flowers dismayed him.

Miranda said helpfully, 'Little things.'

'In the context of an international airport minor incidents tend to be exaggerated.' He knew that he sounded pompous and was aware of the coin in his shoe. It was cutting into his instep.

The aunt cried, 'Oh do look at that woman! How

ridiculous to wear a kaftan for travelling! Miranda, have you decided on your wedding-dress?'

'Almost.'

Novalis said, 'We have almost exhausted the subject.'

'Indeed?'

'We have discussed it at length.' Seeing an opportunity for a little light relief, he added, 'In fact it is only the question of length which remains unresolved.'

'What do you mean?'

'We cannot decide whether the fabric could sustain a train.'

'I shouldn't have thought that need concern *you*.'

'I am concerned in all that concerns Miranda, we are concerned in each other.'

'Take care. One must beware the imposition of one's own opinions on one's nearest and dearest. I have been married and I know.' Perhaps it was sight of the relentlessly revolving luggage on the carousel which provoked the aunt to fatalism. 'It is asking for trouble to assume that another person is having your same thoughts and emotions at precisely the same moment as yourself.'

'I like to think that Miranda and I complement rather than duplicate each other, that we are the two halves of one whole.'

'One whole what? A lemon?' The aunt burst out laughing. 'What a droll fellow you are!'

Miranda smiled. 'He can be very funny when he chooses.'

BIOGRAPHICAL NOTES

GRAHAM GREENE was born in 1904 and educated at Berkhamsted School and Balliol College, Oxford. He worked for four years as sub-editor of *The Times* and established his reputation with his fourth novel, *Stamboul train*. In 1940 he became literary editor of the *Spectator* and worked for the Foreign Office in Sierra Leone from 1941–43. In all, he has written some thirty novels including *Brighton rock* (1938), *Travels with my aunt* (1969), *The honorary consul* (1973) and *The human factor* (1978). He received the OM in the 1986 New Year's Honours List.

PAUL SAYER was born and brought up in South Milford, near Leeds. Until recently he worked as a staff nurse in a large psychiatric hospital in York. His first novel *The comforts of madness* (Constable 1988 and Doubleday 1989) won three awards – the Constable Trophy, the Whitbread First Novel Award and the Whitbread Book of the Year Award. His second novel will be published in 1990. He is married with a small son and lives in York.

DAMON GALGUT was born in Pretoria, South Africa, in 1963. His first novel *A sinless season* was published in 1982 and has been reissued by Constable in 1989. *Small circle of beings* was published by Constable in 1988. He has worked for the Performing Arts Council of the Transvaal as Resident Playwright and Literary Adviser. His play *Echoes of anger* was first produced in 1982.

WILLIAM TREVOR was born in County Cork in 1928

[289]

and spent his childhood in provincial Ireland before attending Trinity College, Dublin. Among his many books are *The children of Dynmouth* (1976; Whitbread Award) and *Fools of fortune* (1983; Whitbread Award). He has also written many plays for the stage, radio and television. In 1977 he was awarded an honorary CBE in recognition of his services to literature.

LAURA KALPAKIAN is the author of many short stories published on both sides of the Atlantic, as well as three previous novels: *Beggars and choosers* (1978) available in the USA only, and *These latter days* (1985) and *The swallow inheritance* (1987) which are both available in softcover from Headline. A native Californian, she currently teaches at Western Washington University, Bellingham, USA.

PAUL PICKERING was born in Rotherham and educated at the Royal Masonic School and Leicester University. He has been a columnist for *The Times*, the *Sunday Times*, the *London Evening Standard* and *Punch*, and has worked as a journalist all over the world. He lives in London and loves Berlin. *The blue gate of Babylon*, his third novel, was published in 1989. His next novel, *Charlie Peace's treasure*, will be published in 1990.

MURIEL SPARK was born and educated in Edinburgh. She travelled in Central Africa and returned in 1944 to work in the Foreign Office. She then entered the literary world, first in publishing and editing, then as a poet, story-writer and a novelist. Her work has been read and appreciated all over the world for the past thirty years. Her most recent novel, *A far cry from Kensington*, was published by Constable and Houghton Mifflin in 1988.

DAVID UPDIKE, the son of the novelist John Updike, teaches English and lives in Boston, Massachusetts. His stories have appeared in the *New Yorker* and in the volume *Twenty under 30*. He is the author of a children's book *A winter's journey*. His first book of adult fiction, *Out on the marsh*, was published by Constable and David Godine in 1989. The *New York Times Book Review* described him as 'a young writer whose intelligence and good-hearted sensibility promise to reward us for many years to come'.

GEORGINA HAMMICK had her first collection of stories, *People for lunch*, published by Methuen and Abacus. It was extremely well reviewed by Bernard Levin, Blake Morrison and Christopher Wordsworth, and the title story was the winner of the *Stand Magazine*'s short story competition in 1985. She lives in Wiltshire, has three children and is currently writing another collection of stories.

JORGE LUIS BORGES (1899–1986) and ADOLFO BIOY-CASARES were friends and literary collaborators for over fifty years. Together, they invented the first Argentine detective, whose adventures appear in *Six problems for don Isidro Parodi*, and the bombastic critic (and putative author of the *Six problems*) Honorio Bustos Domecq, whose collected papers appear in *Chronicles of Bustos Domecq* and in a forthcoming volume of tales, *The monster rally*. Bioy-Casares lives in Buenos Aires, where he was born in 1914.

LAWRENCE SCOTT is from Trinidad and Tobago, now resident in Britain. He has had short stories published in the *Trinidad and Tobago Review, Chelsea* and *The PEN*. He was awarded the 1986 Tom-Gallon Award for his short story 'The house of funerals' which was published in 1988 by Constable in *Winter's tales 4*. He divides his time between teaching Literature at a London Sixth Form College and writing. He has completed his first novel and has a collection of short stories prepared for publication.

A.L. BARKER left school when she was sixteen and, after the war, joined the BBC. Her debut collection of stories, *Innocents*, won the Somerset Maugham Prize, and her novel *John Brown's body*, was shortlisted for the Booker Prize in 1969. She is the author of nine novels, including most recently *The woman who talked to herself* and seven short story collections.